PHILIPOVNA
Daughter of Sorrow

MIROLAND IMPRINT 20

**Canada Council   Conseil des Arts
for the Arts   du Canada**

**ONTARIO ARTS COUNCIL
CONSEIL DES ARTS DE L'ONTARIO**

an Ontario government agency
un organisme du gouvernement de l'Ontario

Canadä

Guernica Editions Inc. acknowledges the support of the Canada Council
for the Arts and the Ontario Arts Council. The Ontario Arts Council
is an agency of the Government of Ontario.

We acknowledge the financial support of the Government of Canada.

PHILIPOVNA
Daughter of Sorrow

Valentina Gal

MiroLand
publishers

MIROLAND (GUERNICA)
TORONTO • BUFFALO • LANCASTER (U.K.)
2019

Connie McParland, series editor
Michael Mirolla, editor
David Moratto, cover and interior design
Guernica Editions Inc.
1569 Heritage Way, Oakville, ON L6M 2Z7
2250 Military Road, Tonawanda, N.Y. 14150-6000 U.S.A.
www.guernicaeditions.com

Distributors:
University of Toronto Press Distribution,
5201 Dufferin Street, Toronto (ON), Canada M3H 5T8
Gazelle Book Services, White Cross Mills
High Town, Lancaster LA1 4XS U.K.

First edition.
Printed in Canada.

Legal Deposit—First Quarter
Library of Congress Catalog Card Number: 2018962476
Library and Archives Canada Cataloguing in Publication

Gal, Valentina, 1952-, author
Philipovna : daughter of sorrow / Valentina Gal.

(MiroLand imprint ; 20)
Issued in print and electronic formats.
ISBN 978-1-77183-369-1 (softcover).--ISBN 978-1-77183-370-7 (EPUB).--
ISBN 978-1-77183-371-4 (HTML)

1. Gal, Valentina, 1952-. 2. Philipovna, Vera. 3. Victims of famine--
Ukraine--Biography. 4. Ukraine--History--Famine, 1932-1933. 5. Ukraine--
Biography. 6. Autobiographies. I. Title. II. Series: MiroLand imprint ; 20

DK508.835.G35A3 2019   947.7'0841   C2018-906224-X   C2018-906225-8

*To my Mother
Vera Philipovna*

Contents

✼✼✼✧✼✼✼

Character List

#:#:#:#:#:

Vera Philipovna: daughter of Philip and Barbara Kyslenko

Godfather: Philipovna's uncle and godfather, name otherwise unknown

Vera Xenkovna: cousin and oldest daughter of Uncle Misha and Auntie Xena

Dmytro/Mitya: Philipovna's distant cousin and best friend

The Unravelled One: Mitya's mother

Auntie Xena: Philipovna's aunt

Uncle Misha: Auntie Xena's husband

Michael, Alexander, Viktor, Maria and Marta: the rest of Misha and Xena's children.

Taras: Xenkovna's young man

Auntie Lena: Philipovna's aunt

Uncle George: Lena's husband

Auntie Liza: Philipovna's aunt

Comrade Zabluda: Communist Party Boss, head authority in village

Comrade Asimov: school teacher and Communist Party enforcer

Uncle Paulo: older neighbour and friend of Uncle Misha

Uncle Simon: more distant neighbour and friend of Uncle Misha

Uncle Ivan: acquaintance of Uncle Misha and Party member

Dr. Bondarenko: doctor from out of town

Slavko: doctor's servant

Comrade Svetlana Ivanovna: Communist head of the orphanage and children's doctor.

Comrade Marina Nikolaiovna: orphanage worker and doctor's helper

Gregory: Marina Nikolaiovna's nephew and helper

Katerina: neighbour

Auntie Anna: neighbour and close friend

Glossary of Ukrainian Words

❉❉❉❉❉

Artil—the name of the original state farms that were established
before the revolution of 1917

Babas—a colloquial term for older women. It also denotes Grandmother when used to address an older woman.

Babushka—familiar term for Grandmother, equivalent for Grandma

Babusya—diminutive form of babushka

Baba Kutsya—the Ukrainian version of hide and seek

Baba Yaga—a witch or enchanted old woman who lives in the
woods, often in a cottage standing on four chicken feet

Borscht—a type of soup made with beets, usually served with sour
cream. It can be made with other vegetables and is made without
meat on fast days and other holy days. There is a large variety
of borscht depending on where in the country it is made. It varies
from the bright red beet *borscht* that is familiar to North
Americans to green and yellow versions made from the vegetables
available at the season or upon the place and what grows there.

Chekists—Stalin's enforcers

Cholera—a mild swear word meaning devil or pest

Chort—the word for devil. It isn't Satan the devil but a lesser more
benign devil who is often mischievous.

Did Moroz—Jack Frost

Diedushka—familiar word for Grandfather, equivalent for Grandpa

Holodets—A jellied meat dish, served cold with horse radish or hot
mustard.

Hospodi pomilui—Lord have mercy, a phrase that is used very
often in the Ukrainian Orthodox liturgy

Kalach—ceremonial bread usually baked for a holiday or special occasion. It is sweetened and contains raisins. It is decorated according to the ceremony that it is required for. When it is baked for weddings, it is elaborately decorated with birds and other wedding symbols. On holy days, it also has crosses and other Christian symbols.

Kalyna—the Ukrainian name for the Highbush Cranberry, a plant that grows naturally in parks and wilderness areas across the region. It is believed to have many healing properties and is heavily laden with Ukrainian symbolism. It is easily recognized in the art, poetry and song of traditional Ukraine. Girls are often named for this beloved plant.

Kolhosp—Ukrainian word for the collective farm.

Krasawitsya—a beautiful woman

Kutya—a dish cooked specifically for Christmas Eve. It is basically a porridge cooked from buckwheat and garnished with a sauce made with honey and ground poppy seeds. Fruit compote can also be served with it.

Pan—the word for Sir or Lord

Paska—special bread made only at Easter

Platok—the name for head kerchief warn by Ukrainian women, especially married women. A man is expected to show respect to a woman wearing this kerchief. They usually are either embroidered or painted with intricate flower designs. When a woman is in mourning or older, she will wear a black kerchief to express her status.

Philipovna—Vera's patronymic name, meaning the daughter of Philip. Traditionally, Ukrainians are known by their given name, followed by their patronymic name, followed by their family name.

Pyrizhky—buns that are filled with either sweet or savoury stuffing. They can have meat or cheese filling for the main course or apple and raisins if they are used for dessert.

Pysanky—intricately painted Easter eggs. The root word is the word for write so Ukrainians say that they will "write" the egg rather than colour it. The design is more important than the colour, beautiful as it may be. The idea is to have each egg look as individual as possible.

Rushnyk—literally meaning towel. Culturally, it is like a linen scarf, usually heavily embroidered and is used for ceremonial purposes. Ukrainian Christian households have an icon, a religious picture which is hung in a place of honour and draped with a *rushnyk*. *Rushnyks* are also used to wrap food in for ceremonies. They are part of the hand-binding at Ukrainian wedding ceremonies, a custom going back to pre-Christian times, and are symbols of home and harmony.

Sharik—the word for ball. Used as the dog's name here.

Smetana—sour cream

Varenyky—stuffed dumplings. Can be made with sweet or savoury filling. The dough is rolled out, stuffed and dropped into boiling water till the dumpling floats.

Verochka—diminutive for the name Vera

Tahto—the Ukrainian equivalent for Daddy

Tsarevitch—the title for the son of a tsar

Tsarevna—the title for the daughter of a tsar

Zaraza—word meaning pest or pestilence

The Legacy

I STAYED AWAY from other children. I preferred my own games of picking flowers and long processions that ended with me and the rag doll Mama made sitting on my parents' grave and talking to them. I can't remember any of the funerals or what my Mama's face looked like. But I still hear the memory of her singing a lullaby. Though Mama was gone, I could always feel her close to me.

My Godfather, who was also my father's brother, took me to his house after all of the ceremonies were over. They say that every time the door opened, I ran straight back to my parents' cottage. They would find me holding my father's tools, spinning the wheel of my mother's sewing machine or curled up on their feather bed by the hearth. If it was a nice day, I hid in our garden, finding bugs or leaves or stray flowers that struggled up through the untended mass of vegetation.

One day, a group of strangers approached my father's house as I was playing with some twigs and a cocoon in the empty garden. I was frightened at first but I recognized my Godfather and Auntie Xena so I didn't run away.

"Verochka, there you are. Come and say 'good-morning' to your Aunts and Uncles," Godfather called to me. "Auntie Xena has brought you a sweet."

I studied the group cautiously. Strangers did not come here unless something very important was happening. What could be so important that a whole group of people was visiting me? My parents were dead and couldn't invite them in.

Godfather drew me forward and, there beneath the frosty blue of the autumn sky, I first set my eyes on my father's sisters. They were robust women with rosy cheeks and bushy eyebrows. Beneath their embroidered *platoks*, their heavy brown hair was plaited in braids that were fashioned into buns on their heads and their sharp eyes looked right through me. They were not like my mother's sister, Auntie Xena, at all. I loved her smile and those soft hazel eyes that wrapped you in a warm blanket of welcome.

"Come, Child," she said. "Let me give you a big hug." She kissed me on both cheeks and presented me to the other aunts. Lena lived one town farther away from Auntie Xena. She sniffed and looked me over from head to toe with disdain. Liza was rich and lived in Kiev. She wore a fur collar even though the day wasn't very cold. Their full names were Olena and Elizabeth. I was too scared to look at the Uncles; they were so strong and tall with their big moustaches.

"Your Aunts and Uncles are here to settle your parents' business," Godfather explained.

For what was the longest afternoon of my short life, I sat on the hearth in the one room cottage that used to be my home. As the men talked through my father's affairs, I rocked the cradle that my mother had laid me in and had prepared for the sibling that should have been sleeping there. I watched as the strangers looked over my father's tools which were in a nook lit by the natural light of a window facing the village square. I remember *Tahto* sitting at his bench on the day I found the ducklings.

In Ukrainian villages wagon wheels made deep ruts in the dirt road. One spring day, when I was playing, I saw a mother duck walking with her ducklings. She led them from the field into a rut and walked along with them lined up behind her. The mother duck stepped out onto the road calling for her family to follow across to the other side. The little ducklings could not climb out of the rut. She quacked and quacked, but they could not get out because they were still too small. I felt so sorry for them that I gathered them up in my skirt and took them to show my father who was working at his cobbler's bench.

He was a master cobbler with two apprentices and was well known throughout the whole county of Cherkassy. Everyone loved him.

"Look, look," I shouted. "I found these little ducks on the road, *Tahto*."

My father's face darkened with an unfamiliar expression.

"We have to drown them in the river, right now," *Tahto* said. He stood up and put those little ducklings into his leather work apron.

I started to cry.

"They must go back into the river," *Tahto* insisted.

I screamed harder. He walked towards the river with me and my tantrum following his long strides.

"Please don't drown them! Please, please!" I begged. I didn't want those pretty ducklings to be dead like my mother and her new baby.

When we reached the river, *Tahto* squatted by the water's edge. He gently picked up the first little duckling and dipped his large cobbler's hand just below the surface of the cold water. The bird's fragile wings fluttered. How beautiful it looked. I watched *Tahto* as he took each duckling from his apron and freed it. I watched each of them spread their tiny wings and swim away.

"Remember, this is where ducklings belong," he said sternly. "A bird can't sing if it isn't free. And you can't survive if you aren't free either."

His blue eyes sparkled like the water in the river. That is the only memory I have of my father. He was so tall and handsome with his dark curly hair. He did not starve in the famine like the rest of them. He and his student were taking a shortcut across the river and were ambushed by thieves. They were robbed of the shipment of expensive leather boots which had been commissioned by the local dance school. He was beaten so badly that he bled to death before the doctor got to him. At least he left me his name, Philip. Back home the father's name was our legacy. It really meant something, not like here in Canada.

The Uncles paid the apprentices with the remaining leather and the cobbler's tools they couldn't use themselves. They promised letters of introduction to any new master that the sad-looking young men might find. The apprentices said goodbye and patted me on the head before leaving.

My new aunts went through every corner and crevice of the house separating out my parents' modest belongings. The pots, the crockery, the brooms and even the sack of wheat that was used for baking bread were accounted for. My mother's trunk was taken apart and the aunts went through her clothing piece by piece.

"Xena," Liza said, "you might as well take the dresses. They're too small for both of us and, besides, we can make nicer dresses than these anytime."

She tossed my Mama's clothes over the trunk as if they were a pile of filthy rags.

Auntie Xena shushed her with a finger on the lips and a sympathetic look in my direction.

Everyone except Auntie Xena had been ignoring me. She would gently look over from the conversation that was going on or come and pat my shoulder in passing. Finally, they converged on my Mama's only treasure.

My Mama had been a dressmaker. Apparently, she was a good dressmaker as she had been able to acquire a Singer sewing machine, all the way from America. The aunts stood around it and discussed. They discussed and discussed till their voices were so loud that I became frightened and started to cry. Godfather came over to see what was going on.

"Good God!" he shouted. "See what you old hens have done."
I cried harder.

Godfather walked over to the hearth and swung me up to his shoulder with one of his muscled arms. He stood me on the cabinet of the sewing machine with one arm around my waist. He brushed my hair back from my face. He wiped my tears with his handkerchief. He looked hard at me with his blue eyes that were so like my father's and said kindly: "Don't cry, Child. You'll have to ask God for strength. He's given you a hard road to walk and you'll need His help. Remember that He gives much suffering to those He loves best. Your name is Vera. It means truth. If you look for truth, you'll always find your way. Don't ever forget that."

He turned to my aunts and glared.

"The one who takes the Child takes the machine. It is her mother's legacy. She may need it to earn her own living."

The room was silent. The two new aunts stared at my Godfather while Auntie Xena stood with tears in her downcast eyes.

"I'll take her," she said quietly and reached out her arms as she stepped closer to the cabinet of the machine where I still perched like a helpless baby bird on the branch of a tree.

Godfather raised his free hand to stop her.

"The one who takes the Child, takes the machine," he commanded.

The new aunts acted as if he wasn't in the room.

"But you can't even sew a straight seam," Lena exclaimed, shaking her finger in Auntie Xena's face.

"I'm the one who makes my living with the dresses," Liza said. "I'd get much more work done with that excellent machine. I have more talent than the two of you put together." She ignored Godfather's thunderous stare.

"That's my loving sister!" Lena said, scoffing. "Never enough for you, is there?"

"Xena," Godfather said. "You and Misha already have six

5

children. It would be much easier for one of the others to look after her."

"Anyone can look after her. Someone has to love her. She needs to be safe, in a good home."

"But I need the sewing machine," Liza said.

"You can afford to buy one," Lena said. "Your husband has a good position with the Party. I need it more than you do."

Godfather's fist pounded the top of the sewing-machine cabinet.

"I am her Godfather. By the Lord's holy name, I promised to stand in her father's stead if it were required. The one who takes the Child takes the machine. Otherwise, no one shall take a thing from Philip's home — over my dead body."

The Uncles stood in silence while the new aunts exchanged vicious looks.

"I said I would take her," Auntie Xena said again.

"You have the least to offer," Godfather said.

"I have God's word. The Child will survive. I swear on my sister's name and on her Bible." She picked up my mother's Bible which was on top of the smallest pile of household goods and hugged it to her breast. Her shoulders shook and the tears ran unchecked down her cheeks.

"Lena, Liza, speak now or forever shut those caverns of yours."

The aunts were silent.

"All of the food stuffs and linen shall go with Philipovna," my Godfather said. "Xena and her brood will surely need them."

On that day, I had a new name. Everyone continued to call me "Philipovna" because my Auntie's daughter was also named Vera. In time, she became "Xenkovna" especially after Uncle Misha died. There was a lot more arguing and discussion but, in the end, Godfather held his own. I was packed into Uncle Misha's wagon with my sewing machine and taken to Auntie Xena's home in Zyladyn.

Christmas in Zyladyn

ZYLADYN WAS MUCH like the village of my birth, like most small villages in the Ukrainian countryside. It was on a tributary of the Dnipro River. The church, store and government buildings were built around the central square and the peasant homes encircled that. The more prominent families also built their larger houses close to the square. Beyond the houses the black soil lay exposed and rolled away for kilometres till it met the blue sky. After the cold winds and white frosts of winter these fields would be planted with grain and turn into oceans of green which would mature into the golden abundance of wheat for which our land is famous. One could have lived forever with a glass of vodka in his hand and a belly full of bread and potatoes the way our ancestors did for thousands of years before us.

Auntie's house was on the edge of the village, not near the central square. It had a dirt floor which was always swept clean and its roof was thatched because, although Uncle Misha had some land, he was not one of the richest farmers in the village. The rich farmers had tin roofs on their houses and boards of wood on their floors.

My aunt and Uncle lived in a bigger house than the one my parents had, though it was just as sparsely furnished. It was square. On the east side was the room in which all our living was done. An

7

icon, adorned by a red-and-black embroidered *rushnyk*, hung on the wall. The other side was divided into two smaller rooms. Auntie Xena put my sewing machine into one of them. Whenever no one was looking, I would go and take off the white cloth that covered it. I'd sit and spin the wheel or push the treadle and watch the needle go up and down. I wondered if Mama could sew as fast as the wheel could turn. Auntie Xena would find me and gently coax me back to the family or conveniently find a task for me to do; but when I returned, the machine was always neatly covered again.

"When you are old enough, we will both learn to use it," she said.

The wall with the fireplace in it divided the house in half. In Ukrainian homes, the fireplace is the heart of the home. Uncle Misha built the platform of his with enough room for a couple of little children or an old person to curl up on should they need warmth or comfort. The stronger members of the family slept on benches along the wall. There were three of them who were younger than me. Maria and Marta were the baby twins and Viktor was a rosy-cheeked little boy whose eyes shone with mischief from the moment I first saw him. I wondered if my dead sibling would have looked like the twins or Cousin Viktor. I hoped he or she would have been like Viktor, as I really wanted a brother. There were also two older boy cousins, but they were mostly occupied by the endless chores that were required to keep a small farm going. Their names were Alexander and Michael.

Auntie Xena put my parents' feather bed and pillows on the sleeping bench where my cousin, Vera Xenkovna, slept. She was six years older than me and had the same hazel eyes as her mother.

"Your Mama and *Tahto* watch you from Heaven and will help you to stay on the right track if you will say your prayers and open your heart to them," Auntie said.

"We can sleep together like real sisters," Xenkovna said. "And you'll be less frightened at night." As she stroked my heavy brown braid, I wondered how she knew that I cried myself to sleep most of the time.

We rose to the smell of bread that each morning Auntie pulled out of the oven in the fireplace with her wooden shovel. My mouth waters even now when I remember waiting for my portion as Xenkovna lathered it with the butter we churned. It was pleasant drinking tea with my Uncle and cousins, playing in the square and memorizing Bible verses and prayers by the fire at night. Of course, we also had to know the patriotic poems of our national hero, Taras Shevchenko. Sometimes, Uncle Misha played his guitar and sang for us. I liked the stories of *Did Moroz*—you know him as Jack Frost —and how he came around at night to paint beautiful pictures of frost on our windows.

As the autumn of 1930 descended into winter, I settled into my new family. The dark nights and frost brought the promises of St. Nicholas Day and Christmas celebrations. Auntie taught us about St. Nicholas and how he gave his gold to those who were poor and really needed help.

"We should pay attention and use him as an example for our own generosity," she said.

Uncle Misha supervised my lessons in the First Form Lexicon. The lexicon was a book with stories in it that were followed by quizzes to see how well the student learned the words and ideas they expressed.

"Make sure you write neatly," Uncle Misha said as he watched me practice writing my letters on the slate. "If you aren't going to write neatly, how will anyone be able to read it?" I was to start school after Christmas. No niece of Uncle Misha's would be ridiculed for not knowing how to read, write and recite the complete lexicon before she started school. Even the poorest in our village were fiercely proud of their intellectual achievements if they could find a way to be taught.

Auntie Xena also found chores for me. I learned to milk the cow and carry water, a job that seemed never-ending with so many people to clean and cook for. I swept the floor and arranged the bedding each morning. As I was sweeping the doorstep one day, a gangly boy with ragged clothes and wild curls appeared from behind the woodpile.

"Are you the orphan?" he asked abruptly.

"I—I don't know. My name is Vera but they call me Philipovna now." I didn't want to admit that I didn't know what an orphan was.

"It doesn't matter," he said. "You look about the same as anyone else."

He picked up an armful of wood from Uncle Misha's pile.

"That's Uncle's wood."

"I guess they haven't told you about the 'Unravelled One'. I'm her son. Your Uncle says I can take as much wood as we need. Ask him, if you don't believe me."

"The 'Unravelled One'? Sounds more like a skein of wool than a person."

"That's how my Mama is," he said with a scowl.

How could anyone look so angry at the mention of his mother, I wondered as I continued sweeping the doorstep. I knew if my Mama were alive, there would be nothing but smiles if I should have talked about her.

"I'm as much your cousin as most of the rest of the village is." He half-sneered down at me and turned to go on his way.

"Wait," I said, my curiosity unexpectedly giving me the words to speak. "I don't really know anyone in the village."

"If you want to find out the really fun stuff, come mushroom picking with me when you're finished sweeping. I'm sure Auntie Xena won't mind."

"I don't know how to pick mushrooms." I blushed.

His grey-blue eyes widened in disbelief.

"Then you'll have to learn. We'll pick enough for everyone. Which is it, Vera or Philipovna?"

"Philipovna, I guess."

"My name's Dmytro, but you can call me Mitya," he said. "Auntie helps me and my Mama whenever I can't figure things out for us."

We walked out of the village, past Uncle Misha's field and, with our footsteps crackling on the fallen leaves, we entered an orchard.

"This is Uncle Paulo's cherry orchard," Mitya said. "You'll love the cherries next spring. We can climb up into the trees and eat as many as we like. Uncle Paulo doesn't mind."

I didn't have the nerve to tell him that I had never climbed a tree.

"There are no mushrooms here," he said. "We have to go into the woods."

"But aren't there Baba Yagas and goblins in the woods?"

"You mean I'm going mushroom picking with a baby?" The sneer from the woodpile was back on his face.

"I'm not scared," I said, resisting a strong temptation to run back to the warmth and safety of Auntie's kitchen. "I'm just wondering if there are any around here."

"That stuff is for babies," he said. "If you want to know about the good stuff, forget about those stupid stories. I can show you where mushrooms are. And rabbits. In the springtime, I can even find some crayfish and nightingale nests. We can build a little fire and cook the crayfish, right by the river."

"What about bears or wolves?"

"Are you picking mushrooms or should you be going back home and hang onto Auntie's apron strings?"

I didn't say any more. We walked through the woods of silver birch, pine and willows that grew close to the river, our steps crunching through the pungent masses of rustling leaves. I breathed in the tangy scent of the pines and the dusty aroma of the drying vegetation. The touch of the crisp air coloured Mitya's cheeks and the late autumn sun cast the last of its warm rays onto our backs. He showed me how to find the mushrooms under trees and in the sheltered places by the river. He knew which were good to eat and which were poisonous.

"It's a good thing we came out here today," he said. "These mushrooms are going to be the last of the season. It's getting too cold for them."

We filled our bucket in no time. When we returned to Uncle's woodpile, the shadows of the afternoon were long and blue in the approaching twilight. It was almost time to milk the cow.

"I can show you some other stuff whenever you want," he said.

I smiled. From that day, I had my first friend. He didn't like Children any more than I did, so before very long, we had our own friendship with our own secrets and special places. I found myself hurrying to finish my work for the day, so we could wander in the woods or skate on the river after it froze. If Mitya was late I was impatient and if he didn't come I felt lonely. Is this what having a real brother was like?

In the final few weeks of the year, strange men appeared in our village. Some were dressed in military garb and stirred up much excitement when they came through the square. Others were fashionably dressed men with pale faces and polished shoes who tried not to get them messed up in the snow. They looked out of place amongst the villagers in their heavy, homemade clothing and felt boots. Mitya loved to swagger like them stepping deeper and deeper into the snow until he would feign losing his balance and fall down on his face and start swearing in Russian. I would laugh and laugh till Auntie Xena heard us in the yard one day and put an end to it.

"You must not show such disrespect," she said. "You don't know what you're playing at and you never know when the Comrades will show up. Can't you play a game of *Baba Kutsya*, like good Children?"

"That's for babies," Mitya said. "I'm almost a man."

When the Comrades did come to our village, Uncle Misha said that they came to look at how many animals we had and how much grain we grew. He wasn't concerned, as the grain quota had already been collected by the bread procurement committee and the army. One day, one of these men stopped at Uncle Misha's barn and inspected his fields.

"Camarad," Uncle Misha said mockingly over tea in the early evening after Comrade Zabluda had gone away. "He can't even speak in our language. How can he call me 'Comrade'?" Uncle lingered on each syllable. "What is the Party thinking anyway—sending out these city know-it-alls to tell us how to farm? You know he called the new colt a calf. When I tell the fellows at the square, they'll laugh him out of the village. It's hard to imagine that they made him a twenty-five Thousander, isn't it?"

"Be careful who you tell," Auntie said.

"Woman, you don't need to worry. The Party can't be serious about the *artil*. If they were, they'd send someone out who knew what he was doing. They tried it in the war and you see the state farms that are left. They've learned that communes are not the proper places for any self-respecting farmer. If I have to, I'll defend this piece of land the way my father did."

"And you may have to pay for it the way he did if you tell the wrong person." She sighed and crossed herself.

I stared at my Uncle. I had heard stories of how, during the war which ended three years before I was born, his father wouldn't surrender his land or livestock, how he was tortured and finally died in prison and how his mother went to beg for his body so that he could have a proper Orthodox burial. But this was the first time Uncle had ever referred to them himself.

"The Party isn't so stupid that they would try the collectives after what went on here in the war. Simon and Paulo don't intend to give their land away either. Simon says that he will try to reason with them but Paulo thinks he can stick it out on his own."

"That's what those *choleras* say now," Auntie said. "But you never know who will bend or even break under pressure." Uncle Misha was about to speak but Auntie cut him off.

"Enough!" she said, and with her soft, hazel eyes shushed Uncle because she could see that I was shivering.

I didn't have the courage to ask them about the revolver that I had seen conspicuously displayed on Comrade's shoulder holster. I didn't even know what a shoulder holster was until Mitya explained that it was used for carrying a gun. It was the first weapon I had ever seen because, after the war, the Communists had completely disarmed everyone in the village and there wasn't a single gun left to shoot a rabbit should one need to find game for his cooking pot.

"What is a Thousander?" I asked.

"Don't concern yourself with things like Thousanders," Auntie said. "You are too young for such evil matters."

This time Uncle shushed her.

"Comrade Zabluda is called a twenty-five Thousander because he is one of the men that supervises twenty-five thousand families for Comrade Stalin," Uncle Misha explained. "But it's easier to say 'Thousander'."

"And who is Comrade Stalin?"

"He has set himself up as our new tsar and father." Uncle Misha went on. "But he knows nothing about being a tsar, especially being the tsar of the Ukrainians. The only father we need is God, our Holy Father. Comrade Stalin hasn't learned that we are an independent sort and will die for it if we're put to the test. We don't need any tsar."

"For the love of God, enough of this!" Auntie exclaimed. "What if they come and make trouble again? You shouldn't be saying such things to her. Philipovna, are you ready to recite?"

After that evening, Auntie and Uncle often had quiet conversations in the barn or in the corner by the icon. They wondered what the Thousanders like Comrade Zabluda were going to do and warned us to stay out of the path of the men who called themselves the Propagandists. They couldn't believe that the rumours of the collective farm were really true.

"After all, they've been tried and they failed," Uncle said.

"There might be war again and then how will we survive?" Auntie crossed herself and wiped tears from her eyes.

But the city men kept coming.

"Philipovna, come and see what's happening in the square," Mitya shouted one December morning when he passed me as I swept off our doorstep.

I finished and leaned the broom in its place by the door.

"What's the hurry?" Auntie asked.

"There are men in the square," I said, calling over my shoulder without stopping for fear that she would not let me go.

The square was full of villagers. Comrade Zabluda had taken over our small government building. A team of workmen was unloading some strange-looking machinery.

"What are they doing?" Mitya asked as he pushed his way to the front of the crowd with me in tow. He was two years older than me and, because he was a boy, wasn't afraid of anything. He would fix those steel blue eyes of his on a person so intently that they just couldn't help but answer any question he would ask.

"We're installing telephone lines, now get out of our way." One of the workers tried to brush him off.

"What's a telephone?"

"Vasel," the worker said, grinning at his colleague. "This bumpkin doesn't know what a telephone is. Imagine, the Comrades are wasting time on such stupid peasants. Putting in a telephone for jokers that don't even know how to use it. Is this what they mean by progress?"

"If you don't tell us what it is, how will we know how to use it?" Mitya said, red with embarrassment and anger.

"Let him alone," Vasel said. He was a kind-looking man with greying hair and heavy moustache. "Come here boy."

We stepped closer to Vasel as he pulled out a black box with a wire hanging from it.

"You use this machine to talk to people who are far away," he explained. "It works on wires like the telegraph but you can hear the other person's voice and they can hear you. See, here's the part you put to your ear."

Mitya put the receiver to his ear.

"I don't hear anyone talking. Here Philipovna, maybe they'll talk to you."

The men roared with laughter.

"You stupid boy," the first worker said. "It isn't connected to the wires yet."

We watched them unravel the wires from large spools and attach them to the building. Then they pulled the spools down the road until they disappeared. As the men moved away, the villagers wondered why Comrade couldn't go talk to a person directly and who was important enough to need a telephone.

We hurried back to report on what we had seen.

"I don't know why we need a telephone either," Auntie said. "Why can't they just send a telegram? Oh Dear God, there will really be big trouble." She sighed and crossed herself.

She tried to keep things going the way they always had. It was easier in the day because my cousins and I could play and study as normal but the evenings were different. Uncle Misha was called to meetings along with all the other men in the village. We read less and prayed more. We didn't recite or sing as much either.

Auntie was conserving food as she was afraid that we wouldn't have enough till the vegetable garden could be planted but, on Christmas Eve, we worked from daybreak to cook supper. She measured the buckwheat down to the last grain and fussed over the grinding of the poppy seeds that would go into the *kutya*. She charged me with stirring the mixture of poppy seeds, dried fruit and honey which was simmering on the fire to be reconstituted as its garnish. The fruity steam made me hungry and when Auntie Xena wasn't looking I licked my finger so I could retrieve a few stray poppy seeds from the cheesecloth they had been stored in.

"Mind you don't nibble at the raisins or poppy seeds, Vera Philipovna," she gently chided. "We only have enough for one portion each and remember, the *kutya* is the most important part of the supper."

"Have you got your spoon ready for this evening?" Uncle Misha asked of Xenkovna when he came in for his tea.

"Why does she have to have a spoon ready?" I asked.

"Because she is old enough to knock on the window tonight. If a man's voice answers, she will be married this year. If it's a woman, she'll have to wait."

"*Tahto*," Xenkovna said, blushing. "I'm not thinking about any of that. There's enough to do here without worrying about such things."

"Never mind," he said, chuckling. "If she's old enough to bake a good loaf of bread, she's good enough for other things. Knock! Knock! Don't tempt fate and stay an old maid."

"Hush," his wife said, wiping her hands on her apron. "We don't want to tempt fate and have her gone too soon either. She's got plenty of time for that."

But Uncle Misha kept grinning.

"I've seen Taras peeking over his accordion at her. She may not have anything on her mind but I'd bet my boots he does. Don't be too surprised if he's sweet on her. And, if I say so myself, I don't blame him either. She's a fine catch."

"You're saying far too much," Auntie said in an unusually sharp tone.

Xenkovna blushed again.

I helped Auntie spread the cloth which her mother had embroidered with the red and black fine cross-stitches that were the special design of our area of the Ukraine. The table was then set with the three layers of *kalach* that, under Auntie's watchful eye,

Xenkovna had braided into rings. She had brushed them with egg white so that their surface would be shiny and baked them that morning. These rings of bread were stacked in three layers to represent the Holy Trinity and were round to show the eternity of God's love and faithfulness. My stomach churned with their fragrance and, as the smell of each successive dish blended with the one that preceded it, I thought I'd never live to taste supper.

Auntie reminded me to never forget the empty place setting for the ancestors. I wondered if my parents were sitting at God's table too. Would they be angry with me if they knew that I couldn't remember having such a Christmas with them? Would they really watch me from Heaven? Did they know I had found my good friend Mitya? I could hardly wait for the first star to appear because we couldn't start the Christmas Eve Feast till it did.

We knelt beneath the icon and crossed ourselves before reciting the Our Father. Auntie Xena read the prayers for our departed ancestors asking for continuing peace for their souls and praying to The Holy Mother for a special boon of health and safety for all of us. Uncle Misha stood a small sheath of grain by the fireplace and thanked God for the many gifts he gave our family. We spread some hay under the supper table to remind ourselves of the hay on which Our Holy Mother laid the Baby Jesus so many years ago. Uncle Misha led us in the singing of a few of our favourite Christmas carols. We lit the candle in the centre of the *kalach* and sat down to eat.

"Mmmm," Uncle Misha said, smiling, "Xena, I swear that you make the best *kutya* in the whole country."

"Thank God that we have enough food to make it," she said.

"Don't worry so much, Woman. We've always made it. It won't be any different this time should there really be trouble."

There was meatless borscht that tasted sweet from all the beets from which it was made served with a generous dollop of *smetana*, some spicy fish in tomato sauce with eggplant dressing and my favourite *pyrizhky*, you know those buns with apple filling. I can still feel my mouth watering when I think of them and their cinnamon smell. Auntie didn't make any extra, as she would have done in the past, because none of the neighbours would be coming to visit. Only Mitya and his mentally ill mother joined us.

"I couldn't live with myself if poor Mitya and the Unravelled One didn't come to eat," Auntie said.

Mitya's father was the last casualty of the war. The Unravelled One was newly pregnant when he was taken. After the birth, instead of thriving and living "for the sake of the boy" the women said, the Unravelled One had sunk into a deep depression that never lifted. She lived with her son in a one-room cottage at the edge of the village surviving on the good will of her neighbours. She only spoke to Mitya and Auntie Xena and never looked anyone else directly in the eye. The other Children were afraid that she had been put under the spell of some Baba Yaga that had wandered into the village from the woods one night, but I liked her. She would peek at me when Mitya and I brought wood from the woodpile or water from the well, and when I brought bread from our house there was a hint of a smile at the corner of her mouth.

We were not allowed to go carolling either in case one of the propagandists would report us to the Party as "an enemy of the people." That was the first time I heard that phrase. Uncle Misha told us that the propagandists were the men that Comrade Stalin had sent to teach the new way of life he designed for us. I wondered who "the enemy" was and of which people was he an enemy. My cousins and I moped by the fire feeling deprived of our Christmas pleasures of sweet treats and drinks that would have been enjoyed had we been free to roam and sing our way through the village as usual.

"Be patient, Verochka," Auntie said. "School will start soon and your heart will be full of Uncle Peter's wonderful songs and stories."

Uncle Peter was the village schoolmaster. He was loved by

19

everyone as he had been our teacher for years. Long before the war he had built a little house where, each day, those who could, came to school and worked their way through the lexicons. He was a fair but strict teacher. When school started after the New Year celebration which was January fourteenth, I would go with my cousins and finally be like the rest of the Children.

At last, New Year's Eve arrived. It was even more subdued than Christmas Eve.

"Uncle Misha says we can't go scattering," Mitya said. "That means I won't be able to get my first drinks with the men. It's not fair. It's the first year that I'm old enough to go round the village with them."

On New Year's Eve, the boys would fill a little sack with wheat and visit their neighbours. At each house they would sing:

I sew and blow and scatter
A wind of blessing, good health and plentiful harvest
And greet you with good fortune for the coming year.

As the blessing was recited, one of the boys would toss a small handful of grain around the door of the house in a sewing motion. He would be rewarded with a glass of liquid cheer which was offered by the womenfolk who remained at home to serve the men and sing a carol with them as they went through the village. We couldn't spare the grain and we couldn't trust Comrade Zabluda's propagandists so my cousins and I sat by the fire and moped ourselves into 1931.

Going to School

"**F**OR THE LOVE of God! Stand still so that I can braid your hair properly." I fidgeted impatiently as Auntie Xena tied the end of my braid with a piece of red wool and wrapped me in a heavy winter shawl.

"Yes, Auntie."

"And don't forget to take this bread for lunch." She handed me a little bundle wrapped in a piece of cheesecloth.

I ran after my cousins who were already halfway up the path that connected our house to the central path of the village.

We walked towards the square and the schoolmaster's house. Other Children joined us, happy to be out in the crisp air and brilliant sunshine. We breathed in deeply and blew out white clouds as our breath froze in the cold morning. The smell of the smoke that curled up from the chimneys teased my nose with its pleasant bitterness. Mitya met us where the path from the other side of the village joined the main one. He greeted me with a snowball on the shoulder.

"Stop that!" Vera Xenkovna said. "Philipovna has to be good or I'm in trouble."

Mitya tossed the next snowball at her back.

"I'll take the switch to you when we get home," she said.

She dropped her few books and was just about to cuff his ears when we saw Comrade Zabluda coming towards us.

"Are you idle brats out to cause some trouble?" he demanded.

Xenkovna picked up her books and brushed the snow off our shawls. The rest of the group moved close to her like a frightened flock of geese clinging to their mother.

"No, Sir," Mitya said. "We are on our way to school."

"Now listen here, you stupid boy," Comrade Zabluda said. "There are no 'sirs' in the Party. Everyone is an equal and you ignorant farmers will be taught to call us 'Comrade'."

"Yes, Comrade." Mitya flushed and hung his head.

I bit my lower lip. What was Comrade Zabluda going to do to him?

"There's no school today. Go home and find something useful to do or I'll give you some important papers to distribute for Father Stalin. Hopefully, there will be someone smart enough in your house to teach you what's in them."

Comrade Zabluda waved us on. Our little group was so stunned by what just happened that we started walking towards Comrade's wave even though it was in the opposite direction from home. As we passed through the village square, we saw that Uncle Peter's door was ajar.

"Uncle Peter?" Mitya called.

He stepped into Uncle Peter's house. I felt my heart pounding in my ears.

There was no answer.

"What on earth is this?" Xenkovna asked, stepping in behind Mitya. I started to cry. Where were the rest of our schoolmates?

There was no fire in the hearth. Uncle Peter's belongings were strewn all over the room and his slate and chalk were tossed about in pieces. A pile of his precious books lay in shreds on the floor. It looked as if there had been a scuffle. This was particularly strange as no one had ever heard the master so much as raise his voice, never mind his hand. Uncle Peter was nowhere in sight.

"I wonder where he is," Mitya said. "Who made such a mess of this place? If I find out who it was I'll punch his face off."

"We better go home," Xenkovna said. "Mama will tell us what to do."

As we passed the open door of the village's only store, we could see that the whole building was a shamble. What wasn't smashed or broken lay helter-skelter half off shelves or was thrown reck-lessly onto the table and floor. Uncle Anton who regularly sat at-tending to his customers was also gone. We stared in silence, for what seemed a long time.

"What is going on?" Mitya asked. "Who's wrecking everything around here?"

"I don't know," Xenkovna answered. "Let's go home." I could see her eyes glittering with tears. This kind of thing never happened in our village. We never touched property that belonged to another person and were taught to take care of things as they were usually expensive and hard to get in the first place.

Auntie bundled herself up and told Xenkovna to look after Vik-tor and the twins.

"We'll go to Anna," Auntie Xena said when we were outside again. "She would know best since she is Uncle Peter's sister."

The crunch of the snow echoed ominously as we made our way to Anna's house. The wind was picking up so the cold which felt so refreshing earlier in the morning was biting at my cheeks and nose. When we arrived, we were met by many of the villagers. Some stood praying; some were crying and others were wringing their hands in despair. Anna sat weeping.

"What's going on?" Auntie asked. She tried to hug the weeping woman, but Anna shrugged her away without saying a word.

Uncle Anton's brother spoke first.

"At midnight, Comrade Zabluda and his Chekists came and arrested Peter and Anton," he said. "Those devils took fifteen men off into the night and God knows where they are now." He looked like he was going to retch and two of the men caught him in their arms as he was about to faint away in grief. Someone found Anna's bottle of vodka and poured him a glass. Uncle Paulo held it to his lips.

"Take heart, brother. This will warm you for the present. The police have no business with him. There must be a mistake."

Mitya and I hung back from the grownups. We had never seen them look so bewildered. We were terrified, but what was it that we were afraid of? If the elders didn't know why these respected men were plucked from their homes, what did we Children know?

As the morning dragged on into the afternoon, villagers from the whole area came and went. We learned that the new village officials had helped to round up our own Soviet Party Council along with some of the prominent farmers. At dawn, more military men came and removed the families of the men who had been taken away. With barely the clothes on their backs, the women and Children were piled into sleighs. It was a terrible scene with all of those adults milling about in confused grief. Would I have to go away again? Where would I go and with whom? Later, we heard that the villagers were transported to the railway station and went on north to concentration camps in Siberia. We never saw them again. Siberia, the sound of that word could set one's bones a-shivering. Uncle Misha fashioned a wooden latch for inside of our door and insisted that Auntie Xena should keep it locked.

"What do you think that would do to help?" she said. "They can make anyone disappear if they should decide he is 'an enemy of the people'. Have you forgotten what they did in the war?"

"The latch will keep out strangers and could buy you a few precious minutes, should you need it, woman," he said.

These short, tense exchanges were becoming more frequent. Uncle Misha came home later and later from the endless meetings that took him away from the hearth in the evenings. He and Uncle Simon discussed a lot when they met with Uncle Paulo for their chess games on Sunday afternoons.

"If you look like you're co-operating with them," Uncle Simon said, "they may leave you alone. Besides, it might not be as bad as it was in the war. After all, we have all learned something since then. You should look at their new ideas. They are promising us that every man will get his share."

"I'm sticking to myself," Uncle Paulo said. "I'm an old man and surely they'll let me keep my orchard and the little garden I have left."

"We have to stand up to them," Uncle Misha shouted. "I'll not provoke them, but I won't allow them to confiscate my land."

And so it went until Auntie would threaten to take the vodka away and throw them and their chess board out into the snow.

"They can persuade all they want," I heard Uncle Misha say to Auntie one night when they thought we Children were asleep. "I'll never give up my land. What kind of man would I be if I gave up the land that my father and grandfathers farmed for generations ... and died for? I'd be nothing without it."

One Sunday morning when we arrived at the square for service at church, we were greeted with a carnival complete with a military band and merry-go-round. The music was strange, but its military rhythm was compelling. I found myself marching in time to its beat in spite of myself. I heard about merry-go-rounds from my cousins who had gone to the city, but I'd never seen one before that day. I wanted a ride on one of those beautifully painted horses. Up and down, round and round they went hypnotically calling me.

"Just one little ride, come!"

I could see Mitya close to the group of Children who were pushing towards this splendid wonder. Of course, he would be one of the first to check it out. I started to push through the crowd myself.

"Xenkovna, hold Philipovna tight," Auntie said. "Stay close together. I don't trust this thing. I'm getting Mitya away from it too."

But my eyes were glued to the circling horses—black, white and bay—with their beautifully adorned leathers and brasses. I stared at that merry-go-round till it felt as if the ground was spinning beneath my feet. I tried to pull Xenkovna closer for a better look, but she and Auntie, who had retrieved a yowling Mitya by grabbing his ear, held their ground and kept our family well back at the edge of the crowd. Suddenly, the music stopped; the merry-go-round stood still.

A man's voice boomed over a microphone and its echoes reverberated over the frosty village. In one move the crowd turned towards a platform that had appeared in the square during the night. We had all been so enthralled with the new attraction that we didn't even realize it was there.

Comrade Zabluda stood in the middle of the platform with his handful of underlings who patrolled and inspected the village to his left. To his right was a group of about eight men dressed in city clothes. They stared at us with harsh eyes and the carnival-like atmosphere in the square fell instantly under an invisible shroud.

I shivered in the cold. I was dressed in my woollen skirt with my embroidered blouse, for going to church, not for a morning out in the blowing wind. My Mama's shawl, that Auntie only let me wear for special days, was made of fine wool which didn't keep me as warm as the homespun one I used every day.

Comrade Zabluda didn't introduce the newcomers immediately. Instead, he wagged his neckless head and gave a speech, a long speech about how fortunate we were to be living in this beautiful country and how lucky we were to have Father Stalin and his Party to look after us and our affairs. Comrade Zabluda paced back and forth with stilted steps, occasionally interrupted by an awkward gesture of his short, stocky arms.

"You are not like the poor farmers in the west who are abused and exploited. They work long and hard only to end up so poor that their families don't have enough to eat," he said. "You are the luckiest and happiest farmers in the world. Father Stalin and the Party will make sure that you and your families will be safe and have more than you need."

I didn't understand a lot of his political talk because I was too little, but even so, I could see that his words and his gestures didn't match up.

As I stood with my teeth chattering in the frosty wind, Comrade Zabluda introduced the city folks. The group consisted of several men in full military dress with their shiny buttons and gleaming leather boots. The rest of the men looked just as important in their store-bought overcoats and big fur hats. After we got home, Auntie told Mitya and me that they were most likely officials of the Communist Party who were sent out to make sure that Comrade Zabluda was doing his job properly. Comrade Zabluda told us that they were here to help us learn about what Father Stalin and the Party expected. They would replace the council that had met its unfortunate demise and help us to form a proper village council which would guide us to a more prosperous life in a new system of collective farms.

"We will be good Comrades," Comrade Zabluda said. "He who is not with us is against us."

As if by some magic, the band started to play again.

Then the strangest thing of all happened. From all sides of the square people dressed in city clothes poured in. Some were dancing and twirling to the music. They carried red banners with different slogans written on them. I remember reading something about collective farms and "Long live the Party." I was numb with cold and overwhelmed with all of the commotion which had overtaken our normally quiet village. I stood frozen in place until I felt a sharp tug on my shawl.

"Come quickly! Don't say anything." Auntie Xena took advantage of the chaos and shepherded us back to our home. "Mitya, get in here so that no one sees you. And for the love of God! Keep quiet." Tears were streaming down her cold cheeks.

We learned later from the other villagers that Comrade Zabluda blocked the square off just after our family slipped away. He kept the people standing out in the cold till past nightfall and many were suffering from frostbite and exhaustion.

But Auntie could not keep us away from the inevitable. The movies came to our village soon after that Sunday. No cartoons or Charlie Chaplin like in Canada—just long tirades featuring happy workers in productive factories. We never knew when the army would come to our village with cannons and full manoeuvres. On such days, I would crawl under my parents' feather bed listening to the shells sail over our houses and fall and explode in the river. I would stick my fingers in my ears to try to get rid of the horrid sound. Other times, bands of city workers ensconced themselves in the village square and bombarded anyone they could find with their slogans and ready-made speeches which always extolled the virtues of Father Stalin and his new collectivized way of life.

"Didn't we want to be equals with the city workers?" they asked. One learned to anticipate an unwelcome knock at the door only to find a propagandist who would push his way in, day or night, harass our family for hours with more personalized barrages about the value of being a good Communist and then expect to be fed for his effort.

"That was close," Mitya said as he blew into Auntie's house one cold afternoon. "I thought I was in for it till I lost them in Uncle Paulo's orchard."

"Lost who?" I asked.

"The Propagandists again," he said. "They're trying to catch another fish to use for spreading a new batch of pamphlets. Can I hide out here for a while?"

Auntie nodded her consent. We were getting used to these un-expected visits.

Comrade Stalin charged everyone over the age of eight years to be part of the movement. A Child like Mitya or me would be given a bundle of pamphlets and then be escorted round the village as he distributed them to his family and friends. He was then paraded around the square and held up as a good example for the other Children. In March, it was announced that school would begin again.

"I don't want to go," I cried. "Uncle Peter won't be there."

"Be a good girl," Auntie said. "These are difficult times. If you don't go and if you don't obey your teacher, Uncle and I will have to answer for it. Put on your shawl and go with your cousins. You'll catch up with Mitya. I'm sure that by the time he pulls a few faces, you'll be fine."

Our classes were no longer conducted in Uncle Peter's small home. Comrade Zabluda had given the new schoolmaster one of the larger confiscated houses in which to set up a nine form school. The inner walls of the house had been taken out to make it into a hall of sorts and everything that had made the main room of the house look like a home had been removed. It was furnished with a few hard benches and tables.

The icon which would have been hanging in the eastern corner was gone and the walls were plastered with propaganda posters. A blackboard was crudely nailed onto the far end of the room. Our new textbooks from Kiev had not arrived yet. For the first term, all of the Children would learn the same lessons so that Comrade Asimov could assess where they should be placed. He wrote our lessons on the blackboard. We brought our own slate from home to write on. Students like Mitya who didn't have a slate would share with those who did.

"You might as well start learning the Party concept of sharing," he said. "We'll all be better once we understand that everyone owns everything equally." We were given some time to study and memorize the lesson. Then, one by one, we were called up to the front to recite it back. I could remember and recite quickly so I never stayed at the front of the room for long.

Comrade Asimov was a tall, thin man, dressed in black. We called him "The Snake" from the first day that he came to our school. His heavy spectacles hung precariously over his long nose and bushy black eyebrows. His voice was high and nasal. He would linger a bit on the S sound that whistled through the gap in his teeth when he spoke. When I stepped too close to him, I could smell a sour odour, something like stale vodka. He was ready to pounce at the first hint of a mistake a student would make. Mitya and I found that out by receiving a strapping after we were late because we stopped to look at a nightingale's nest that was unusually close to the path that branched off to the river.

"There'll be no bourgeois fairy tales in this classroom," Asimov proclaimed. "And forget about your precious Shevchenko, too. You are Little Russians. You will learn about the glory of Mother Russia, her history and her language—and most importantly, you will be trained to serve Father Stalin so that you can take your place in our better way of life."

I discovered that, in spite of Comrade Asimov, I loved the Russian language. The G that replaced the H of Ukrainian bubbled deliciously up from my throat and the different accent flowed easily off my tongue. My handwriting was beautiful even though I was the youngest and newest student. I soon became as much of a favourite as the curmudgeonly Asimov would allow.

Xenkovna often came home crying with humiliation, especially after Asimov belittled her for being so slow at answering, and particularly because she was the oldest student in the class, a fact that The Snake would never let her forget. She missed the patient Uncle Peter. She often lamented the loss of the stories of the Fire Bird, Olga and the Magpie, and Shura sowing her poppy seeds. She hated the lessons about being a good Party member and didn't know why we had to learn about Russian history.

For poor Mitya, school was a nightmare.

"Your Uncle ought to know better than to let you associate

with such a buffoon," Asimov said to me one day. "He'll bring you nothing but trouble."

Asimov took an instant disliking to Mitya. He hurried him through his recitations; he badgered him any time Mitya shifted on his too small bench and mimicked his wrong answers in front of the whole class. On the days that he couldn't hold his temper and answered back to the teacher, Mitya came home with bruises on his biceps or welts on his hands from Asimov's punches and metre stick. The other Children wouldn't play with us because they were afraid of what The Snake would do if he found out we were friends, but I didn't care about what The Snake thought. Nothing would separate me from my best and only friend.

"I hate that stupid bastard," Mitya said to Auntie one day. "He's nothing but a snake in the grass."

"Hush, Child. Those are adult words and you are still a boy. I know he is a bad man but you can't let anyone hear you speaking like that. They can do worse things to you than Asimov does."

One spring afternoon, I sat staring out of what used to be the living-room window. As usual, I had given my recitation and was waiting for my classmates to do theirs. The sun looked so inviting as it warmed the greening fields beyond the edge of the village. A nightingale was singing somewhere. I wished I were a boy like Michael and Alexander and old enough to be out in the fields helping Uncle Misha with the ploughing. I wanted to be out there, rolling down the hill of fragrant grass, behind Mitya's cottage or splashing in the creek, trying to catch some crayfish for Auntie to cook for supper. A fly buzzed by the window. I followed it with my distracted gaze.

If it comes near me, I'll catch it, I thought. *Then, what would I do? Hmmmm.*

As if by magic, the fly buzzed over in my direction. I stared at its eyes, at its wings and legs.

Could I tie you up and show you to Mitya without Comrade Asimov seeing you?

I carefully pulled out a piece of long hair from my braid. I made a little slipknot in its end and, to my own surprise, slipped it over the fly's leg on the first try. It was amazing! The fly moved away but could only go as far as the end of my strand of hair. I nudged Xenkovna.

She made a disapproving face and shook her head.

Mitya had just returned from the front of the room and was settling down into his seat. As he sat down, the fly buzzed up and tickled his cheek. I jerked it out of his sight. The next student began her recitation.

I let the fly move again. It tickled Mitya's arm. He flicked his hand at the fly. Again I pulled it away. He saw my hand move and was staring at the fly when it landed on the desk by Xenkovna's hand. She swatted at it and missed. I started to giggle. Mitya laughed out loud.

"What's so funny back there?" Comrade Asimov asked. He slammed his book down on the table.

I sat in terror, too stunned to let go of the strand of hair. The fly buzzed in circles around me. From the corner of my eye I saw Xenkovna grow pale.

"I'll teach you ignorant Children that school is a serious business," Asimov shouted. He ordered us to the front of the room. He handed Xenkovna the waste paper basket. "Bring some gravel from the path."

Mitya and I waited at the front of the class while our schoolmates stared at us in startled silence.

"Pour it out onto the floor." He gestured to the corner of the classroom when Xenkovna returned. "I'll teach you how to behave properly since your stupid parents don't know how to raise cultured Children." We were forced to pull up our skirts and kneel on the gravel with our bare knees. To make sure we got the message, Asimov came and put his hands on our shoulders in turn. He bore down hard so that we could feel his full weight and held for what seemed a good ten minutes.

"That is women's punishment," Asimov said as he returned to Mitya. "Men are dealt with more directly."

He took off his belt and right there, in front of the class, administered such a beating that Mitya's shirt was stained with blood. Mitya's face turned to grey, but he would not let one tear drop fall. For an hour, we knelt and cried; Mitya stood. The class sat, not daring to look at us directly. Some of the smaller Children were sniffling. I wasn't sure if I cried more for me or for the pain and humiliation I caused for poor Mitya.

"Class is over now," Comrade Asimov said. "Make sure you come back tomorrow with a better attitude."

"I can't wait till I grow big enough to kill that bastard," Mitya said through clenched teeth. "My father died fighting men like him and I will too."

"I don't want you to die!" I started to cry all over again as we walked home in the spring sunshine.

"My God!" Auntie cried when she saw Mitya. She crossed herself before grabbing a cloth and basin of cold water. "I'll clean you up before your poor mother comes all of the way undone. That's all she needs to see—you covered in blood."

"I hate those Party bastards!" Mitya shouted. "I hate them."

"You must never let anyone hear you say that. I told you already not to use that word," Auntie said as she washed Mitya's bloody back. "You don't know who their friend is. You can think what you like, son. Just be very careful who you share it with. I'm sorry if I'm hurting you." She found an old shirt of Uncle's and threw Mitya's damaged one into the fire.

"It doesn't hurt," Mitya said. But he winced as she applied the iodine to the open wounds on his shoulder.

"Don't tell your mother what happened either," Auntie said. "You don't know what she will say to anyone or what they would do to her if she did. Come to Uncle or me if anyone says anything to either of you—and for Heaven's sake, don't forget to say your prayers. Now go home. It's time for supper."

When Auntie recounted what had happened, the usually quiet Uncle Misha flew into a rage. He picked me up, put me over his knee and spanked me.

"As much as I love you," he said, "you must never ever misbehave again. You can't afford it. My family can't afford it. The only way we can survive is to be inconspicuous. You can think what you want but you can't say it. You can't do what you want either. These are dangerous times, Child."

"Enough!" Auntie shouted through her own tears. "We've had enough unpleasantness for today."

"She and Mitya better pay attention," Uncle Misha said. "I can only do so much to protect them, and we have enough with our own Children to keep safe. We don't know what these idiots are capable of."

I sat sobbing, my bottom sore and my knees still peppered with stubborn bits of gravel that refused to come out. Yet a part of me knew that this whole thing was my fault. If I hadn't caught that fly, none of this would have happened.

"If my father were here he would never spank me," I cried. I went to my sewing machine and moved the treadle. I wished my *Tahto* were here because I was so sure he would have done something to that awful Comrade Asimov. I cried and watched the treadle go up and down—the wheels of the machine go round and round—till my head swam and I fell asleep on the floor beside what was left of my mother.

Our Last Easter

W HILE THE MEN from the city, with their new rules and
ideas were changing our village, spring arrived with its pro-
fusion of cherry blossoms and nightingale song. As soon as the terrible
Asimov dismissed the Children from class, Mitya and I headed for
the river to play. He said that it was too early to catch crayfish so
we crawled through the willows to look for birds' nests and pretty
stones which we threw into the water. He could always throw further than me because he was a boy, but I enjoyed trying to beat him
just the same.

Sometimes, I sat staring into the rushing cold river, mesmerized
by the way the sunlight sparkled on its surface like jagged bits of
fractured mirror. I breathed in the rich smell of awakening earth or
I laid back on a mossy patch and stared at the puffy clouds floating
in the brilliance of blue above wondering if my parents could see
me and if they knew that I was all right. There weren't as many of
the Party men around either. There were no more evening meetings
and Uncle Misha said that the men were needed for ploughing and
sowing or making sure that the collectives were being managed
properly. So, we could take it a little easier.

"How long are you going to lie around in dreamland?" Mitya
said, interrupting one of my meditations. "I found some pussy willows

that haven't opened into leaves yet. Let's cut them and bring them to Auntie. She always likes it when I bring these." He took his little knife and cut an armful of willow branches from the dense growth of budding trees.

"It's so soft," I said as I stroked their furry, green-grey pods with my index finger and rubbed one against my cheek. I had never picked pussy willows before.

"We'll be really quiet," he said. "I'll get some water from the well and you can make them look nice. She'll be so surprised."

But it was Mitya and I who were surprised. As we sneaked up to the doorstep of my house with our pail full of willow branches, we heard voices in the kitchen. They weren't the quiet voices of Auntie and Uncle Misha in one of their discussions; they were shrill voices, raised in argument.

"You've enough Children to feed," one voice said.

"Did I ever bother you for food?" Auntie Xena responded. "We've all had enough even though it was a hard winter."

"But you already have six Children and besides, I could use her help in the garden."

"I see, now that she can be used to work in your garden you remember that you have a niece, and more food than your poor sister. Where were you when the snow was deep and the wind was blowing?"

"You know I have my sewing to do. Be reasonable, Xena. I'm sure you won't miss the orphan with all of the Children you have of your own."

It was Auntie Lena. Why was she here?

"So that's how it is with you!" Auntie Xena was shouting. It was the first time I heard her raise her voice. "So now she's the orphan Child—not your niece or your sister's daughter? Your own flesh and blood!"

My chest felt like someone was squeezing the air out of it.

"What's an orphan?" I asked Mitya.

"Someone with no parents."

"It sounds so bad."

"Don't worry, Philipovna," he said with a little smile. "You'll get used to it. People say things about me all the time."

"ORPHAN. It sounds like something a Baba Yaga would leave behind."

"Only if you listen to it. So don't listen."

My pail bumped on the step distracting the women.

"There you are, Vera Philipovna," Auntie Xena said. Her voice was now smiling but her face was wet with tears. "I was about to send Viktor to find you. Come, I have a special surprise for you."

I followed her into the kitchen with my eyes lowered.

"Do I have to go with Auntie Lena?"

"Isn't that a fine way to say 'hello' to your aunt? Xena, you should teach her some manners," Auntie Lena shouted.

"Don't be silly," Auntie Xena said lightly. "It's Willow Sunday so Auntie has come to help me make some new dresses and get ready for Easter, haven't you, Lena?"

Lena looked down her nose at Mitya and me and said nothing.

Auntie Xena looked at my pail.

"Good Children, we need fresh pussy willow branches to take to church tomorrow," she said. "Comrade Zabluda has given us permission to hold church services and we found a new priest to minister for the holy days."

Our old priest had disappeared shortly after Uncle Peter, the schoolmaster, and was thought to be among the villagers that were taken to Siberia. I shivered at the thought of Siberia. The sound of that word made me feel cold even on this warm, spring day.

"But the church isn't a church anymore," Mitya said.

He was right on that account. During one of the military exercises the brigade destroyed our beautiful little church, breaking windows and pulling down the crosses. They shot bullet holes into the icons, toppled the precious bells and took away the altar. It was now the centre for the military from which our area was watched and controlled. In the evenings, it doubled as the theatre where we would be forced to watch propaganda movies. Eventually, some of the villagers would come to terrible ends when the Comrades turned the sanctuary into the *kolhosp* court that could try and sentence anyone it pleased with no oversight from any government.

"We're having the service in the school house," Auntie Xena said.

Many of the village families came the next morning. The willows were blessed in the traditional Orthodox way. It seemed to be a sad service considering the event that was being celebrated. We ran about after church smacking each other with the willow branches and chanting the age-old verses: "It is the tree that hits you, not me that hits you." And: "Soon there will be a red Easter egg for you." Auntie said that we could be happy for Christ's arrival, but we had to do it quietly. Hopefully, the Comrades wouldn't be here forever. When they would go away maybe we could even walk through the village waving the willow branches just like the disciples waved their palms.

"In your dreams," Auntie Lena said.

When we came home from the service, Auntie Xena put the willows into a china vase with the embroidery design of our village painted all over it. She placed it under the icon of the Last Supper.

"Never disrespect the blessed things," she said. "Once something is blessed, it is sacred. It is no longer like the everyday things of this world even though it still may look like it is."

We ate some borscht and rye bread rubbed with garlic and butter. I loved the sweet beets in the borscht and the pungent smell of the garlic, but when Auntie Xena spooned out generous scoops of *smetana*, I begged for more. The Children went to play while the adults sat out in the afternoon sun with their tea and glasses of vodka. Uncle Simon and Uncle Paulo came with their chessboards so that all of the men could play. Taras, a young neighbour of Uncle Simon, came with them, lugging his accordion. I could see Xenkovna blushing whenever he looked at her, but when he asked Uncle Misha for permission to take her walking, Xenkovna agreed warmly. Some of our neighbours stopped by to visit Auntie Lena but Uncle Misha reminded everyone to keep the festivities down so as not to attract too much attention.

The following week was a flurry of preparation. I stayed home from school to help Xenkovna watch the Children while the aunts measured and cut some of my Mama's cloth for new skirts for Auntie and Xenkovna. The wheel of my Mama's sewing machine whirred as Auntie Lena treadled and refitted their old skirts for me and my little cousins.

"What a miracle this machine is. Pretty soon Philipovna should start learning how to use it," Auntie Lena said. The aunts exchanged knowing looks and Auntie Xena went on ironing.

The embroidered sashes and vests with their red and black cross-stitching and lattice work of grape vines were taken out of the trunk. The smell of the mothballs in which they were stored burned my throat and nose as I spread them out on the bushes to air.

"Xenkovna can wear your Mama's vest and sash till you grow into it yourself," Auntie Xena said. "She'll take good care of it. You can wear the one she's grown out of till then." I stood in my traditional Ukrainian outfit and spun around so that the skirt would flare out like an umbrella. A rare smile managed to squeeze across Auntie Lena's sullen face as she watched me.

"We'll have to tame that wild hair of hers," she said. "She's got enough for two—and so curly."

"Don't mind that. Once I'm done with it she'll have a braid that'll be the envy of the village," Auntie Xena said. "When she's grown, she'll even be more beautiful then Barbara was."

"If you can control her. Since I've been here all I've seen her do is run wild with that Mitya instead of learning something about her mother's craft. She can't even stand still long enough for me to see that the hem is straight."

Uncle and the boy cousins' shirts were also remade and mended. After a storm of words, Auntie Xena convinced her sister-in-law to mend an old shirt for Mitya.

"He must present himself decently before the Cross on Easter Sunday," Auntie Xena said. "Surely, The Good Lord will reward your kindness."

Auntie Lena sniffed her usual distaste.

On Thursday the cooking began. The aunts made a *holodetz* from pork hocks and meat Auntie Lena brought, while I sat on the back step and grated the last of the horseradish.

"Sit with the breeze blowing away from you," Auntie Xena said, wiping her hands on her apron. "And for the love of God, don't touch your eyes while you're grating. They'll feel like they're on fire." She went to her cold cellar to check on the progress of her present batch of *smetana* and cottage cheese. We had churned the butter before Auntie Lena's arrival.

"And don't dawdle," Auntie Lena said. "There's lot of work to do when you finish."

I grated till the muscles in my arm were burning, but I didn't mind the pain. At least I didn't have to sit in the kitchen with Auntie Lena's stares and nasty comments. Meanwhile, they made *varenyky*, some with potato and cheese and others with fried sauerkraut and onions. The whole house was filled with spicy steam that made my mouth water. Xenkovna helped with the *paska* because she loved to bake bread. She particularly liked to fashion the little birds and flowers that would decorate the top. When the *paska* cooled, Auntie Xena chose the best one for the Easter basket and the second best to save for the following Sunday when we all would go to the cemetery to celebrate Memory Eternal. We would cut small pieces of this special *paska* and give them out to anyone who came to our graves for the blessing of the remembered ones.

On Saturday, I woke up to the aunts bustling around the kitchen.

"Where did you find those?" Auntie Lena asked.

"Katerina's chickens always seem to lay white eggs," Auntie Xena said. "They'll make beautiful colours, won't they?"

"I'm sure you'll have to do more than your share to repay the old witch," Auntie Lena said. "You know how that old baba can hang on to an obligation."

The aunts giggled like schoolgirls as they boiled first onion peels and then beet and carrot peelings in pots of water. Then, they cooked eggs till they were sure they were hard-boiled and dipped them into the pots of boiling peelings. They added small amounts of vinegar to the pots to help keep the eggs from cracking.

"Can I try?" I asked, wrinkling my nose over the smell of the sour steam.

"Be very careful," Auntie Xena said. She gave me an egg balanced on a big spoon and I dipped too.

"Make sure you turn it," she said and gently guided my hand so as to turn the egg in the simmering water till the shell absorbed the colour evenly.

"Look, look, it's such a pretty golden colour," I shouted. It was the first time I ever coloured an Easter egg.

"Stop dancing around with it. You might drop it—and for Heaven's sakes, don't splash the colour around the kitchen."

"Does that girl ever stay still?" Auntie Lena said. But she did have one of her rare smiles on her face. She gave me a cloth with a little piece of butter in the centre of it.

"When each egg is completely dry," she said, "rub it till it shines. Be careful not to crack any of them. We won't have any extra."

I rubbed for hours and then arranged and rearranged the amazing eggs in different patterns on a big platter. Meanwhile, the aunts laid a beautifully embroidered cloth into the basket that would carry our breakfast for its blessing. Great Grandmother had stitched the cloth with her own hand and it was only taken out for special occasions. They put a *paska* in the centre. Around it they placed some of everything we would eat for the holy breakfast, a piece of smoked ham, a hunk of cheese, some sausage, a small container of salt, butter and even a little glassful of the horseradish I grated on Thursday. When all of that was in, they took some of my eggs and decorated the top of the basket. I thought it was perfect until Auntie Lena reached into her bag and pulled out a carefully wrapped bundle.

"This should do it," she said. "I hope none of them are broken."

There on her white cloth lay four fancy designed eggs. They had little birds and sprigs of flowers on their sides with different squiggles of colour between the pictures. Two of them had flowers on their ends and interlacing designs sprouted out from between the points of each petal. I thought my eyes would pop just from looking at them. A new candle was stuck into the centre of the *paska* and the basket was ready.

"If you like colouring eggs so much," Auntie Lena said, "come home with me and I'll teach you how to write *pysanky*."

I looked hard at her but the word "orphan" still rang in my ears. I couldn't answer. I felt dirty or was it different? Then it was time for all of us Children to wash and go to bed.

"The sun is still up and it's not even supper time yet," my cousin Viktor said.

"You'll be happy for the rest when we wake you at midnight," Auntie Xena said. "The service lasts all night and you have to be there for as much of the liturgy as you can."

"Why can't we go like at Christmas?"

"Because it's Easter and it's more important than Christmas."

"Why?" I asked.

"Vera Philipovna, everyone is born just like Jesus was, but no one rises again. If you don't remember anything else I ever teach you, Child, remember, Christ suffered for all of us—for every sin we all commit. On this day he rose as we must all rise from beneath anything that comes our way. Suffering purifies our soul and we all need to learn to do it with His Grace. When we die and go to

Heaven we'll be perfect and we won't have to suffer any more. Now, go to sleep."

"Will Mama be watching?" I asked.

Her hazel eyes glittered and she rubbed them with the back of her hand.

"Yes, Child. Now do what I ask." She gently stroked my mass of brown hair.

I was so excited that I thought I would never go to sleep. But sleep I did and, in what seemed a very few minutes, I was awakened by enthusiastic voices in the kitchen. Uncle George, who couldn't leave the ploughing for the whole week, arrived to join his wife for Easter. He brought Godfather with him.

"Why is Godfather here? Is he going to make me go home with Auntie Lena?" I asked Auntie Xena as she braided my hair.

"Good Heavens, Child! Don't carry on so," she said.

"You look just like your mother," Godfather said, tearfully, when Auntie presented me to him in my grown-up Ukrainian outfit. "You'll be a lucky woman if your character is as much like your mother's as your looks are."

It was past midnight when we all walked to service. There were no more fancy icons. I wondered what happened to the beautiful ones that used to hang in the church. The men stood, bareheaded on the right facing the priest and the women stood on the left, their heads wrapped in embroidered *platoks* as was the custom since the days St. Vladimir brought Christ to the Ukrainian countryside almost a thousand years ago. Only the very old or sick were allowed to sit through a service that would last all night.

The aunts whispered about who was there and who was not, noting that most of the families who worked on the collective were absent. So were a lot of the young people who normally sang in the choir. I loved to hear the music. It wasn't lively and dancing like Uncle's music when he played his guitar. The notes were drawn out and full with big words that I didn't really understand. But the *hospodi pomilui* was a special thread between Jesus and me and if I hung on to it and the words of the Lord's Prayer, I would surely see my parents someday. I pictured myself floating up on that beautiful sound, like the chimney smoke does on a winter's day. Up, up, I could go right to my mother and father on that swell of sound if I could only be good enough. But I was an orphan now. Did God want orphans in Heaven? Would He let me in?

The service went on. Kneel, then stand; stand, then kneel. The schoolroom that had become the church for this night got hot and stuffy with the smell of sweat, mothballs and incense. I started to feel tired. I tried not to yawn, but soon I couldn't hold it back, and once I started, I couldn't stop. I tried to focus on the candles at the front of the room. I imagined the faces of people I knew in the clear spot of the candle flame. Auntie said that a dead person's soul could go there when they wanted to be remembered by the living. If I concentrated, would God put my Mama's face in one of those candles so that I could finally see what she really looked like? Did I really look as beautiful as she was supposed to have been? A gentle tug on my sash broke into my contemplations.

I don't know how, but Mitya had squeezed between the praying women and, without making a sound or sudden movement, motioned for me to follow. I whispered to Auntie Xena that I had to tend to a call of nature and quietly slipped out from among them. The cool spring night woke me up immediately.

"What are we going to do out here?" I asked.

"Aren't you bored with all of that praying yet?"

"Yes," I said, lying. I wouldn't dare tell him the truth in case Jesus would get angry and keep me away from my parents if I died someday. I also didn't want anyone to go into that special place that opened when I prayed at church.

"Well, I am, and I want to go to the river so that I can see it at night."

"The river? Won't the Baba Yaga and her goblins be out?"

"Stop being a big baby. We'll just have a quick look and come back before anyone notices."

I hesitated for a moment. The sky was so black and the stars so bright. The air was damp with its springtime smell of awakening earth. It was quiet. The only sound was the song of the river, low and compelling.

"All right, I'll come but we'll just take a quick peek. I don't want to get in trouble."

We tiptoed through the village. Its houses seemed unfamiliar, dark and still in a fairy tale landscape. Even the dogs were asleep. The birch trees glistened in their silver ghostliness casting their branches in fingers of shadow in the moonlight. We didn't speak till we passed Auntie's house.

"Let's go round that woodpile and across the field," Mitya said. "If we cut through Uncle Paulo's orchard, we can make it faster."

"No, we can't. Your white shirt will get dirty and I can't get mud on my new skirt. Auntie Lena will kill me if I do."

Mitya shrugged his shoulders and held to the main path that would bring us to the riverbank. I followed behind like the page in the song of Good King Wenceslas. The twigs that snapped under my feet seemed to echo like thunder claps through the silent village. The path skirted the orchard whose opening cherry blossoms looked as if they were glowing in the moonlight. Their fragrance beckoned to me on a breeze that seemed to be stirring because we were disturbing the quiet night. Mitya's longer legs covered the distance more quickly than mine so I soon was breathless. Suddenly, he stopped. I almost made him lose his balance when I bumped into his back.

"Be still!" he hissed under his breath.

"Why?" I whispered. "There's no one here."

I stared at the silver ribbon of moonlit water that cut through the land below the bluff on which we stood. It wasn't far from the spot where we found the pussy willows just one week ago. The scene was familiar, but eerily beautiful. Mitya was not looking at the river. He stood rigid, his arm gesturing for me to look upstream. The acrid smell of smoke had taken the place of the smell of cherry blossoms. There on the bank, not far from the water's edge, was a roaring bonfire with people around it.

"Who could that be?" I asked.

"I don't know," he said. "We'll go and check it out." He moved toward the fire.

I grabbed at his shirt.

"You can't go there. What if they catch you and take you to Siberia."

"I'm just having a look."

"But they could hurt you. They'll see your white shirt."

"I'm not going right up to them, silly. I'm going to look from between the trees. You can wait here if you're too scared to come along."

I didn't want to go with Mitya but, as he moved away, the darkness seemed to be coming toward me from out of the willows. If there were some evil spirit hiding in the tangled bushes, I wouldn't see it until it caught me with its claws or teeth. Auntie wouldn't even know where to look if I should suddenly disappear. By the time Mitya was just ten metres ahead of me, the weight that was rooting my feet lifted and I put my hand over my mouth to keep from crying out his name. I scrambled through the bushes after him. He moved nimbly, without a sound until we approached a little lookout directly above where the fire crackled.

"You've been here before?" I whispered. "Who's down there?"

He put his finger to his lips. The more I looked, the more questions I had. There, right under our noses, was Comrade Zabluda. His usual companions from the Party weren't with him. There were some strange men that looked like farmers, but also there were men we all knew. Uncle Paulo, whose orchard we had just passed on our way, Uncle Simon who liked to talk to Uncle Misha about politics and Uncle Ivan whose nostrils turned up like a pig and flared when he was angry. What were they doing here? And who were the strangers? We could see that they passed a flask as they talked.

"I'm going to slide down a bit closer," Mitya said, "so I can hear what they're saying."

Before I could make a protest, he moved forward. We slid down the sloping side of the bluff just out of the range of the firelight.

"How easy it is to bait their trap if you get to know their weakness," Comrade Zabluda said, snickering. "The Comrades in Moscow say that the buffoons who pray the most are the ones that are the most attached to their land. That priest better have his wits about him. I'll have lots of questions about who was at his service."

"They better be praying well," Uncle Ivan said. "They'll need their prayers by the time I'm through with them."

"You'll wait for instructions," Comrade said. "No tricks till I give the word."

Uncle Ivan leaned back, sighing and sipping again from the flask.

"Remember, tonight is a set-up. The ones who pray the best will be the most difficult nuts to crack. Some of them will die before they surrender their land to the *kolhosp*; I'm sure of that. We'll start the friendly way. Paulo, your job is to persuade them, if you can. When that doesn't work, Ivan, you'll put your men on them. Once your men have all of the land, we'll switch groups and you will go to other villages. The word is that the grain quotas are going to be higher this fall so we have to get a handle on things sooner than later. Now, let's have the names of those who're praying rather than working for the Party."

Simon started and followed by Paulo and Ivan, they named the heads of all of the families we left in the schoolhouse. How long could I crouch without crying? Were we all going to Siberia? I touched Mitya's arm and signalled that we should go, but he wouldn't move. When he finally did look, I saw my fear reflected in his moonlit face. Then, one of the men rose and started walking toward where we were hiding.

"I'll toss one last load onto the fire," he said. "We'll drink one more toast in honour of those praying church mice and then I'll have to be heading home, unless you have more duties for us, Comrade."

He started towards the spot where we sat. I don't know how, but I snapped a branch with my foot.

"Did you hear that?" Uncle Ivan asked. He scanned the bushes above him. "What's that white there?"

"It's probably a patch of moonlight—or maybe that extra swig of the flask. Nobody in his right mind would be out here at this time of night," Uncle Paulo said.

Mitya and I started like frightened animals and scurried through the brush.

"Ho, what's up there?" Comrade Zabluda roared.

"Don't know," Uncle Ivan said. "We're going to check it out."

The willow growth was dense with many branches growing low to the ground. Mitya pulled me under and through the brush with a well-practiced hand.

"Don't worry," he whispered. "They're too big to get through here."

I couldn't answer. My vision blurred with tears and my throat closed. I followed or was pulled like a lifeless thing without knowing where I was going. The branches grabbed at my hair and my clothes and I could feel the sting from a bleeding scratch on my cheek.

The roots sprang up from the ground like magic booby traps. The men crashed like great bears behind us. I had to work hard to keep my feet moving. We crawled up to the top of the bluff over the fire. Then Mitya stopped. He took a stone from the ground and threw it hard. It hit Uncle Ivan's head. He grabbed another and pinged it off Uncle Paulo's shoulder. The distraction stopped the men. We scrambled away again. We ran away from the bluffs through Uncle Paulo's orchard, across the field without stopping till we were behind the safety of Uncle Misha's woodpile.

"Now what are we going to do?" I whined through my tears. My breath came in sharp bursts.

"We're going to wash up and go back to church."

"Are you going to tell everyone when we get there?"

"Does Uncle Misha know that Uncle Paulo and Uncle Ivan are friends with those men?"

"I don't know. I think I should wait and tell Uncle Misha first. I don't want to get us into any more trouble than we're already in." He looked down at the twigs on his newly laundered shirt. We brushed each other off and walked back toward the schoolhouse. We tried to sneak into the service unnoticed. But it was too late.

The dawn was just beginning to blush pink when we arrived on the village square. The congregation was marching out behind the priest and his choir which was still singing its hallelujahs. The women carried their baskets and discreetly jockeyed for the best positions around the priest for the ritual of blessing the food they would soon serve to their families. The more holy water that actually touched the basket, the happier they would be. Their greetings of "Christ is risen" and "Truly He is risen" rang like silver bells through the morning air. I longed to be safe among their mothball smelling vests and sashes, muffled within the safety of my family.

Auntie Lena's eyes shot lightning bolts at us when she spotted us slinking towards the group but Auntie Xena looked sadly down at my dishevelled skirt and put her finger on her cheek as if she were touching the scratch on mine. Mitya and I had no option but to stay where we were. We watched the congregation from the edge of the square. The magic of the celebration was gone. My shame for getting my skirt dirty branded my cheeks and the newly discovered danger weighed more than any water I had ever carried. My eyes kept searching every inch of the square to see if the men from the fire followed us. There was nowhere to hide so we stood there till the ceremonies were over.

As each family passed us on the way home, they either pointed or looked away. We knew we'd be "present" at every table in the village over this Easter breakfast. Uncle Misha motioned us to join as his family approached. He walked as if nothing had happened till we got to the path that forked off to our house. When the rest of the family turned off the main path, his hands clamped down hard, one on Mitya's shoulder and one on mine. Godfather stayed behind, too.

"There better be a good reason for the two of you to be looking the way you are," he said. "I don't want to spoil this blessed day, but by God, I'll tan the both of you if I have to."

I was too frightened to cry. The memory of the last spanking was never far from my mind whenever I was in trouble. To make it worse, Godfather was here to watch my humiliation.

Mitya stared at his muddy shoes.

"We're waiting," Uncle Misha said.

Slowly, Mitya pushed back his shoulders and met Uncle's blistering gaze.

"It was my fault," he admitted. With a stammer in his voice he told Uncle Misha and Godfather about how he squeezed through the women and enticed me out to the river. But as he recounted the story he gained confidence. By the time he described the men by the fire, Uncle's face softened.

"Are you sure about Paulo? I knew that Simon and Ivan were sympathizers, but Paulo? Are you absolutely sure?"

"We've got a much bigger problem than this little bit of mischief. Did they get a good look at who threw the stones?" Godfather asked.

"No, I don't think so," Mitya said.

"Say nothing to anyone," Uncle said. "I need to take some time to figure out what to do. The Comrades won't let this pass lightly. Let's hope nobody says anything about seeing the two of you after church. And there's no mistaking that Simon and Paulo were both there?"

"Yes, sir," Mitya said. "And Uncle Ivan, too."

"Philipovna, you better be especially good," Uncle Misha said. "Lena won't be feeling kindly for the job you've done on that outfit after all of that work she's done for you."

"I'm sure any punishment we can dream up won't match what you'll be suffering till she goes home tomorrow," Godfather said, chuckling. "Now, Mitya, go fetch your mother for breakfast."

"Will I have to go home with Auntie Lena?" I asked.

Uncle Misha shook his head. He put his hand gently on my arm and I walked between the two men toward the house where breakfast was already on the table.

Easter Sunday

❋❋❋✦❋❋❋

MY HAND HADN'T dropped from the door latch of Auntie's cottage before a storm of questions confronted me from within.

"Where did you go?"

"Why did you sneak out of church?"

"How did you get that scrape on your cheek?"

But it was Auntie Lena's stare that glued my feet to the threshold. Her eyes said it all: *I should know better than to make nice clothes for an orphan!*

I could hear her words screaming in my ears and could see fire in the disdain that blazed in her eyes, even though she hadn't uttered a word yet. I tried to back out of the doorway, but Godfather put his hands on my waist and lifted me in. I stared at the streak of April sunlight that stole across the white tablecloth, turning Xenkovna's *Paska* into an even more beautiful shade of rosy golden brown. The candle which had been blessed at church flickered in the little breeze of cool spring air that accompanied us in.

"Is all of the blessed food on the table?" Uncle Misha asked.

"Is that all you can say?" Auntie Lena said, shrieking. "No wonder that filthy little orphan runs wild and has no respect for her elders. Just send her home with me for a month. I'll show her a thing or two about how a young lady behaves. Poor Barbara. What would she be saying if she were here today?"

"Today is to the glory of God, our risen Saviour," Uncle Misha said calmly. "Christ is risen." His eyes matched Auntie Lena's with equal fury.

"Truly, He is risen," the family chorused.

"But ..." Her finger wagged frantically in my direction.

"Today is for the glory of God," Uncle Misha said again. He took his seat at the table which was positioned in front of one of the sleeping benches by the fire so that the Children could sit on them while the extra adults sat on the chairs.

"Sit here," Xenkovna said as she beckoned me over to her and squeezed the rest of the cousins more tightly on the bench.

"At least that beggar and his crazy mother aren't here to crowd an already full table," Auntie Lena said.

"Lena, remember your Bible. As you have done it for one of these, so you have done it for me." It was Godfather who spoke this time. "Mitya and the Unravelled One have nowhere else to go. You know they are part of the family."

Auntie Lena sighed loudly.

"Let us pray." Godfather crossed himself three times with his right hand as all faithful Orthodox men did and began to recite the Lord's Prayer. We prayed with him in a subdued, but hurried, mumble as everyone was anxious for breakfast. But Godfather crossed himself after the "Amen" and kept on praying.

"Blessed Father. You know we are living in difficult times. The wolf is knocking at our door; the Enemy hungers for our land. We beg, in Your Son's Holy Name, for your help and protection even as you held the Children of Israel in your hand and led them through the bondage of slavery and wanderings in the desert. Spare us from the wrath of evil masters and save us from the weakness of a divided house. Bless us with your bounty as you have blessed our ancestors for these past thousand years. We thank you for our health, our family and for the abundance of this table on this Your Holy Day. Amen." He crossed himself again.

"Isn't that a lot of praying?" Auntie Lena said. "We've just spent the whole night in church."

"We should probably be spending every night in church these days," Uncle Misha said.

"Enough gloom," Auntie Xena said, wiping her hands with the corner of her apron. She forced a smile and began cutting up Xenkovna's bread into little pieces.

"That daughter of yours seems to have inherited Barbara's hands for bread-making," Auntie Lena said. She smiled approvingly at Xenkovna. "It's so light and fluffy. Too bad her own Child is so backwards."

"Lena, for the love of God, it's Easter Sunday. Could we not just have a pleasant breakfast?"

Mitya and his mother came in while we were praying. Auntie Xena found room for them at the corners of the table. The Uncles poured glasses of wine which they brought from town — even a small taste for every Child. Auntie Lena began filling up our plates with the blessed food.

I was hungry, but when I tried to eat, it wouldn't go down. Xenkovna's bread stuck in my throat. The spices from the sausages teased my nose, but I sat playing with them, pushing pieces of them through the horseradish that I had so laboriously grated. I didn't crack the blessed egg that was set aside for me.

"Philipovna, you must eat your blessed food," Auntie Xena said. "We can't throw it out. That would be a sin."

"I'll have her holy egg, if she's not going to eat it," Viktor said from the bench.

"Speaking of sins, so is sneaking around behind everyone's back when you're supposed to be in church," Auntie Lena said, waving off Viktor's offer.

Mitya hung his head.

"Lena, may I remind you that you are in my home and I am the one looking after our niece." Auntie Xena flung a piece of the holy bread onto her sister-in-law's plate.

"Maybe someone else could do a better job. Look at the beautiful new clothes I made her. A field rat looks better than she does right now. Besides, her bad behaviour can put all of you in danger."

Uncle Misha pushed his chair back with a clatter and stood over her with his fist clenched.

"I will deal with our niece. I have six Children; you have none. Who do you think has more experience? You are not to say another word about this matter as long as you are here." He sat back down gulping his wine while everyone at the table stared in silence.

The Unravelled One started to cry.

"That's enough," Uncle George finally said, fixing his dove grey eyes on his wife. "There are so many ill winds blowing around our villages. We can't allow this little incident to destroy our family. The Children will have to own up to what they did, whatever it is, and we'll do our best to protect them."

"Well, I'm not taking an ungrateful wretch like her home with me, that's for sure," Auntie Lena said. "She'd be a disgrace. No matter what I would do with a wilful Child like her, she'd never be good enough to take out into a civilized world."

"It's just as well if that's how you feel," her husband said.

The adults went on with their discussion but I no longer cared what they said. As long as I never had to go home with Auntie Lena, I would be able to deal with anything life could throw at me.

After breakfast, the younger Children were wrapped in blankets and tucked up on the hearth to catch up on their missed night's sleep. The adults took their tea and vodka out onto the grass in the brightening day.

Mitya and I wanted to go to the river. It was too early for crayfish, but there would be a nightingale's nest or maybe the last of the pussy willows. We didn't dare ask. We didn't have to speak to each other to know that last night's campfire discovery would come back to our door. We finally went to the room where my mother's sewing machine was stored and sat around moping. Out of habit, I started to spin its wheel.

"Do you ever wonder what she was like?" Mitya asked.

"No," I answered. "I'm sure she was like Auntie Xena. No one could be nicer than her. But I do wish I had my own parents. Then no one would be fighting about me or scolding like Auntie Lena always does. I'm sure my *Tahto* wouldn't let her say all of those horrible things about me, either. Do you miss your *Tahto*?"

"Yes, all of the time. I can't wait to grow up and kill all of the men that killed him."

"But that would be scarier than last night."

"Maybe so, but life is always scary and if he were here my Mama wouldn't be so sick either."

I could see him swallow hard. I never saw him do that before.

"Mitya, don't ever talk like that." It was Auntie Xena. She came into the room with a steaming dish of pale gold liquid. "You never know who might be listening. I can't begin to imagine the sadness you have in your heart for your *Tahto*. He was a wonderful man and we all loved him. He would be so proud of you, especially of how you take care of your poor Mama. Please, Child, for your good and for the good of your Mama try not to say such things. Ask God to heal your heart."

"I don't want to," he shouted. "I want to kill every one of those idiot Comrades. Their Children have their *Tahto* to come home to each day. They don't have to beg for food or chop wood or steal from Uncle Paulo's orchard and other people's fields just to survive."

"Hush, Child! Uncle Simon is outside asking questions. We can't let him hear such terrible things." Auntie Xena put a gentle hand onto Mitya's shoulder. He pushed away and turned his back to her. His thin shoulders shook violently as he tried to swallow his tears.

She dipped a clean tea towel into the bowl of liquid she had brought and wrung it out.

"Philipovna, Here's some camomile tea for your face. It's looking angry. I don't want you to get an infection. We'll bathe it well and keep an eye on it. Do you two think you could tell me whatever possessed you to leave the church? It must have been something big."

"Uncle Misha said not to tell," Mitya said.

"Are there any of the other men with Uncle Simon?" I asked. The thought of the men around last night's fire made my stomach feel funny. I tried not to cry. Auntie Xena put the compress that she made with the hot tea onto my cheek. I'm not sure whether it was the heat from the tea, the ice in the stare of Mitya's blue eyes that now gave them a steel grey cast or the terror of Uncle Simon's name that made me do it. I found myself sobbing on Auntie's shoulder confessing last night's whole adventure. Reluctantly, Mitya filled in the details I missed.

"You two must not come out till Uncle Simon goes away. Don't be afraid. Uncle Misha knows what to do. He'll make sure you two are safe."

Auntie Xena left the room. Mitya and I glumly sat on the floor leaning against the sewing machine. We strained our ears, trying to make out what was being said in the discussion on the grass outside. We could only catch the odd word of the muffled conversation till it became a low drone. We must have fallen asleep listening. It was late afternoon when the brightness of the sun's rays woke me. My cheek was stinging and the skin felt like someone was pulling at the scrape. I was stiff from the awkward position in which I had gone to sleep. It seemed strangely quiet except for a bustling sound that was coming from the big room of the house.

"Wake up." I nudged Mitya. "I'm starving. Let's go see if there's anything left from breakfast."

He curled himself up into a tighter ball and rolled away. Lying there on Auntie's floor, he looked so small and helpless—like one of the younger cousins that Xenkovna would rock to sleep in the evening as her mother mended. His rich brown curls had settled down a bit and framed the face that now looked like an angel as his eyes were closed and not shooting blue sparks of rage or defence.

He is so beautiful, I thought as I sat and stared at him breathing peacefully. I had a strange urge to put my arms around him, but couldn't find the courage.

"What are you staring at? Is Uncle Simon gone away yet?"

He woke up so abruptly that I jumped back.

"I don't know. We'll have to go out and see. It sure is quiet. Do you want to eat anything or not? I'm hungry."

We went back into the big room of the house. The table was pushed back into its customary place under the east window. The remnants of breakfast were neatly stacked on the big platter under a clean, white tea towel. The holy candle still flickered in the breeze which was coming in from the open window and the embroidered *rushnyk* around the icon moved a little. The scent of new grass and cherry blossoms sweetened the room. I could see Auntie Lena in the sleeping corner but she had her back to me and looked like she was doing something with her own blankets.

"I'll get us a drink from the pitcher," I said. "They've probably gone to the pasture to show Uncle Simon the new calf." I brought two glasses of water and two plates to the table. We sat down and ate from the platter as if we had never seen the food before.

"I'm going to build a house just like this one day," Mitya said.

"And I'm going to marry someone just like Uncle Misha, He'll have a house like this too."

"Not if you keep on with your wild antics." Auntie Lena emerged from the sleeping bench in the corner, her tied bundle of clothing in her arms. "You'll be the downfall of all of us and bring ruin onto this home—you wait and see." She didn't look at me but gave Mitya the evil eye. I swear she was the Baba Yaga herself, just for a moment. When I looked away, I saw Mitya's fingers crossed in his lap as if to find some protection from the woman in front of him.

"Why don't you just go home," Mitya said. "You're a hateful old biddy that's mad because she has no Children of her own. I hear the Babas talking about you at the well every day. They know you want Philipovna to work for you—we all do. None of them can figure out how Auntie Xena even lets you step a foot into her house."

She charged across the room and slapped his face with all of her might.

"You'd better watch it, boy," she said. "The Uncles have decided to protect you, but I don't have to. You're lucky we're leaving first thing in the morning or we'd be having more to say to Simon and his little helpers. At least they have their heads on straight and have already joined the *kolhosp*. If Misha had any brains, he'd give up this independence nonsense and do what's best for his Children, his family and his country. And you'd better keep a good eye on that crazy Mama of yours too."

She grabbed me by the shoulder and leaned right down into my face. Her hot breath felt like it would burn my other cheek.

"Just remember one thing, you ungrateful little wench. If you ever need a piece of bread, I'll eat it in front of you and watch you drool before I ever offer you one more thing."

She took her bundle and was gone.

"Uncle Simon is part of the collective," Mitya said.

"I thought he and Uncle Misha were friends ... on the same side." I sat in my chair, stunned, watching the print of Auntie Lena's hand appear red on Mitya's cheek.

"Oh, your poor face," I finally whispered.

"Never mind, we'll both have to use Auntie's medicine bowl now." He touched his fingers to the handprint on his face dramatically. And for some unknown reason, we started to laugh—not a fun happy laugh—but one that releases feelings the likes of which one doesn't even know one has. I was the first to recover.

"I better put these things away," I said, covering what was left on the platter. "Do you want more water?"

"No, we should go see where everyone is. It's very quiet."

We stepped out onto the grass where the adults' tea things still sat on the table. Auntie Lena was rummaging around in her wagon, but no one else was in sight. I wanted to ask where everyone else was, but I didn't want to look into those eyes of hers in case she really would do something terrible to Mitya and me.

"Where could they have all gone?" Mitya asked. "What about Mama?"

"It's milking time soon," I said. "Look how low the sun is. They must have walked with Uncle to get the cow."

"All of them?"

"Maybe Xenkovna took the cousins for a walk in the orchard to look for nightingale nests or to the river to hunt for tadpoles."

"Maybe, but the Uncles wouldn't go for that."

We walked toward the pasture. The warmth of the sun felt good on my shoulders. I breathed in deeply. I could smell the wild flowers that bloomed by the path. The fragrance of Uncle Paulo's cherry orchard and the river mixed into the familiar scent of our village in spring. Just as we reached the pasture, we met Xenkovna and the cousins. They were carrying an old tin full of water with at least a dozen tadpoles swimming in it.

"I ate your holy egg," Viktor said. "I hope you're not mad at me."

I laughed and pinched his rosy cheek.

"Did they find her?" Xenkovna asked.

"Find who?" Mitya and I asked at the same time.

"The Unravelled One—sorry, I mean your Mama."

"What do you mean?" Mitya asked.

"Your Mama. Uncle Simon and Uncle Paulo came while you were sleeping. They asked a bunch of questions and wanted to talk to you. They said that someone tried to kill Uncle Ivan with a stone at the river last night. *Tahto* said that the two of you were asleep and that, since you were Children and they were adults, they should speak to him. He would tell them what they wanted to know."

Mitya's face paled.

"What does all of that have to do with Mama?"

"Nothing," Xenkovna said. "Except that she tried to tell them that you didn't know anything and that they couldn't take you away from her. She was crying and making those strange sounds that she does—you know the ones that make her look, you know how she looks. Uncle Simon told her to shut up because this was man's business since you were trying to be such a big man. Mama took her around to the well and bathed her face to try to calm her down, but the Children came out just then, and we had to figure out what to do with them. We decided that I would take them for a hike and Mama would look after your Mama. By the time we collected the Children and got ready to go, your Mama disappeared."

"Disappeared?"

"Yes, one minute I saw her by the well with Auntie Lena and the next minute, after I tied Viktor's shoe, she was gone. Mama told me to keep the Children busy while she went to get the Unravelled One back."

"Maybe she went home," I said.

"I'm going to look," Mitya said. "You stay with Xenkovna."

"Oh no. I'm coming with you."

"Maybe you'd better not," Xenkovna said.

"I'm going. What if something happened to her? Mitya might need me to help him."

"I think Mama wouldn't like you to be wandering around the village after last night," Xenkovna said. "You'll get in trouble if you do."

"I'm going anyway. If something happens, Mitya can stay with his Mama and I can run for help."

She could see that I was determined to go and that Mitya was barely able to stand still while we argued. She waved her hand in acquiescence and turned back to her other charges who were already starting to scatter in all directions.

Mitya and I cut across the pasture towards his home.

Memory Eternal

❋❋❋❖❋❋❋

MITYA RACED THROUGH the fields like one running away from a *chort* who would steal his soul. As I scrambled after him, crawling under the fences he jumped over and through the bushes he pushed aside, my breath came in hot bursts and the taste of panic burned my throat. The delicate sunset behind us faded and the moon rose again. I was sure the spirits would catch me, unless Uncle Paulo or Uncle Simon did first. A cool breeze stirred the budding branches with a clammy breath that conjured every ghost that lived in my childish imagination. The magic of the night before had gone and the black shadows of the branches pointed their accusing fingers at us as we rushed toward the Unravelled One's cottage. We almost ran into Auntie Xena who was coming down the path from the other direction.

"Is she here?" Mitya said, gasping.

"Bless you, Child. Take a breath," she said. "The Uncles are looking all over for her. Does she have a place she likes to hide? We've searched the gardens and pastures—and she's not in the old shed where your *Tahto* used to keep the cows."

"Did you—did anyone check *Tahto's* grave? She likes to talk to him when she's scared." Mitya rubbed his eyes with the back of his hand.

"Uncle Misha is looking there now. The others have gone into the woods. Does she have a special place there?"

Mitya's face contorted with the effort of trying not to cry.

"Oh my darling boy, you're far too young to suffer so." She put her hand gently on his shoulder. "God will keep you if you have faith."

"What happened to Mama?"

"Simon and Paulo were asking so many questions. She was getting shaky; you know the way she gets before she starts crying. I knew that wouldn't do so I took her for a walk. It seemed to make her feel better. When we got back, I took her to the well to bathe her face and get a drink. Uncle Misha called for more food and drink so I sent Lena to look after her while I put more bread and vodka out. When I came back, the little ones were awake and she was gone. Lena said that she just got up and walked away from her."

"Did Auntie Lena say anything to Mama?" Mitya asked. "She doesn't like us, you know."

They stood there for what seemed a long time, saying much more with their eyes than I could have possibly understood, then he jerked his shoulder away roughly.

"I can't just stand here, snivelling like a baby. I have to follow them."

"Get your coat before you go," Auntie said. "And let's find a shawl or something for Philipovna. I'll take a lantern."

I had often played in the unkempt yard of the Unravelled One's cottage but was never invited in. Though I had wondered what was inside, on this night, beneath the rising moon, I didn't want to find out. The weathered old cottage with its thatched roof was surrounded by a tangle of blackcurrant bushes. The wayward birch tree that shaded the broken-down bench on a summer's day stood ready with its skeletal arms hungry for some Child to grab and give to the forest demons as a tasty morsel for a vernal feast. The door hung crookedly on its hinges and the darkness behind the glint of the cracked glass in the only small window offered no welcome as I stood shivering in the cool evening. I was sure the chicken feet that Baba Yaga's cottages were built on were hidden by the pile of wood that was stacked by the door.

Auntie Xena stepped inside while I hung back at the threshold. The moonlight coming through the small window illuminated what could easily pass for a Baba Yaga's cottage. A pile of old blankets lay strewn in the corner of one of the sleeping benches. I could see the eerie shadow of a broom leaning precariously in the corner. An old looking glass hung over the small table showing a spotty reflection of moonlight.

The fire was out and dirty dishes with dried out chicken bones still on them stood scattered on the table.

"What if the *chort* came and sucked out her heart?" I blurted.

"Hush Child, you mustn't speak of such things at a time like this. You might tempt the evil spirits," Auntie Xena said. "God will protect all of us." She quickly crossed herself three times as if to make sure God would.

But Mitya didn't hear; he was flinging things about, trying to find his coat as if looking for things in the dark was something he was used to.

"Where's the lantern?" Auntie Xena asked.

"Behind the door. It might not have kerosene. We haven't used it for at least two weeks."

Auntie rummaged behind the door and managed to coax what kerosene was left out of a rusty can. "That's better," she said as the feeble flame finally blossomed in the lantern. "Is there anything missing? If she took something with her, it might give us a hint as to where she's gone."

Mitya shook his unruly curls.

"Now what can I find to put around Philipovna?"

I didn't want to be wrapped in anything from this place. Everything was covered in dust. Spider webs hung from the corners; the embroidered *rushnyk* framing the old icon on the east wall was torn and yellow with age. Dirty rags that filled large cracks in the wall to keep the cold away splayed out like tentacles trying to grab me. Uncle Misha's stable smelled more fragrant than did this cottage that my beloved cousin called home.

"Look on the nails by the sleeping benches," Mitya said. He was rifling through a wooden box.

"I'm getting *Tahto's* knife," he said. "If I see either of those two old pigs, I'll run them through if it's the last thing I do. *Tahto* would expect no less."

"Please, my son, don't speak that way. I'm sure your Mama just wandered off into the woods and lost herself."

"She loves the woods. She would never get lost, especially at night. The night fairies are her friends. They give her protection wherever she goes."

Auntie picked through some dark garments which were carelessly tossed onto the nails. She shook out a black triangle shawl and bits of thatch flew about her head like a swarm of fruit flies round an over-ripe apple.

"This will work. Come, Philipovna."

I stayed where I was, still on the threshold, shivering.

"I don't want that! It belongs to the Baba Yaga."

"Don't be silly. It's just a wool shawl and will keep you warm. Please be good and put it on so we can move on and find Mitya's Mama."

I shook my head.

She sighed.

"All right. Take mine. I'll wear this one. It's probably left from the time the Unravelled One still lived in her own home, before the soldiers kicked them out."

She took off her shawl and put it over my shoulders. I snuggled into it, but I didn't feel warmer. My skin felt creepy and I was afraid that some bugs or spiders that I didn't see in the gloomy light of the lamp may have fallen on it. Auntie picked up the black thing and put it around her own shoulders.

"We're ready to go," she said, turning to Mitya. As she turned, I caught a glimpse of her in the looking glass—but it wasn't her reflection. I saw Mitya's Mama. Her face was smashed and pussy willow branches were placed behind her. The sound of the river roared in my ears. It felt as if my screaming would never end. I started running.

I don't know what possessed me or gave me the strength to run but run I did, down the path from which we had come, across the pasture that was now lit by the rising moon. I didn't hesitate when I came to Uncle Paulo's orchard, but kept running, straight into Uncle Misha who was returning from the graveyard.

"Ho, Philipovna, What's the hurry?"

"I saw her. I know where she is. I saw in the mirror—her face —her head—all blood."

I stumbled into his big arms and sputtered into his chest, my sobs coming so hard and fast that I lost my balance.

"Easy daughter," Uncle said. "I can't understand a word you're saying. Is the Unravelled One hurt? Did you find her?"

"No. We didn't find her—but ... but I know she's bleeding. I saw her, saw her in the mirror—she's by the river."

I huddled closer to him, shivering and sobbing while he tried to make sense of what I was saying. I didn't hear Auntie and Mitya approach.

"What's going on?" Uncle Misha asked.

"I'm not really sure," his wife answered. "One minute I was wrapping her up in my shawl and the next minute she was scream-ing and running away. Any sign of the Unravelled One yet?"

"No, nothing," he said, shrugging. "She disappeared into thin air."

"No, she didn't," I said. "I saw her."

"After you left the cottage?" Mitya asked.

"No, in the mirror."

"You couldn't have. Just you, me and Auntie were there."

"I did! I did! I saw her bleeding by the pussy willows. I could hear the river. We have to go get her."

"We should wait for the others to come back from the woods," Uncle Misha said.

"If we do it'll be too late," I cried. "She's bleeding—I saw her."

"How could you see her by the river if you were at her cottage?" Uncle asked.

"I did! I did!"

"Philipovna." His face hardened into the face that meant business. "This is not the time for childish fairy tales."

"I saw her." I was shaking again, the tears flowing like the river I had heard in that spotty looking glass.

"Vera Philipovna." It was Auntie this time. "Are you sure? Tell me everything."

"She was in the glass—so clear. Her eyes told me to come to her." I started sobbing again.

"See," Uncle Misha said. "She's telling stories."

"Maybe she really did see—maybe she's a seer like Babushka was."

"Not here, not now," he said. "We have to find the Unravelled One."

"If Philipovna's right, we can all save ourselves a lot of time and trouble by going to where she thinks the Unravelled One is."

"Woman, I don't have patience for this nonsense." His usually quiet voice was starting to get very loud.

"Well, it's worth a look, even if only to calm Philipovna down."

"It's not a good idea to go by the river after last night's goings on," Uncle Misha said. "They're probably watching to see if anyone comes to finish what they started. I wouldn't have expected Paulo or Simon to do something, but now I don't know who to trust anymore."

"Where else would you look then? They haven't found her in the woods yet."

"I'm not afraid to go back," Mitya said. "I've got *Tahto's* knife. If anyone gets near me, he'll sure know it."

"Son, you're playing with fire," Uncle Misha said. "Your little knife didn't help your *Tahto* and it won't help you if they decide to finish you. Keep your nose clean and your eyes straight. Give me the knife."

"Not till we find my Mama. If you don't want to come then I'll go myself." He turned to me furiously. "Lead the way if you know where she is. We've wasted too much time already."

"By the river," I said. "Where we got the pussy willows."

He started retracing our trek from the night before. My family went after him with Uncle Misha stopping now and again to make sure we weren't being followed or watched. The night deepened; the wind stopped and we cautiously moved toward the spot where Mitya and I found the now sacred willow branches for the Palm Sunday service. There was nothing; no sound, no movement and no smell of smoke from a fire either.

We almost tripped over the Unravelled One who lay, bathed in moonlight on the mossy spot from which I had so often gazed up at the fluffy clouds or down at the sparkling river. The dark shadow of blood was clearly visible on her face. Her hair was as wild as that of any night demon who might roam the woods, and in her hand was a rudely-fashioned cross made of pussy willows.

I put my hand over my mouth to stifle a scream. I stepped closer to Auntie hoping that she could protect me from whatever was out here.

"Mama, Mama, are you all right? Please don't die. Not now. Not here. Please." Mitya dropped to his knees and held his mother's hand.

"What's this?" Uncle Misha bent over the body.

"Is she alive?" Auntie asked, kneeling by the fallen woman to have a closer look. "She's so still. Where did that cross come from? It must have been a nasty fall. Do you see what she tripped over?"

He put his hand on the Unravelled One's chest.

"She's warm and barely breathing," he said. "She's taken a serious knock to her head. It's pretty swollen. This was no tripping or falling."

"We'll have to take her home," Auntie said. "She might bleed to death out here."

"We have to find out who did this to her," Mitya said. He jumped to his feet. "I'll kill him myself."

"You'll do no such thing," Uncle Misha said. "You're lucky that it isn't you lying here."

"I'm going to find out, no matter what you say."

"You'll do what you're told. I'm as close to a father as you've got. We'll try to find out what happened, but we'll do it my way. Your foolish temper will bring nothing but trouble to all of us."

"Your way is getting my Mama killed," Mitya shouted.

He started to run, but Uncle Misha bounded after him like a nimble bear. He grabbed him by the shoulder, turned Mitya to face him and landed a resounding slap across the boy's face.

"I told you earlier, boy. You're playing with fire. Get it through your thick head that I'm your only help, your only hope and your only protection. Those animals know you threw the stone. They're waiting for you to act—to do something that they can really nail you with. Whatever you do will come back on all of us. We can't afford it and I won't allow it. By God and for the love of your mother you'll do as I say or I'll give it to you worse than they ever could. Now put your strength to good use and help me get your Mama back to our house."

"I want to take her home."

"Son, there's nothing there to help her with," Auntie said. "We have blankets, a warm fire and my medicine box. If you go back to your house, she'll certainly die."

"But that's our home."

"You can go home when we get her put back together. Please do what Uncle asks."

Uncle Misha took the knife from Mitya and cut some willow branches. They tied them together with their shirts and Auntie wrapped the Unravelled One's head in the black shawl that she had taken from the cottage. Uncle and Mitya shouldered the makeshift sling. We started for home with me following them. We slowly retreated from the riverbank towards Uncle Paulo's orchard. We couldn't take the shortcut that Mitya and I had used the night before because it was too rough. As we came near the pasture, I could see some shadows moving toward us. I tugged on Auntie's hand, pointed to them and swallowed hard.

"Stop," she said.

Mitya and Uncle Misha put the Unravelled One down and waited.

"Can you see who it is?" I whispered.

As they came closer we could see that they were men who knew the village since they moved easily across the pasture.

"What if Uncle Paulo and Uncle Simon find us here?" I whispered to Auntie Xena. My heartbeat was so loud in my ears that I was sure they all could hear it.

"We'll just tell them that we are looking after the Unravelled One."

"Will they do anything bad?"

"Let's hope not. You never know these days." Auntie crossed herself.

As the men approached we heard a low whistle. Uncle George and Godfather joined our little group.

"We've searched all around the grave; she's not anywhere in sight. Maybe she's hiding and just not answering," Godfather said.

"We found her," Uncle Misha said. "You can help us carry her home."

"They know what's going on. I'm sure they did this," Godfather said, leaning down to pick up one end of the sling. "We ran into them at the fishing spot on the river. Simon asked how the stone-throwing was going and Paulo just sat there like a slug. The pig Ivan wished the crazy woman a fast recovery. It was all I could do to keep from permanently wiping the smirk off that fat jowl of his. I just don't understand how they got to her so quickly. And what in the name of Heaven was she doing out so far from home anyway?"

"You see, boy. I told you this is messy business," Uncle Misha said.

"Stay close to your Uncle," Uncle George said. "You're a marked man. Ivan has no conscience and will tear you to bits just for his own satisfaction. We must decide what to do with you."

"I'm not leaving Mama," Mitya said. "No matter what."

"We'll decide in the morning," Uncle Misha said.

"We have to tend to her first." Auntie nodded her head in the Unravelled One's direction and we continued towards home.

A candle burned in the window, beckoning to us as we came to our house. Xenkovna and Auntie Lena had put the little ones to bed and lit a fire, but when Xenkovna tucked me into my parents' feather bed, I couldn't feel the warmth it offered. I lay shivering, watching the Uncles carry in wood and water. The women undressed and bathed the Unravelled One. Auntie Xena got out her special box of herbs. She set herself to boiling and mixing potions that would speed healing and keep the fever down, not to mention frighten away any evil things that may have clung to the Unravelled One out there by the river. It was clear that all of her healing skills, both the practical herbal ones and her grandmother's spiritual ones, would be needed for her patient to survive.

Meanwhile, Mitya sat or knelt by his Mama's side. He smoothed her hair like a man much older than his years, promised that he would be good if only she wouldn't die and sang songs that only the two of them understood. When the women ordered him away so they could do their ministrations, he knelt beneath the icon and prayed. But in all of what went on that night, Mitya never cried—not one tear. His face changed and his eyes changed so that I never saw them sparkle again.

I cried myself to sleep.

Easter Monday dawned into a grey drizzle. Uncle Misha read the Bible and prayed again before breakfast. It was a tense affair. Those of us who hadn't slept sat dazed and lifeless while the little ones whose sleep had been disrupted complained fitfully.

"You should go back to your farming and stay as inconspicuous as you can before the whole family is marked," Uncle Misha said to his brothers-in-law at the breakfast table. "The Thousanders talk to each other these days so you can be sure that they'll find out when they realize you were here."

"We will. But we have to take care of business first," Uncle George said. His face, which was usually soft and without expression, was stern and determined.

"Get Mitya. We should have reined the young fellow in before this. We're partly to blame."

"I'm not taking him with me." Auntie Lena's chair went back almost landing on top of the Unravelled One's sick bed.

"No, you're not," her husband said in an unaccustomed air of authority. "The men are going out to the barn to decide the boy's future. I should have spoken up much earlier. You will have our things packed in the wagon and ready to go by the time I get back."

"She already did that," I said.

Everyone turned to look at her.

"I don't know what you're talking about." Auntie Lena glared at me.

"She doesn't want to help. She says that Uncle Simon has already given his land to the *kolhosp* and that, if you were smart, you would do the same. She told us that if it were up to her, she would give Mitya to Uncle Ivan and be done with him. You won't let her do that, will you?"

Everyone gasped.

The Uncles stared, dumbfounded, as if someone had punched them in their stomachs.

"Lena, is this true?" Uncle George asked.

"You're not going to believe the brat's lies?" she screamed.

"The Unravelled One was with you when she disappeared," Godfather answered.

"And I did see you gossiping with Simon while Xena was getting out food," Uncle Misha said. "Did Simon join the collective? What else did he say?"

"It is as the Good Christ said." Auntie Xena looked tearfully at the icon and crossed herself three times. "Neighbour against neighbour and brother against brother. The end times are here. How will we ever survive?"

"Our clothing and blankets," Lena's husband said. "Go pack them."

She turned on her heel, grabbed her shawl from a sleeping bench, and went out.

With no further discussion, the men took Mitya to the barn. I tried to sneak out to spy on them, but Auntie Xena wouldn't let me. She kept finding a Child for me to mind, a dish to put away or a compress to replace on "the poor Unravelled One's" fevering head.

"How is anyone supposed to recover from anything with such unpleasantness in the house—and on Easter Week to boot?" Auntie lamented. Xenkovna gathered the younger cousins around her and told them stories while I flopped restlessly from corner to corner unable to find a comfortable position or place. Finally, I took the shawl that had comforted me on the way home last night and hid by my Mama's sewing machine.

It was mid-morning when the men returned. Mitya was carrying an old wooden box and the men hauled a battered wooden trunk between them. They were covered with fine soot and smelled of smoke.

"What happened?" I asked, running to greet them.

"They decided that I would live here," Mitya said glumly. "They said that our house wasn't fit for living in even if Mama does get better. They might make us live in Godfather's town away from Uncle Simon, Uncle Paulo and Uncle Ivan."

"No, you can't do that!" The tears squeezed out from the corners of my eyes, no matter how hard I tried to hold them back.

"We went to the cottage and took out some things," Mitya said. "Then Uncle Misha and Uncle George put all of the wood in the middle of Mama's cottage. We poured kerosene on it and set it on fire. You should have seen it burn. I have nowhere to go now." He dropped his box at my feet and stood, tired and bedraggled with head and shoulders drooping.

"Yes, you do. Auntie and Uncle will let you stay as long as you want." I bent over to pick up the contents of the box which were scattered at my feet. I carefully replaced his family's Bible which was wrapped in the embroidered cloth they would have used to cover their Easter basket, a worn leather pouch that held a golden cross on a golden chain, a silver pocket watch which must have belonged to his *Tahto* or *Diedushka* and a knife with a *kosac* insignia etched into its blade. There were a few other personal things of his *Tahto's* which I don't remember. This was all that my cousin had left other than his Mama.

Uncle George got into his wagon where Auntie Lena had been waiting since breakfast.

"I'll find out what Simon said to her," he said with a nod in her direction. He shook hands with Uncle Misha and cracked the whip over his horse's back. The last I saw of Auntie Lena was her tearful face looking back to her sister-in-law who couldn't stop crying herself. I didn't see how things could get any worse.

After the wagon was out of sight, Godfather took Mitya to the barn. He and Uncle Misha helped him build a little corner and sleeping bench since Mitya said that he didn't want to stay with us in our house. He would be there for his mother, but refused to actually live with us.

"It's all for the best. He'll come around in time," Auntie said. She helped Mitya make a bed out of some blankets from the battered trunk they brought from the cottage and some old ones of her own.

"This will do till we figure out what's going on," she said. "The barn is very warm."

The next three days dragged on even more slowly than Monday. The Unravelled One got worse and worse. We Children were sent to the river for fresh strips of bark from the *kalyna* or to the woods to pick this herb or dig that root so that Auntie Xena could cook up a new concoction to try to break her fever. Still, the Unravelled One moaned or flailed about in incomprehensible dreams till Auntie could settle her down again. There was no doctor for some kilometres and, even if there were, no one had enough money to pay him.

"You must learn which plant is which," Auntie said to me patiently. "Since it looks like you are the next one in the family with the gift of seeing and healing, I must teach you everything I know. When this is all over, we'll have plenty of time to talk and learn. Remember, you should never be afraid of what you know and must always pay attention to what you see—even if others around you don't understand. You'll understand as you grow."

The priest was sent for to pray and neighbours dropped in quietly to bring a loaf of bread or a dish of food or just sit and drink a cup of tea. They all found something good to say about the sick woman—even the ones who would have shunned her a week ago should she have tried to borrow a cup of sugar or ask for a potato. Most of the neighbours came in the evenings since a lot of their farms were already turned over to the *kolhosp*. Mitya was oblivious to all of it. He sat by his mother or slept by her when his eyes wouldn't stay open any longer. Finally, on Thursday, the Unravelled One breathed her last breath and her spirit crossed over to join her ancestors.

The women took her to the river. They gave her a ritual bath and dressed her in her Ukrainian dress which Auntie Xena found in the old trunk from the cottage. I was shocked to see how beautiful it was, made of pure silk and embroidered with much finer thread than our linen ones.

"She earned this from the mistress when she was a servant at the estate," Auntie Xena explained. "She used to do all of the fancy stitching for the estate so the stitching on it is all of her own work. I wish I could do it that well."

Because the Unravelled One had been so sick, it was decided to hold her burial as soon as possible. Uncle Misha and Godfather fashioned a wooden bier where she was laid, her hands folded in prayer. Xenkovna and I went to Uncle Paulo's orchard where we cut an armful of cherry blossoms which we used to cover the departing one. The priest came and led the procession to the graveyard. We sang the ancient hymn of Memory Eternal. I listened to its haunting echo coming back to me in the fading sunset and breathed in the smell of the sweet cherry blossoms and the scent of the freshly opened earth. Was it like this when my own mother died? Would my Mama be waiting for Mitya's mother when she got to Heaven? I wondered if the Unravelled One could hear us singing to her.

We walked sombrely back to our home in the evening chill. Everyone squeezed into the house and Auntie cut up the *paska* which was baked for the Memory Eternal that would be celebrated on Sunday. We ate food that the villagers brought and the adults raised a glass in the Unravelled One's memory.

"Let's hope she's happier now," Auntie Xena said with an exhausted sigh.

"Of course she is," one of the old *babas* answered. "You can't be more fortunate than to suffer and die the same week as Our Blessed Saviour, can you?" She crossed herself three times and bowed her head in a hasty prayer.

Planting the Garden

❈❈❈◈❈❈❈

MONDAY MORNING FINALLY arrived. Uncle Misha said that we should go back to our normal routine as soon as possible in order to escape the attention we were attracting. But, when my cousins and I came to school without Mitya, the gossip was flowing as abundantly as the river itself. Some of the Children said that a witch had come and killed The Unravelled One while others had gone to see the burned-out ruins of the hut that had been their home. Could it be that Mitya was as possessed by demons as his mother had been? Was it the devil himself that burned down their house—on Easter Week? Would Mitya become as "unravelled" as his mother was? They even kept their distance from the beloved Xenkovna.

"My cousin won't be coming to school for now," Xenkovna told the terrible Asimov when the class assembled. "*Tahto* needs him for ploughing and sowing." She pushed back her shoulders, trying to look confident as Asimov's snake-like eyes slithered over her from top to bottom.

"Here," Asimov said, "is a perfect example of why the *kolhosp* is good for the farmers. If your father would use his brain correctly, he would see that the *kolhosp* would ensure that he had enough adults to help with the planting and that little pig of a cousin of

81

yours would be able to attend class as he ought. How does your father expect that wild boy to ever become civilized? Hands up those of you whose families have joined the *kolhosp*. Tell the class how well the collective is working for your family."

Half of the students in the school timidly raised their hands. The rest of us shrugged our shoulders or hid our faces. Asimov paced up and down the room in his agitation, gesturing with his metre stick. He called several members of the class to the front where he cajoled or prompted them to declare how much fun it was to be part of a large communal family and how much more they had now that their parents had a part of the collective farm—and their own garden too.

"The rest of you, go home and tell your ignorant parents to give their land to the *kolhosp*. We will be welcoming the Young Pioneers soon. I expect all of my eligible students to participate." He pointed his metre stick directly at Xenkovna and me.

I wondered who the Young Pioneers were but was too afraid to ask.

"You will learn how Papa Stalin will give you a joyous childhood and new songs like 'We will increase the harvest on the *kolhosp*.' If you are good enough you will sing at the celebration on Red Army Day." With that he burst into a chorus, in a high, clear tenor voice which we had never heard before: "Sing more merrily, sing to the harvest on the collective fields."

If it hadn't been Asimov singing, I would have liked his voice. How could such a man sing with such a beautiful sound? Maybe he was a demon sent by one of the witches from the forest with a sweet singing voice that would charm you so that the *chort* could steal your soul when you were sleeping. I couldn't sit still after hearing him sing.

The lecture continued for at least an hour and the rest of the day dragged on even worse than the week before. I soon put aside my wondering and tried to concentrate on my mathematics. Xenkovna wouldn't dare raise her eyes from her books and my bench felt very empty without Mitya. I caught myself making faces towards the place he used to occupy. Xenkovna nudged me back to attention quickly before my slacking could be noticed. When it was my turn to recite, I stumbled over the words and couldn't remember my work even though I had read it at least ten times. I received a sound rap from Asimov's metre stick for my troubles.

When school was mercifully over, I let the others walk ahead while I sulked my way home alone. I didn't stop to catch a butterfly or look for snails as Mitya and I used to do, nor did I listen for the chirping of the nightingales which were nesting as they always did. I felt tears welling up behind my eyes, but couldn't really say why I wanted to cry. I don't know how or why, but I do know that it was on that day, on the way home from school, that I felt my new world had shifted forever.

I looked for Mitya as I approached the birch that was in new leaf in our yard, but it was Auntie Xena who was waiting for me.

"Vera Philipovna, put your things away and have some bread. I want you to come and help me in the garden. We have lots of work to do before the sun goes down."

In the house, Xenkovna was already peeling potatoes and chopping vegetables for the boiling pot of chicken soup that was hanging over the fire. The little ones were gathered around her as usual.

"Where's Mitya?" I asked.

"In the field with the men," she replied. "The folks decided that it's best to keep him close to *Tahto* and the other men."

"I want to go to the river with him. It's so sunny and warm today."

"You can say 'goodbye' to that," Xenkovna said in a practical voice that seemed more like her mother's than her own. "He has to earn his keep and *Tahto* can't afford to take chances, especially when he hears about what the snake Asimov did at school today."

She told me that Uncle Misha decided that it wasn't worth going to the constable to try to find out who had beaten The Unravelled One. The constable and judge were from the city now. Uncle Misha felt that asking too many questions would bring on more trouble.

"We'll find out in time. The truth always has a way of coming out," she said. "At least that's what Mama says."

"Philipovna," Auntie called from the yard.

I stuffed the last bite of bread into my mouth, gulped my milk and went out to join her.

"We're planting potatoes first," she said. She was shaking some sand off the seed potatoes that she had brought up from the root cellar. While we were at school, Auntie had dug up a section of the garden. She made a couple of clearly marked rows.

"Uncle Misha made you your own hoe." She handed me a hoe with a shortened handle and a matching rake.

"First we'll hoe these rows again. Then you will take these potatoes and cut them into pieces," she said. "Make sure that you leave two or three eyes on each so that they can start growing. Then we'll put them into the ground and hill them up. It's best to plant things in the morning or evening with a little watering so that they can settle in before the hot sun dries them out in the middle of the day. Let's see if things grow as well for you as they did for Babushka. It looks like you are taking after her, God rest her soul." Auntie crossed herself with the blessing.

And so the spring days went on—lengthening into early summer. Each day we got up early, went to school, came home, planted and hoed. There were the potatoes first, then rows of beets, carrots and spring onions. As it got warmer, we planted hills of cucumbers and beans, rows of radishes and lettuce greens that seemed to pop out of the earth before our eyes. The food was fresh and meals were deliciously interesting. I learned to husk strawberries without squeezing them too hard and soon shelled peas as quickly as Auntie Xena.

Once the vegetables were established, Auntie took me to the

river where we gathered a variety of herb plants and roots for the herb garden. We would collect the various parts from the *kalyna* as it grew through its life cycle throughout the year. She carefully showed me which plant did what and quizzed me on their properties till my head swam.

"We'll put the poppies on the cool side of the house," she said. "We need plenty for baking, tea and medicine, God forbid that we should need it." She quickly crossed herself lest the sickness was lurking around the corner just waiting to pounce.

"We can plant the gladioli and hollyhocks in the bed at the front of the house," Auntie said one afternoon, "and that should do it for this year. We want it to look nice, don't we?"

I collapsed into unconsciousness every night for the first few weeks as I had never worked so hard. It was my first year in the garden. My hands soon cracked and blistered. But Auntie washed my wounds with her herb potions and applied her creams. Before long, the protective calluses developed.

Mitya, tired and hungry, came home with Uncle Misha and the boy cousins each evening. He too, learned about planting, not the garden because that was woman's work, but the fields of spring barley. The men who hadn't given their land to the collective shared the village horses for ploughing. Uncle Misha taught Mitya how to sow.

"I tell you, Xena," he said one day as the men came in when the chores were done, "this boy's a natural. I showed him once; the seed falls so evenly from his hand. He'll make a fine farmer someday, I swear. He's every bit as good as Michael and Alexander."

Mitya grinned at Uncle, but wouldn't look at me. He attacked his meal in silence.

"Did you see any nightingale nests in the field today?" I asked.

He waved me off like an unwanted mosquito.

"We're too busy for nightingale nests," he said, reaching for another boiled potato. "Uncle, did you tell Auntie about Uncle Paulo?"

"Uncle Paulo?"

Everyone stopped eating.

"What about Uncle Paulo?" she asked.

"Rumour has it that he's given his cherry orchard to the *kolhosp*," Uncle Misha said.

"He can't do that." Auntie almost choked on her bite of bread. "His orchard is right next to our land."

"He does talk about working with the Party," Uncle Misha said. "But I don't think he's that far gone. Anyway, he's always been a good neighbour so I'm sure he'd tell us. You know how rumours fly these days. Don't fret till you have to, woman. We've got our hands full as it is."

"But what'll we do if he gives in? The Comrades will never give us any peace. They'll want our land next. Oh dear God, how will we ever survive?"

Everyone was quiet for the rest of the meal. The supper things were put away under an invisible cloud and we all went to bed early.

To make matters worse, the distance that started between Mitya and me the week of the Unravelled One's death was growing. Auntie said that he would get over it, but I could see that the Mitya I knew was gone. On the rare occasions that he looked at me, he did not do so as an equal any longer. He treated me more like the little ones. He looked down his nose at me and, rather than getting more comfortable with us, he grew more and more sullen. If I asked to go to the river, he was too busy—always doing something for Uncle Misha. If I found him, as I sometimes did, sitting under our favourite tree, he snapped at me or simply didn't answer.

One day, when he came home with Uncle, Mitya carried a little black and white puppy in his arms.

"What's that?" I asked.

"Can't you see? It's a dog."

"Sure," I said. "Whose dog?"

"Mine. His name is Sharik."

"Where did you get him?"

"One of the farmers' bitches had babies and he had too many dogs."

"Does Uncle Misha know?"

"Yeah, he said I could have him."

"Can I play with him too?"

"Only when I say so. He's my dog—my own dog."

I stepped back from them and stared.

"He's going to live in the barn with me and Uncle Misha says that he's my responsibility."

"You're so mean," I screamed at him. "I always share with you and was your best friend. Now that you live in Uncle's barn and think you're a man you're mean and ugly ... just like Asimov says ... a pig. You'll never be like Uncle Misha."

He reached out to slap me, but I was quicker. I didn't stop running till I was in the house, safely crying behind Auntie's skirts.

"What on earth is going on with you two?" she asked.

"He won't let me play with his dog."

"I'm a man now," Mitya yelled. "I don't have time for little girls. I work like Uncle Misha and the other cousins. I'm not a kid anymore."

Uncle took Mitya out to the barn while Auntie dried my tears.

"Be patient," she said. "I know he loves you. Give him time."

"I hate him now," I said. "I'm never talking to him again."

But I didn't hate him. I watched as he walked, the dog following him. He talked to Sharik the way he used to talk to his mother. They went to the pasture for the cow together; they did the chores together and, one day, I even followed them to the Unravelled One's grave. He sat on the grass, stroking the puppy and talking—talking to the dog—maybe it was to his mother. I didn't get too close. The Unravelled One might come and pull me in with her if she thought I might be disturbing the visit with her son. What if Mitya really did become unravelled like she had? I remembered the nasty things that the Children said in the schoolyard. I shivered in spite of the warm sunshine.

On Sundays, we prayed and read the Bible in the morning. It was the one day of the week that the men weren't in the field. Church services were only held on holy days now. We ate our big meal at noon and rested or visited the neighbours afterwards. Uncle Paulo still brought his chessboard for a game with Uncle Misha, but Uncle Simon had not come since Easter Sunday. Sometimes, Taras came alone and took Xenkovna for a walk. Other times, all of the older cousins joined the rest of the young people in the village square or on a crossroad and sang the songs they knew. Xenkovna liked the singing very much because Taras would often bring his accordion.

I wandered down the path which skirted the orchard or picked wild flowers to bring home for Auntie. I went to the river to the places that Mitya had shown me in the spring, but it wasn't as much fun without him. Once, I went to the little place by the pussy willows, but the memory of the Unravelled One's face wouldn't let me stay to enjoy it. I wandered further up the river, hoping to find a new spot—a spot of my very own.

As I made my way up the riverbank, it widened into a meadow of sorts, full of vibrant blue forget-me-nots and white lily-of-the-valley whose fragrance filled the air with the sweetest scent I have ever smelled. The *kalyna* was budding with the promise of summer flowers and bitter berries in the fall. The sun was warm and the fast flowing water beckoned. I stuck my bare toes in. Auntie had warned us to stay away from the river in spring. I could see why. The water was as cold as ice.

I'm not really going in, I thought. But the pebbles were so interesting and there were places where there were little pools that were made by rocks and plants that didn't look dangerous. Some of the pools had insects floating on their surface. I moved closer. Maybe, I could find some crayfish to bring home. Maybe then,

Mitya and I could be friends again. I don't know how long I was there. I remember being fascinated by the stones in the bottom of the clear water and my fingers clutching at a particularly silver looking pebble before I found myself falling into the river.

I called Mitya's name out of habit but no one answered. The water grabbed at my skirt and the current would have pulled me all of the way in had I not been fortunate enough to hang on to the trunk of a little willow tree which had rooted itself onto the river bank. My feet were numb with the cold water. I dug in with my toes and slowly worked my way out and, to my surprise, I found myself still clutching the silver thing. It wasn't a pebble; it was the rounded bowl of a silver spoon that had caught my attention. I had never seen anything like it before. On its handle were carved initials and a beautiful scrolled design. I sat looking at it till my clothes dried and, after picking some of those beautiful flowers, I went home.

"For Mercy's sake, what have you gotten yourself into now?" Auntie Xena said when she saw me with my muddy skirts. "You'll wear your clothes out from washing before you can grow out of them." She crossed herself as if she were offering a prayer of thanks.

I held out the spoon.

"Where did you find that?" She dropped her bread knife onto the wooden table.

"In the river."

"You mean you went in after it?"

"No, I saw something shining. I thought it was a pretty stone till I almost fell in."

She looked it at carefully for a long time. Then I noticed her eyes glistening with tears.

"Do you know who it belongs to?" I asked.

"You see these initials?" She wiped the spoon with her apron. "A.K. They belong to Anastasia Kalynowich, the mistress I used to work for, the one who gave me my blue wool skirt, the one I wear to church. She was a distant relative of ours. Look at the pattern on the handle. I used to polish it when I was her servant. Where did you find it?"

I told her about the spot I found on the riverbank.

"Yes, I know the spot. We used to have picnics there in the old days." She took the spoon and wrapped it in a tea towel. "We'll put this away and not say anything to anyone. We could get into trouble for having such an extravagant thing in our house."

"What? A spoon?"

"No, this particular spoon. It's made of real silver and has the special design that only the old families used to have. If the Comrades find it here, they'll accuse us of all kinds of things, just like they did in the war."

I watched her put the little package into her decorated trunk in the spare room. Life was confusing. What kind of trouble could a little spoon bring? Why should the Comrades know anything about her spoons? Her stern face told me not to ask. She went back to cutting her bread.

The following Sunday I returned to the spot by the river. I looked and looked, but there were no more spoons to find. As I walked back towards Auntie's house, I met Mitya. He was unusually cheerful.

"The cherries are ripe in Uncle Paulo's orchard," he said. "I'm going to pick some."

"Did you ask if we could?"

"We?" He scrunched up his face in disgust.

"I could help you."

He hesitated.

"I guess you could if you could reach them."

"You could pick me up like you used to," I said tentatively. "Or I could hold the bucket for you so that you could drop them in."

"I guess two pairs of hands are better than one," he said, trying unsuccessfully to imitate Uncle Misha.

I followed Mitya and Sharik around the field and through the familiar path on which we had shared so many pleasant hours. Despite the fact that the sky was blue and the white clouds were turning pink with the onset of evening, something didn't feel right.

At the orchard, we chose a tree heavy with ripe cherries. The first few handfuls we picked found themselves stuffed into our mouths. They were still warm from the sunshine and the juice ran sweetly down my chin. Mitya laughed when he saw me.

"We can't just eat," he said. "We'd better get picking. Maybe, Auntie and Xenkovna will make some *varenyky* with these."

The bucket was bigger than we thought. Since the cherries were just beginning to ripen, Mitya was careful not to pick the greener ones. We found ourselves working our way off of the path by the edge of the orchard and into the interior trees.

"Look at that bunch." I pointed to a luscious branch over his head.

"I can't reach it," he said.

"Hoist me up then."

He bent down so I could stand on his shoulder. I swung up easily into the tree and squealed in excitement.

"We've got a treasure." I pushed through the branches and dropped the shiny fruit into his waiting bucket. I dropped so many that I missed and hit him in the head. I thought he'd be angry as was his habit of late, but he took a handful and flung some back. I answered in kind and, before we knew it, he had also swung himself up into a tree and was whipping up a sweet and sticky storm of his own. It was only when Sharik began to bark furiously that we paused and listened.

"Do you here bells?" I asked.

"Yeah, I thought I did."

We sat still but heard nothing. Sharik barked again.

"Stop that," Mitya said, leaning down toward him.

"There they go again," I said. "Where could they be coming from?"

"There are no bells," he said. But as he swung himself down, I heard them again.

"Who would put bells in the orchard?" I wondered out loud.

Sharik would not stop barking. From my perch, I saw them, Uncle Paulo and Uncle Simon, hurrying towards where we were.

"You better run," I screamed. "They'll get you."

Mitya froze.

"Hurry," I hissed. "I'll tell them I climbed up into the tree and can't get down because my skirt's caught."

He grabbed the pail and ran with Sharik close at his heels.

I stayed in my crook of the cherry tree, hoping that the men wouldn't notice. I watched Mitya bound over the fence and cross the pasture. My chest felt so tight that I could hardly breathe. I waited—right to the moment that they passed under my tree—then, I pretended to fall. I jerked so hard that I would have smashed my head had Uncle Paulo not caught me in his arms.

"We thought someone was picking cherries," Uncle Paulo said.

"I only wanted a little taste," I said.

"You won't be doing that again," Uncle Simon said. "Do you hear those bells?"

"Yes, sir."

"We set up a system of bells that will let us know when someone is picking the cherries." He pointed to some ropes that were interlaced through the branches of the trees. "Whenever anyone puts their weight on those branches, the rope will move and the bells will ring. Where's that cousin of yours? Isn't he tagging along as usual?"

"No, sir. He works with Uncle Misha now," I answered. "He's all grown up. He's got no time for little girls and picking cherries."

"No matter," Uncle Simon said. "We'll catch up with him."

They brought me home to Uncle Misha who was drinking tea under the birch tree with Auntie Xena. They told us that Uncle

Paulo had wisely decided to join the collective and that the orchard belonged to the Party now. No one was allowed to pick anything without the committee's permission—not even Uncle Paulo.

"So this is how you treat a neighbour?" Uncle Misha said. "Give in to the Party behind my back while you play chess at my table and drink my vodka every Sunday!"

Uncle Paulo shrugged.

"Come now, Misha, even you will see the writing on the wall sooner or later. They're squeezing all of us. We will have to give in or die. I didn't want to do it. There's no other way."

"The Party is the best thing that's happened to us since the Tsar," Uncle Simon said. "Listen to your good neighbour. We'll be better off if you die-hards just stop dreaming about an ideal that'll never be fulfilled. The Ukrainians have always been ruled by someone. It's been that way since the Mongols. Forget about being independent. At least Father Stalin will give us enough to eat and will educate our Children."

"And enslave us all once he has our land," Uncle Misha said.

"Misha," Uncle Simon said, "even the Bible tells us to render unto Caesar what is Caesar's. Put your bull-headed ideas aside."

"You dare to blaspheme the Word of the Lord in the name of these devils!" Uncle Misha roared. "Is there nothing that remains sacred anymore? The Lord never asked us to give up our land. Without my land, I won't be able to give anything to anyone. Where has your common sense gone?"

Uncle Misha swung his arm to punch Uncle Simon. But Uncle Paulo was quicker and deflected Uncle Misha's fist with his shoulder before it connected with Uncle Simon's jaw.

"Calm down Misha," he said. "We don't need this to get worse than it is."

Before they left, Uncle Simon insisted on seeing Mitya. He appeared, freshly washed and dressed in his Sunday shirt with Sharik, perfectly behaved at his heel.

The Uncles went away as we stood watching the sun settle over the pasture.

"Imagine that," Auntie said. "The whole village used to pick cherries from that orchard and Paulo's family still had more cherries than they could ever eat." She wiped away a tear with the corner of her apron.

Mitya told them about how I stayed behind and distracted the men. Although we never played the way we used to, he would let me pet his dog on a good day. We made an uneasy peace between us.

The Wheat Harvest

OUR ROOT CELLAR was filling up quickly. There were crocks of pickles, pots of jam and jars of honey. Bunches of fragrant herbs and spices hung from the rafters in the house after we had laid them in the sun to dry. The fields were heavy with their golden burden and Uncle Misha was planning to harvest the winter wheat.

Auntie and Uncle sat drinking tea on the bench under the birch tree in our yard. The little cousins were tucked up on the hearth. Mitya leaned his back against the trunk of the birch with Sharik in his lap. Xenkovna, Michael and Alexander had gone off to meet the neighbouring young people as they did each summer evening. They gathered to sing songs at the place where the paths intersected with the main path to the village. From the stoop of our cottage, I listened to the faint sound of their singing drifting over the pasture:

What a night, so moonlit and bright with stars.
Come with me, though you're tired from your day's work.
Come with me to the meadow just for a moment.
Sit together with me beneath the kalyna as the mist overlays
the meadow.
Don't fear the cold dew on your bare little feet for I'll carry
you home in my arms.

I'll draw you close to my heart and keep you warm as the hearth.

I breathed in the smell of freshly-mown hay. The breeze gently stirred the leaves over my head and streaks of sunset painted the land red, orange and gold in the fading twilight.

What fun it must be to go with those almost grown-up boys and girls and sing those songs. I couldn't wait till I was old enough. Maybe, by then, I could learn to play Uncle's guitar. I strained my ears trying to hear if Taras was out with his accordion.

"It should be an easy winter," Uncle Misha said. "The wheat is full. It should be taken in soon."

"An easy winter?" Auntie said. "What if the army takes more than they did last time? It was all I could do to stretch out our wheat to feed us over last winter."

"Don't fret, woman," Uncle said. "We're in the bread basket of Europe. There's enough for all of us, even the blasted Party. They can't take it all. They need us to live so that we can feed them next year too."

"I hope they remember that when the wind is moaning," Auntie said. She crossed herself as if to remind God that we might need His protection.

"I have no choice but to go over to George to see who can come to help with the harvest. You know that Paulo and Simon won't help. Even if they would, their horses have been taken away when they gave their land to the Comrades—and the others, the others ..." His voice trailed away. I knew he meant Uncle Peter and the other men who would have helped had they and their families not disappeared.

"What happened to all of the horses?" I asked. "I don't see them working in the fields. All I've seen is the new tractors."

"New tractors?" Uncle Misha asked.

"Yes, Uncle. I was walking and heard a rumble so I went to see what it was. It's so big and shiny and the ground shakes when it moves through the field."

"A tractor? You went onto the field of the *kolhosp*?"

I could see a storm brewing in his eyes. They were as dark as the blue shadows of the birch tree stretching out behind him.

"Never, never let me hear you say that you've gone to the *kolhosp*," he bellowed. "No one from this family is to step one foot onto that place. Do you understand?"

"Yes, Uncle, but I heard the sound. I asked what that machine was. I just wanted to see. The men said that it was a tractor, bought by the Party, all of the way from America. They said it is made by the Fordson Company and that it can do the work of many men and that soon all of the fields will be full of these machines so the men on the *kolhosp* won't have to work as hard any more. The driver said that Father Stalin is setting up factories to make our own."

"I don't care what you wanted to see," Uncle said. "Never, never go there to look or to do anything else. Do you understand? And above all, don't disturb any of the workers. You will be in trouble and so will they for talking and wasting time. Someone is always watching."

"But Uncle, I didn't see any army men. There haven't been any around here since early spring."

I hung my head.

"Daughter," he said, trying hard to contain his impatience with me, "you'll never know if someone is watching. The man who watches can be the very neighbour who draws water from the well with you. Uncle Paulo is my best friend, yet he gave up his orchard without saying a word to me. You're still not old enough to understand things as they really are. Do as I say."

Auntie sighed in sympathy.

"I hear that the horses aren't looked after very well," Uncle said. "The talk is that they are over-worked and don't get fed enough. They say that it's so bad that the horses have been let loose to forage for food in the forest on their own. And others say that the animals are dying of some kind of sickness. Some of the men in the village say that they'd kill their horses themselves rather than surrender them to the Party."

"Good God!" Auntie exclaimed. "That's severe, isn't it? That's like killing a member of the family."

"Maybe so," Uncle Misha said, "but it's better than seeing the horses sick or abused."

"Can I come with you to Uncle George's, Uncle?" Mitya asked from his spot beneath the tree. "I've never stepped a foot out from the village. Shouldn't a real man know a little of the world outside?"

Uncle Misha was taken aback by the request, but after a few thoughtful minutes, he nodded his consent.

"I'm sure that Michael and Alexander can manage the chores for a couple of days. There's plenty of cut hay for them to bring in from the field while I'm gone."

"Auntie Lena doesn't like Mitya," I said.

"We're going to Godfather first," Uncle said. "She won't have anything to say about who stays in his house. And besides, Mitya is now one of the men. Women have no business in this matter."

"I can look after Sharik for you," I said.

"He's coming with me." Mitya stared as if he was looking right through me. "I don't go anywhere without him."

"For the love of God," Auntie said, "don't start that nonsense all over again."

The next morning, with a basketful of goodies for Auntie Lena and a picnic lunch, Mitya and Uncle Misha got into the wagon. They took only one horse so that the cousins could use the other.

"Mind that you boys don't try using the scythes without me," Uncle Misha reminded them as they handed him the reins. "Don't think you know it all just because I've showed you how it's done. They're very sharp and you still need an experienced hand guiding you. There's enough hay ready for bringing into the barn. Make sure you help your mother. She'll have more than her share of work when I come back with the men."

He clicked to the horse and they were off. Sharik sat looking back at me from Mitya's lap. They would do what they could in the way of helping Uncle George and then, if they were lucky, return with a couple of horses and some men from around Uncle George's village to help bring in the harvest. Once Uncle was home again, Michael and Alexander would also volunteer to go back to Uncle George's village to help others who were short of hands for the harvest themselves.

The rest of us carried on as usual, hoeing the lettuce, pulling up carrots and beets, and milking the cow. The house felt as if there was a big hole in it. It was so quiet. I missed Uncle and Mitya, particularly at supper, as that was the only time we spent together these days. I thought that I missed Mitya when he stopped playing with me, but to actually not see him at all, and not to be able to sneak in a pat onto Sharik's head made me feel lonely.

Funny, I thought. *He doesn't have time to be playing with me, but I still miss seeing him.* I wished that I was a boy and that I could have gone with Uncle Misha too.

On the day before the men were supposed to return, Auntie killed two chickens and told me to dig up some more potatoes. She and Xenkovna set up a double batch of dough for a baking of bread. We gathered the vegetables for a fresh borscht that she would cook first thing in the morning. When morning came at long last, I was charged with minding the younger children.

"Take Viktor and the twins for a walk," Auntie said. "But don't go too close to the river. You know how your mind gets lost in your wonderings. And don't startle the cow either. All I need is to have her chasing the little ones—and for the love of God, don't go exploring near the *kolhosp*. Come back when the sun is high and we'll have lunch ready."

"Yes, Auntie." I rolled my eyes. I would much rather have

stayed to work in the house and garden because I didn't care for minding the little ones. I knew that Xenkovna was almost a woman and could do much more around the stove than I could so I swallowed my protest.

I took the little ones to look at the cow in the pasture. We stopped on a flat place on the path and I showed Viktor how to write his name in the dirt with the pointed end of a stick. We found caterpillars attaching themselves onto tree branches and bushes. We found soft, brown cocoons. I even took them to the place where Mitya showed me my first nightingale nest.

"Mama says that we aren't supposed to bother the nightingales," Viktor said. "She says that they are special birds. She says that God blesses us with their singing."

"It's all right to look at the nest," I answered. "The babies are all grown up now that it's almost autumn."

We picked daisies from the sweet-smelling pasture for Auntie.

"I'm thirsty," Marta said. "Can we go see Mama now?"

We followed the path back to where it joined the main path of the village. But just as we were about to turn into it, I heard a rumbling sound.

"What's that?" Viktor asked. "Is it a tractor?"

"I don't know," I said. "We'll see it when it drives by. I think tractors drive only on the fields. Don't make a sound till it's gone."

Maria's lower lip quivered. My stomach flip-flopped as Uncle Misha's stern warning replayed itself in my mind. As we stood watching, an army truck went rumbling slowly by. It was full of men with city uniforms like the ones we saw in the winter. One of them smiled and waved to the twins. Uncle was right. The army would be watching somebody—but who and why? We let them pass and then we followed the main path till it branched off to Auntie's house.

As we approached the gate, I heard a bustling sound. My cousins started to run before I could see what was going on. Sharik bounded out of the gate and after licking the little ones came to greet me too. Uncle Misha and Uncle George were tending to our horse and three other strange horses. Godfather was there with three other men whom I'd never met before. Mitya didn't look my way as he helped the visiting men carry their bedrolls to the barn. The yard was buzzing with activity.

"Ho, Philipovna," Godfather called out. "Look at you, Goddaughter! Why, you are turning into quite the young lady." He picked me up in a huge bear hug. "I've brought you a special sweet — but if you keep growing up like this, I'll have to bring something lady-like, a new *platok* maybe." His blue eyes twinkled down at me and he brushed a stray curl off of my face. He reached into his pocket and handed me a little parcel wrapped in brown paper.

"Oh, thank you Godfather," I said. "I'd much rather have the sweet."

He grinned over his shoulder and was gone up the path to the barn with his bedroll under his arm.

Auntie came out from the house with some sheets in her hand.

"Come Philipovna, don't stand there. Help me with these tables. The dinner is ready. No doubt, the men are hungry. They'll want to go to the fields once they've eaten."

"Is Auntie Lena here?"

She shook her head sadly. I didn't dare ask any more questions. The memories of Auntie Lena on Easter Sunday still stung painfully. I helped Auntie Xena spread the sheets over the tables which she and Xenkovna had placed under our birch in the yard. I carried out plates of bread and bowls of potatoes. The borscht was ready and the chickens smelled spicy from the oven. A small crock of freshly pickled dill cucumbers tempted my taste buds and a fresh salad with ripe tomatoes made my stomach gurgle. It felt like a holiday.

"Let us pray," Godfather said once we were all seated.

"We'll eat and then go to see how you two have managed with the hay," Uncle Misha said after Godfather finished praying.

Michael and Alexander were puffed out with pride. They had worked very hard while Uncle was gone.

"You'll see, *Tahto*," Alexander said. "We're old enough to earn our keep." He rubbed the crust of his bread with a clove of garlic.

They ate heartily and were off to the field before I had a chance to ask any questions or say anything about what happened while they were gone. The holiday feeling disappeared quickly as we washed dishes, put the little ones down for their afternoon nap and started on making supper right away. Not only was there more than the usual number of mouths to feed, but also Auntie and Xenkovna made *varenyky* with potato and cheese stuffing like they did at Easter. They baked *pyrizhky* with poppy seeds inside them. I was sent for *smetana*, vegetables, another egg for this or that or anything that was needed to keep the cooking going. The kitchen was hot in the late summer afternoon.

"We can't save on hospitality," Auntie said. "We have opened our homes to strangers since the days of our ancestors and have always offered them the best of what we have. I could never forgive myself if I didn't feed those hard-working men with the best from my kitchen."

While we worked from morning till night, the men were busy reaping the wheat and setting it up into shocks in windrows so that it could dry properly for the threshing. I wished to be out of the hot kitchen, in the fields with the men so that I could see how it was done, but Auntie always found something for me to do before I could slip away. I collapsed into deep sleep from the hard work each night, and so the week flew by, until it was the night before the men returned home.

As we sat down for our after-supper tea, under the early evening stars, I breathed in the fragrant air, sucking in the smell of the newly-mown wheat. It was so peaceful out here after the food was cleared and the dishes were washed. One of the visitors played his accordion and Uncle Misha strummed his guitar. They played as the rest of us sang in the summer dusk. I wondered if the stars looked like this in Godfather's village. A rumbling sound coming up the main path pulled me out of my daydreams.

"Oh, no," I cried. "I forgot to tell you. Oh, Uncle I'm so sorry, I forgot to tell you that I saw some army men."

But it was too late. Comrade Zabluda and some men we had never seen before were marching up the path toward the garden.

"Good evening," Comrade Zabluda called as he approached the gate.

I saw Auntie send a desperate look in Uncle Misha's direction as he got up to greet the Comrade. He did not open the gate.

Uncle George tugged at his moustache.

"To what do I owe this unexpected pleasure?" Uncle Misha's words were civil but his voice was as cold as the winter wind.

"Nothing in particular," Comrade Zabluda answered lightly. "We're driving around, enjoying this summer evening and checking how the wheat grows."

"Well enough," Uncle answered.

"All of these young men," Comrade Zabluda said, waving his arm in our visitors' direction. "Here to help with the threshing, I presume."

"Presume what you will, Comrade. We've had a long day in the field so it would be best for us to get down to business."

"No business," Comrade Zabluda said. "I'm checking out what fields are being worked and how the *kolhosp* will look once you come to your senses and acquiesce."

Uncle Misha's face turned purple with rage.

"Well," Godfather said as he sauntered up to the two men at the gate, "if there's no business, Comrade Zabluda, you'll excuse us. We have an early day tomorrow and you know us peasants, we love to get our sleep."

"I suppose you do," the Comrade said, never taking his eyes off Uncle Misha's face. "Remember, in a couple of weeks we'll be around to pick up our allotments. I can see how much is in your field so don't cheat our glorious Mother Russia." He turned on his heel and was rumbling off in the truck before any of us could say another word.

"Oh Auntie," I sobbed. "I saw the truck drive by the day that Uncle came home, and I didn't tell you. I'm sorry. It was so busy and ..." I sat with the unchecked tears flowing down my cheeks, but I didn't really understand why I was crying or why I felt so guilty.

"Hush Child," she said. "They would have come whether you had seen them or not."

But Uncle was angry.

"You saw the truck and you didn't say anything?" he demanded.

"I meant to," I said, sniffling. "But you and everyone came, and we were all so busy."

"You're lucky all of these people are here," he said. "Otherwise, you'd get a good strapping. Whenever you see anyone around here, you must tell me, and tell me right away."

"Take it easy, Misha," Godfather said. "She's a Child. She doesn't understand it all."

Uncle Misha poured a round of vodka for all. He didn't say one more word to me that night.

The next morning, the men packed the wagons and went off to Uncle George's village to return the favours that we had been receiving all week. This time, it was Mitya who stayed home to look after the chores. There was nothing to do in the quiet fields that they left behind but wait for the wheat to dry. Auntie and Mitya dug out some potatoes and buried them in sand so that they would keep till we needed them for the table. She taught me how to make an onion braid. She and Mitya dug out the onions and trimmed their roots.

"Make sure you braid it nice and tight," she said. I braided the green tops together, with the onions still attached, into a long string that looked like a necklace for a giant. When it dried the tops would contract and harden into a strong natural cord that could support a string of onions up to two meters long. My hands, arms and hair smelled like onions.

"You have good hands," Auntie said. "We will dig the onions and you can braid them so we can hang them from the rafters. Whenever we need an onion, we can cut one or two off and we're on our way. There's a good crop of them this year. When the garlic is ripe, you can braid that as well. Maybe Uncle's right. We'll have plenty to eat this winter."

But seeing my beautiful onion braids didn't cheer me up. I felt restless, like a black cloud was hanging over my head. I went to the river, to the orchard and into the woods, but could find no comfort.

"For Heaven's sake Child," Auntie said. "What's got into you? Find something to do. I can't stand to see you mope around so."

Before long, Uncle and the men came back to thresh the grain. They managed to borrow a threshing machine from one of God-father's friends in his village. This time, I did have a chance to see how the wheat was harvested. It went down the conveyer belt of the threshing machine where it was separated. The grain was forced into two pipes and was put into storage. The chaff was blown the other way and the straw was collected. If you were standing in the direction from which the wind was blowing your eyes and nose burned from its dust.

"It feels worse than smoke," I said to Mitya.

"Then stand up wind from it," he said, "and your eyes should feel better."

It smelled so pungent and fresh and the straw so sweet and welcoming. I knew the cow and horses would be warm and dry this winter. Yet, there was an overwhelming sadness that wouldn't give me peace.

"Good Heavens," Auntie said one day. "What has gotten into you? You haven't been so sullen since you arrived. Are you sick?"

"I don't know," I answered. "It feels sad somehow, like something is going to happen."

"Have you seen anything unusual?" she asked.

"No, Auntie, it just feels scary."

I did see more army trucks in the village. As the days mellowed into early autumn, more trucks and more strange men came. Most of them stayed near the *kolhosp,* but every once in a while a truck would wander up this path or that. Uncle said that, although they were trying to make it look like random visits, he was sure that the army was tallying up the harvest and deciding how much they could take. We settled into our fall activities and prepared for school. I wasn't looking forward to going as the memories of the snake Asimov were just as painful as those of Auntie Lena. Uncle made me start reading and reciting again and made me help Viktor learn some letters even though he wouldn't be going to school for at least another full year.

"You can never read too early," he said.

One Saturday afternoon, Uncle Paulo came to our yard asking for Uncle Misha. He told him that all of the men were ordered to appear in the centre of town.

"They've commanded every household head to be present," Uncle Paulo said. "You can't refuse. If you don't come with me, they'll come down hard on me, too."

Uncle Misha put on his hat and followed Uncle Paulo down the path. What else could he do? Auntie crossed herself and whispered a prayer after him.

The afternoon dragged on, but there was no sign of Uncle Misha. Suppertime came and went, but Uncle Misha did not come home. The boys did the chores without him. The little ones were put to bed and still the rest of us sat around the fireplace waiting. I passed the time by practising my recitation, but I kept making mistakes and even Auntie's endless patience was tested.

"I hope nothing happened to him," I said.

"Keep praying," Auntie said.

I finally dozed off and only realized that Uncle was home when I heard Auntie's crying and Uncle's agitated voice.

"They want more than last year," he said, fuming. "We had hardly enough to survive the winter. We told the greedy pigs that we can't survive with that much of an increase, but they won't listen."

"What if the women tell them?"

"Funny that you should say that," he said. "You know how sharp that old witch Katerina can be. She gave them a piece of her mind. They tried to shut her down and only succeeded when they threatened her with violence. Ivan threatened to knock her teeth out and that dreadful Zabluda only stepped in when it looked like Ivan was really going to do it."

"Oh my God, is Katerina all right?"

"I think so, but there's no doubt that she has been shaken up. The Comrades have also told us that we need a passport to leave our village."

"A passport? Why?"

"I don't know. They said that we can't leave the area without papers now."

"But we've never had papers before. I don't understand."

"I don't either. Let's go to bed. Tomorrow's another day. We'll have lots of time to think it over then."

Sunday morning dawned crisp and blue with a promise of the coming autumn. We started our day with the usual chores and a quiet breakfast. Auntie insisted on Bible readings and prayer although I could see that no one's heart was really in it. We were reading the parable in Matthew, the one about the wheat and the tares.

"I wish the Party would see with their eyes and hear with their ears the way God says we ought to," Auntie said.

"That's asking for too much," Uncle Misha said. "These barbarians are more likely to be the enemy that sows weeds among the good seed, if they sow anything at all. Besides, the Party doesn't acknowledge God. They say He's nothing but a useless myth, a fairy-tale."

"But that's blasphemy," she said. "We should still be thankful for the wonderful harvest this year."

"Let's hope there'll be some of the harvest left for us to enjoy."

"Can I go to play now?" I asked. "It's so lovely out today."

"I suppose so," Auntie said. "You're all not really paying attention anyway."

She tucked the Bible back into her trunk and put on some tea. Before the water boiled, we heard Sharik barking.

"They're coming! They're coming." Mitya burst in through the kitchen door.

Then the sound of rumbling trucks came up the path.

"It's early for visiting, isn't it?" Uncle Misha said.

"You better go see who it is," Auntie said.

A loud thumping on the door let us know that it wasn't a friendly neighbour.

"Hold up your suspenders," Uncle Misha said. "I'm coming." He signalled for the rest of us to stay inside as he stepped out of the door.

We moved closer to watch and listen. I could see Comrade Zabluda coming across the yard.

"We're here for your contribution to the Party," he said. "The men will have it now."

Comrade Zabluda led about twenty men towards the barn. Uncle Misha was quicker and beat them to the door. He stood his full two metre height with his shoulders pushed back and stared right back at Comrade Zabluda with eyes so dark that they were navy blue. For the first time, I noticed that the hair at his temples was tinged with silver.

"This is my barn. You'll have to take me first," he said.

Comrade Zabluda punched Uncle Misha square in the belly. Before Uncle could do anything to fight back, two other men grabbed him and pinned him against the wall of his barn. Michael and Alexander pushed past Auntie and tried to defend their father, but the men who were closer to the house grabbed them and wouldn't let them near the fight. Mitya darted around them but was tripped by a man with shoulders like an ox who pinned him and wouldn't let him go, no matter how much Mitya struggled. Uncle Misha fought like a trapped bear. Two more men hit him with their fists and batons. His nose started to bleed. More blood oozed from a gash on the side of his jaw but he kept on struggling.

"Easy boys," Comrade Zabluda said. "I want him to see whose barn this is. Stand him up so that he can watch."

They hauled out grain and hay till the trucks they brought were full. Then they filled Uncle's wagon.

"What are you doing with my wagon?" Uncle Misha asked.

"The Party needs it," Comrade Zabluda said. "Hitch up his horses." He waved to two of his men.

"I'll drive the hay wherever you want it," Uncle Misha said angrily. "But the horses and wagon are mine. And release my boys this instant." He started fighting with the soldiers again.

"You're not driving any horses anywhere," Comrade Zabluda said. "You had your chance. Now we're driving them for you."

The Comrade pulled out his pistol from its holster so quickly that I gasped in horror. "I tell you the Party needs them. The *kolhosp* needs them and if you're not willing to surrender them, the Party will show you how to do it. Now, do you have any more peasant wisdom to teach those who know more than you do?"

He aimed the barrel of the pistol right between Uncle Misha's eyes.

"Are you brave warriors taking this all in?" He motioned towards the cousins and their captors.

Auntie started screaming. Xenkovna was crying too. The rest of us simply stood rooted in place as if we were made of stone.

"Don't kill him, don't shoot," she rushed out of the house, got down on her knees and begged. "Take the wheat and hay. Just don't shoot. Don't shoot my husband, please! Don't shoot my boys. I have a houseful of Children. Please!"

We stood helplessly watching as the army took most of our wheat, our hay, our horses and our wagon. Meanwhile, Comrade Zabluda always kept the gun pointed at Uncle Misha's head. When Comrade Zabluda was satisfied that we understood his message, he lowered the pistol. He motioned his thugs to release the boy cousins. He slapped Auntie soundly across the face.

"Talk some sense into him, woman, if you value that house and the brats you have spawned in it," he said. He pushed Uncle Misha down to the ground and walked down our path after his men.

Comrade Zabluda wasn't out of sight before we all ran out to see if Uncle Misha was all right. He sat shaking and crying by his barn door where the army had left him. His face was swelling and his shirt was covered in blood. Alexander and Michael were the first to reach him.

"Sorry *Tahto*. We tried to help you," Alexander said. He swallowed hard, holding back his tears.

"All of the hay and most of the wheat," Uncle said. It was so terrible to watch him fighting with himself, trying to get control of his emotions. His shoulders shook and his breath came in uneven gulps.

"All that work," he said. "All of the trouble we went to … to get that wheat in. I don't even know if we'll have enough to eat and what am I going to do for seed? And my horses, my beloved horses. I trust them more than I trust most men." His sobs were no longer controlled. "We've worked together every day for years! What will become of them?"

"Come," Auntie said, unconsciously rubbing her cheek where the imprint of the slap was burning red already. "Let's go in and have some tea. I need to clean up that wound. You look like death has reached out and touched you."

"Maybe it has," Uncle answered. "Those horses! A man couldn't ask for better friends."

"Thank God they didn't kill one of you," Auntie said, crossing herself and muttering a prayer. The cousins helped him to his feet and we all followed them into the house.

We sat around the hearth moping. No one felt like talking, but no one had the energy to do much else. We sat, downcast and miserable while Auntie and Xenkovna tended to Uncle's wounds and cleaned up his bloody nose. Even the little cousins clung to their mother's skirts like frightened little birds.

In the afternoon, when our usual visitors came, Uncle Misha wouldn't come out to see them. Michael told them what had happened. Uncle Misha couldn't face them until they poured out some tea and vodka and made him drink two glasses full.

"There's no shame in it, man," Uncle Paulo said. "What can one man do against an army?"

They told us that our house was the first one that was visited and that all of the others who were not members of the kolkhoz had received a visit from the Comrade too. They all complained about how the army took more than last year and they all wondered how they could conserve the little grain that was left until it was time to sow the winter wheat. Taras and Xenkovna sat apart from the group under the birch tree. They talked together quietly and he kept holding her hand. The day that had dawned so blue and beautiful seemed to drag on forever and, as if God Himself was sympathizing, the sky clouded over so that by early evening the rain started falling.

That week, the fall session of school started up again. It was much as it had been in the spring with the snake Asimov commanding us to the front of the class for recitation and smacking us with the metre stick or worse when we didn't meet his expectations. Xenkovna didn't attend as Auntie said that she was old enough to stay home and think more about women's responsibilities. I missed her terribly.

One day, as school was about to finish, Asimov said that he wanted us to see something special. He took us out into the centre of the village. When we arrived we saw that there was a big pile of grain in the middle of the square. I noticed it looked a little strange as there were also bunches of straw tossed over it. The army stood around the grain and the townspeople milled about them in confusion.

"Make way for the Children," Comrade Zabluda said. "This is a lesson I want them to remember."

We were shepherded into the square and all of the villagers were forced to make a circle around the grain. I noticed that there were a lot more army men than usual. After we got home that evening, Mitya would tell me that they came through the village and confiscated all of the grain that they found in every single barn and piled it there.

"I'm here to say that the Party is very disappointed with you," Comrade Zabluda said. "We've talked and cajoled long enough. From now on you will do what we tell you without dragging your feet. You know that your land will eventually all be collectivized. Make it easier on yourselves by volunteering your land and your work."

"But we've already given more grain than last year," shouted one of the men from the crowd.

He received a thud on the head with a baton from one of the soldiers for his outburst. The crowd groaned collectively.

"You see, it's loudmouths like this that will get you into trouble," Zabluda said. "Today, I've gathered all of you to show you that I mean business. Since you're so greedy that you've held back some of your grain, we'll teach you a lesson that you won't forget."

"But that is our seed grain," another man shouted. "How do you expect us to grow wheat next year?"

Another thud in the back of the man's head. He passed out of consciousness and crumpled to the ground. His family gathered around him, crying.

Comrade Zabluda strolled around the pile of wheat. As he walked, he casually pulled out a box of matches. He struck a match then tossed it right into the pile of grain. Everyone gasped as if they were going to sing together. He took several more steps and struck and tossed again. As each burning match landed, I could hear a whooshing sound. The smell of smoke burned in my nose. A woman screamed. Some of the Children began to cry. Others tried to find their mothers.

The fire grew bigger and hotter. We tried to run away, but the army would let us back only far enough to keep from getting burned. The smoke burned our throats and eyes. I couldn't tell if I was crying from the smoke or from the terror of what I was seeing. Some of the women covered the eyes of their Children. Some people cried while others leaned against the town buildings either staring or covering their faces. We milled about in confusion as we couldn't go anywhere. I tried covering my eyes with the hem of my skirt but that was worse than watching. I saw it all. It is amazing the way a burning fire holds you in its grasp, especially a fire that is not in its accustomed place. I couldn't look away. There was nowhere to look.

Somehow, Mitya appeared and grabbed my arm. He dragged me to where my family stood. Since the straw was dry, the flames flared up high into the air as soon as the lit matches touched it. The matches kept on coming as Comrade Zabluda circled the mound of grain.

Taras and his brother, who were very close to Comrade Zabluda jumped on to his back to try stopping him, but several soldiers grabbed them off. They took them to one side of the square and shot them point blank as we watched. They fell to the ground with blood rushing out of their mouths and heads. They died right before all of their family and friends with no one allowed to help them. Women and Children were screaming. Xenkovna, with tears streaming down her own face, tried to go to Taras, but Auntie held her back as it was clear there was nothing to be done. We were forced to stand and watch our seed grain burn until there was only a pile of smoldering ash left.

I was surprised that none of the buildings around the square caught fire but, as Auntie said later, we were lucky that it was not windy that day.

When the fire subsided, Comrade Zabluda ordered the army to move us a little further down the main path. Before we could go home, he stood on a wagon where we all could see him.

"Remember," he said. "From this day forward, it is the Party and Mother Russia that dictate what you do. Those who don't do what we tell you will pay dearly. Now go home to your supper."

A Hungry Winter

:#:#:#:✦:#:#:#:

COMRADE ZABLUDA JUMPED down from the wagon and, in what seemed a very few minutes, the army was gone. Xenkovna was the first to reach the shot young men and would have thrown herself down onto the ground beside Taras had Uncle not caught her in his arms. I never knew that a human being was capable of making the sounds that were coming out of Xenkovna's mouth. The mothers of the two dead men were hysterical too.

I felt my own chest tighten and my head spin with what I was looking at. Although my parents were dead, I had never actually seen anyone but the Unravelled One die and certainly I could have never imagined anyone getting shot to death. It didn't make sense. One minute the young men were fighting, the next their heads were exploded on the ground. The sight of it was making me want to vomit, but I couldn't look away. All they had tried to do was to protect the precious seeds that would feed us over the winter and that would be used to grow new food next year. Why should they be lying dead on the ground now?

"Come," Auntie said gently. "We're going home." In my stupor, I hadn't noticed that the family had gathered again.

"What about them?" I said, pointing.

"There are plenty of men to help them," Auntie said. "We must take the little ones home as soon as we can."

We walked towards our house. Michael and Alexander led the way, stone-faced and silent, each of them holding one of the shocked little twins. Dmitri and I came after them with Viktor who cried and screamed so that we carried him some of the way. Auntie and Uncle followed with Xenkovna. She tried to loosen her father's arms so that she could go back to Taras, but he held her tight. Finally, she was overwhelmed by her father's strength and her own grief. When we got home, Uncle Misha carefully laid Xenkovna on the hearth and left her sobbing until she passed into blissful unconsciousness.

"It's a good thing I filled the pails in the kitchen with grain," Auntie said. "It'll be enough till we figure out what to do about bread."

Uncle didn't answer.

Auntie made some tea. No one wanted a real supper so we drank tea and ate some bread and butter. The men went off to their chores. We spent the evening sitting by the fire barely speaking to one another. Whenever Xenkovna woke up, she started to cry again.

"We'll never be married," she said. "Oh Mama—*Tahto*! He was going to ask for permission to marry me—at Christmas. Never be married—we'll never be married!" She buried her head in her arms and continued her weeping.

"Hush, daughter, hush," Auntie said. "Taras is with God now. None of us can understand God's plan—especially in such terrible times." With eyes full of her own tears, she stroked Xenkovna's head or cheek and made her drink some tea until she calmed down again. Then we all went to bed.

I tossed and turned on my sleeping bench in a fitful sleep. The images of the fire burned fiercely in my dreams; the exploded heads of the two young men appeared and disappeared. Their eyes looked at me right from inside of that fire as if they would draw me in magically. At other times, the heads came to life. One head would be in front of me and the other behind so that if I tried to run the one behind could grab me and not let me get away. They came so close that I could touch them. I could hear explosions and feel the blood from an unseen gunshot splattering all over me. If I washed it off, it would just smear all over me and cover more of my skin. The harder I rubbed, the more blood there seemed to be.

Meanwhile, Xenkovna's weeping played itself over and over in my head. It was a soft crying at first, but as those bloody heads tried to suck me in, it grew louder and louder till I screamed myself.

"Philipovna, wake up, wake up! It's a dream."

Auntie was shaking my shoulder. It was late in the night, but she hadn't undressed for bed yet. Apparently, I wasn't the only one dreaming. It would be months before a night could pass without Auntie being wakened up by one or the other of the Children and their nightmares.

"Go back to sleep," she said. "Remember, when you start seeing something bad, you can make yourself wake up. You're safe and warm. Uncle Misha and I are here. We won't let anything happen to you. Remember, I promised on your Mama's Bible. God won't let anything happen to you either. You must learn to trust in Him."

"But Auntie, Taras loved God too and, and ..." My voice trailed off. I wanted to ask the question, but I was too scared to actually say the words.

"I know, Child," Auntie said. "It is very hard to understand. We have to have faith that this will all be for the greater good—somehow. God doesn't give those He loves more than they can carry. Now, try to rest. Morning will be here soon enough."

When morning finally came, it was cold and rainy. I didn't want to go to school.

"You must go," Uncle Misha said. "We can't afford any more visits from the thug Comrades."

It took me longer than usual because I went around the buildings of the village. I couldn't bear the thought of walking through or looking at the village square. The smell of burning wheat hung over the buildings like an invisible shroud and the damp air made it cling to my clothes and skin so that I felt like I was being suffocated all over again. I arrived just as the others were filing in.

Asimov was in good form. He wore a big smile and started the day as if nothing had happened. But it didn't last long. We made mistakes in our sums, stumbled over our recitations and weren't enthusiastic enough in our singing of the songs that conjured up happy farmers. By noon, he returned to his usual miserable self and his metre stick was busier than ever. Half of the smaller Children were crying.

When we finished our lunch, Asimov put down his metre stick and said that we were going to have a different kind of lesson that afternoon. What could he possibly do after yesterday's horrific events?

"Today, you will listen very carefully," he said. "This lesson is a lesson that is more important for your parents than it is for you. If we see your parents doing the things we talk about this afternoon, Comrade Zabluda and I will know that you have done your homework."

He reached into his leather bag and produced some propaganda papers like the ones that Children were forced to hand out last winter. He pointed to me and, while I handed them out to the class, he continued.

"Yesterday shouldn't be anything you ought to worry about. It's only a few sacks of grain. Father Stalin has much more grain than your insignificant village can grow. He will look after those who are willing to work with him. If your parents know what is good for them, they will give their land to the *kolhosp* and come to work on it. If they continue to hold back, well, yesterday is just the beginning. You must help Father Stalin, his Comrades and me to convince your families that submitting to the new way of life is best for all of us."

We spent the afternoon taking turns reading aloud through the papers. My head was swimming with the promises of a "better way of life" for "happy farmers free from the burden of having to deal with commerce." Papa Stalin would provide "an opportunity for women to be free of the drudgeries of being tied to the household and the taking care of babies." Asimov said that girls should concentrate on their education so that they would be able to work in a factory or office and make their own living just like a man.

Why should I do that? I thought. When I grew up, I wanted to find a man like my Uncle Misha and be a woman like Auntie Xena.

There was even a section about how God was a useless fairy tale that kept a man's mind locked in the dark ages. I left the school with a pounding headache and a pile of papers full of Party propaganda.

When I returned to our home after school, the rain had stopped. Everyone was getting ready to leave the house. Xenkovna's face was swollen and her eyes were red from crying.

"Oh, Philipovna," Auntie said, "we've been waiting for you."

"Are we going somewhere?" I asked.

"We're going to Taras's funeral. Put your things away and come along. Don't dawdle."

"What are those papers in your hand?" Uncle Misha asked.

I swallowed hard and stepped back from his abrupt question.

"I—I am supposed to give them to you and Auntie," I said in a small voice. "Comrade Asimov gave them out to all of the students and said that our homework was to study them with you."

"I'm not going over any papers," Uncle roared. "Imagine that! The Child teaching his father how to live. What kind of world would that be!" He grabbed the propaganda sheets and threw them in the fire without a second look.

"When you go to school tomorrow, if Asimov asks you, tell him to take the matter up with me directly. This is not a matter for Children. Now let's go to the cemetery before it gets too dark."

We went to the cemetery. The two bereaved families were already there. The women were still crying. Xenkovna was hysterical again.

"I want to look at him," she cried. "I need to have one last look."

"Daughter," Auntie said, "he's all wrapped up and the coffin is closed. You don't want to see him now. Remember him as he was when he looked at you or how he was when he played his accordion. Please Child, for your own sake, remember him as he was."

Thankfully, the young men were covered up in closed coffins crudely fashioned by their fathers and close family members. There was no priest.

Auntie brought the Bible so Uncle Misha prayed over the caskets and read the funeral passages. There was no ritual bread to pass around. I stood back a little and watched as the coffins were lowered into the ground. Everyone helped to fill in the graves but I still stood watching—watching and praying to God and to my dead parents. I wondered if they would take care of these two young men. Certainly my Mama would look after Taras since she must have seen how much Xenkovna loved him. And since the other young man was his brother, I was sure that Mama would welcome him too.

There was no procession, no singing, no food or drinking vodka at anyone's home. The families would grieve alone.

\#\#\#

One sunny afternoon, after school, I found Uncle Misha and the cousins digging what looked like a shallow grave in the corner of our garden.

"Don't look so scared," Mitya said, laughing.

"Who died?" I asked.

"No one," Uncle Misha said. "We're digging a hole so that we can store some of the carrots, beets and potatoes for spring. We'll need something to eat before we can pick from the garden."

I didn't understand.

"Don't we have a root cellar for those vegetables?" I asked.

"Yes," Uncle Misha said. "But this storage space will let us keep more of them longer. If we dig a hole that is more than a meter deep and line it with clean sand, we can bury some of the root vegetables. They will stay fresh without freezing till the ground thaws in the spring when we can dig them up for the table. The trick is to dig the hole deep enough. Then we have to make sure the sand is perfectly clean with nothing in it to make them want to sprout."

I was amazed at Uncle Misha. He was so wise. How did he know all of these wonderful things? We spent the next week bringing sand from the river, sifting through it to make sure it was clean and lining the hole with it. Then we put layers of carrots, beets and potatoes each with a thick layer of sand separating it from the layer beneath. I loved looking at the dark red beets and the glowing orange carrots. I didn't even mind the sand grating on my teeth when I bit into a particularly good-looking potato. Its starch stuck deliciously to my teeth even after I crunched it down. When Uncle was satisfied that all was done properly, he filled in the rest of the hole with the original dirt that he and the cousins had dug out.

"All is not lost," he said with satisfaction at supper that night. "That should fill a few bellies in the spring before your garden grows."

He told us not to tell anyone about the stash of vegetables. "You never know who will become desperate."

Auntie crossed herself with a prayer of gratitude but her face still was shadowed with worry. And so the autumn dragged on. Each morning, she strictly measured and ground just enough wheat to make bread for breakfast. I took a baked potato or apple for lunch and we ate the root vegetables from the garden. Auntie was very careful with the vegetables too. She would cook just enough for us to have one bowl of soup each.

"Don't ask for more," she said. "We have to try to make it last till spring." She didn't know that I heard her say to Uncle that the vegetables might not last. "After all," she said, "there are ten of us eating."

Since there was little food for the chickens and they were laying fewer eggs, she killed them off one by one. She roasted the younger ones and made pots of soup with the older hens. Eggs became something of a treat. And then there were no hens or eggs at all. Mitya took to scavenging again.

"This is nothing," he said to me as I was sweeping the doorstep one late November day. "I used to pick mushrooms, catch rabbits and find all kinds of things when Mama was alive. I'll just have to go back to finding things for us."

But "finding things" didn't prove to be as easy as he thought. It was too late for mushrooms. The army was taking more than their regular share—and "much more than they did last year" I heard Uncle Misha say.

Asimov told us that the army took the food from our village and others like it so that the workers in the city would have something to eat.

"They don't have the luxury of having their own garden and living in paradise like you do," he said before launching into yet another song about happy farmers.

Those who were poorer than our family were already living off the land. The usual places for mushrooms were picked over and farmers were quick to catch any rabbits or other animals that had the misfortune of coming near the village. As the pastures froze and the cow didn't have enough food, her milk dried up. There was no milk or butter. Auntie quit making her cottage cheese.

"How are we going to feed the cow now that the snow is starting to fall and we have no hay?" Auntie said at supper. "She doesn't have any milk these days. We have to do something."

"I'm going to get my papers," Uncle Misha said. "I should be able to borrow some feed and straw from George and the others. "If I can't borrow it, I'll buy some."

"How will you buy it?" Auntie asked. "We have no money."

"I'll offer to work. Someone always needs a pair of hands to do something, even if it's only chopping wood. Let me worry about that. You have enough to do with managing the kitchen here."

Auntie looked as if she was going to question him, but shut her mouth and busied herself with clearing the table.

"*Tahto*," Viktor said. "What if you can't get any work? What will we do with the cow? She'll be hungry."

"We'll see what we do when the time comes," Uncle said gruffly. He went out to sit alone on the stoop in the crisp starlit evening.

"Auntie, what will we do?" I asked.

"I really don't know," she said, crossing herself. "We've always had enough to eat. Sometimes, it was only bread and potatoes, but, by the Grace of God, we've always managed. Don't worry. Uncle Misha and I will make something work. Now get into your bed."

The next morning, Uncle Misha headed toward the house that now was the government office. He was going to ask for his and the older cousins' papers. But when I came home from school, there was another of those invisible shrouds that would come over the household in those days. The Comrades would not give Uncle his papers. He was informed that no one was allowed to leave the town.

"Father Stalin's orders," the clerk said to Uncle. "No one goes in or out for the next two months."

"You mean we're prisoners in our own village?" Uncle Misha said.

"Don't bother saying anything. I'm not the one who gives the orders — take it up with the Thousander."

Uncle came home, angry and frustrated.

"Why are we being held like prisoners in our own village?" he said, raging. "They refused to give me the papers and that was it. I guess we'll have to kill the cow." Then he left the house abruptly.

He didn't talk to anyone or eat anything for days. He didn't kill the cow either.

One cold day, Comrade Zabluda and the army came to the house again. Uncle Ivan was with them. They grabbed Uncle Misha and the older cousins like they did the first Sunday when they took our wheat and hay, except it was a different man that held Uncle Misha at gunpoint.

"We're here for your share of the allotment to the army," Comrade Zabluda said.

"You set it on fire. I have no more," Uncle Misha said.

The Comrade laughed. They went into the barn, tied up the cow and loaded her into one of the trucks.

Auntie ran out of the house screaming again but none of the army men paid attention.

Uncle Ivan grabbed Auntie and twisted her arm behind her back.

"Now give us the food from your pantry," he demanded.

"Why are you asking her for it?" Comrade Zabluda asked. "You've stuffed that fat belly of yours many times at her table. Take the food. You said that you know where it is. I have no time for pleasantries."

Uncle Ivan came into the house pushing Auntie before him. Some of the soldiers followed him into the kitchen while others ransacked the root cellar. They took all of the food they could find, pots of honey, jars of jam, crocks of pickles and all. I started to cry when one of them cut down every single onion string that I had so carefully braided and tossed them onto one of the blankets that they grabbed from a sleeping bench. They tied up all of our garlic and onions into that blanket and took the bundle out onto the truck. They did not even spare auntie's precious sack of berries from the *kalyna*, the ones she had dried for the use of medicinal needs that might arise over the coming winter.

Once Comrade Zabluda was satisfied that he had all of our food. He told the soldiers to let everyone go.

Uncle Misha spat at the Comrade's feet.

The soldier standing closest to him repaid him with a blow on the head with the butt of his gun. Then, they went away. Mitya's head popped up from behind the woodpile just as they were leaving, but he had enough sense to be quiet till they were gone.

"What's going on?" he asked, rounding the woodpile with Sharik following at his heel.

"They took our food," I said flatly. "All of our food—even the onion strings and vegetables from the root cellar." The tears rolled down my cheeks—my precious braids of onions and garlic.

"I guess we could eat this rabbit," he said.

We were too shocked to eat. There was nothing to say. Auntie cried that whole evening and Uncle sat brooding quietly. Xenkovna huddled with the Children. We didn't know what to do.

Uncle Misha opened the stash of root vegetables that was meant for spring. Mitya said that the army put out patrols in the woods so he had even more difficulty finding food because he always had to keep an eye out for soldiers. Uncle Misha suggested that he take the cousins with him, but Mitya said that they would slow him down. I suspected that he just didn't want everyone to know all of his secrets. When I went to school, I learned that the army had gone through the whole village taking any food that they could find and sparing no one.

I learned how it felt to be hungry. I ate my breakfast bread slowly—taking a sip of water or tea and chewing till there was no bread left in my mouth before I took the next, small bite.

"It will feel like you have more food in your tummy," Auntie said. "You have to make it last till supper."

The little cousins were always asking for something more to eat. The older members of the family started saving a portion of their meagre meal for them when they cried with hunger. I went to school, always looking for anything that someone could have left or dropped that resembled food, but of course, there was nothing. Every one of Asimov's students was doing the same. They were just as hungry as I was—maybe worse. We never talked about it. I'm sure they had the same instructions as we did from their parents. Uncle's words kept ringing in my ears: "Don't tell anyone. You never know who will become desperate." I found it hard to concentrate on my schoolwork and didn't care if Asimov smacked me with the metre stick.

The evenings were the worst of all. After eating the small supper that Auntie dished out for everyone, we would try to read and recite like we used to. I often fell asleep while I was reading and couldn't remember the words to recite. The thought of food was never far from my mind. In the end, Auntie got so tired of waking up to the cries of hungry or dreaming Children, that she put small amounts of dried poppy heads and stems into the tea, no honey, just a pinch of poppy plant. It was the only way we could sleep through the night.

On one of these evenings, we heard the sound of a truck rumbling up the path.

"What could they possibly want now?" Auntie said. "We've nothing more to give them."

The Comrades from the bread procurement committee didn't even knock on our door. They tried to come in as if they owned the house, but the latch that Uncle Misha put on the door held until Uncle lifted it.

"So Comrade, this is what you're doing instead of coming to the meetings," Comrade Zabluda said to Uncle Misha. "Lounging rather than being part of the *kolhosp*."

He grabbed the book of poetry that I was reading out of my hand and threw it into the fire.

"Let's see what other nonsense you are teaching these wonderful young Russians."

He turned to one of the soldiers and waved to the corner shelf where all of our family's books were always neatly lined up.

"Sasha, I think the fire's a little low, don't you? Throw some more kindling on it. This second." He motioned to the books. So there went our books, one after the other into the fire. All we could do was watch.

"Now, Michael Ivanowich, get your hat and come along to the meeting where you belong. Bring those fine young men, too." He motioned to Alexander and Michael, but didn't see Mitya and Sharik in the far corner away from the fire.

They did as they were told. What could they do with half-a-dozen or more armed soldiers in their house? After that evening, Uncle and the boys never sat with us by the fire. As the year ground down to a dull, hungry end, they were forced to go to meetings while we suffered through one long day after another. The only reading we could do was the reading from the Bible which was always kept in Auntie's trunk so it had not been thrown into the fire.

The Shadow of Death

I T WAS UNUSUALLY cold in the house. I wrapped myself in my
Mama's feather bed, but the cold still crept in. Despite the fact
that I had all my clothing on when I went to bed, I felt stiff and chilly.
I opened one eye just enough to see that the night had stretched itself into another gray winter morning. I tried to pretend that I was
still asleep, but Xenkovna was quicker than me and greeted me with
a tired gesture.

"You might as well get up, Philipovna. I'll need all of the help
you can give me."

"Are they any better?" I said, yawning. I sat up on my sleeping
bench. Xenkovna was sitting by the three little ones who were
tucked up on the hearth. It looked like she hadn't moved since they
had finally succumbed to the poppy-laced tea she had given them
in the early hours of the morning.

"I'm not sure," she said. "Their breathing is still very rough. At
least they're sleeping."

Auntie was not home yet. Uncle Misha was asleep in his chair
where he collapsed last night upon arriving home very late after yet
one more meeting with the men of the village. Xenkovna had pulled
his boots off and spread his soaking clothes out to dry.

"What on earth were you doing, *Tahto*?" she asked as she sat on a stool rubbing his purple feet. "It looks like you were out in the fields all night."

"In a manner of speaking, I was," he answered, his whole body still shivering from the cold. "They can't persuade us with words so they set up a boot camp of sorts. They walk us back and forth, through the fields, doing military exercises till we're exhausted. Then they ask if we're ready to give in yet. Can you imagine—they wanted to send a telegram to Father Stalin to tell him that we all finally agree to give away our land. As if a silly telegram would make the difference. I'm glad I could still walk home. Some of the boys were carried back to their women. They didn't just have frozen feet. They were so confused by the Comrades' interrogations that they wouldn't have been able to find their way home, I'm sure. I don't know how we'll hold out. It's a good thing that Michael and Alexander weren't there."

Xenkovna had thrown what was left of the wood onto the fire and poured Uncle a cup of tea. He had taken a few gulps and collapsed into his chair where he now sat sleeping. There was nothing to eat.

"No sign of her?" Mitya asked as he staggered in under a load of firewood. He shivered and rubbed his hands which I could see were raw and red from the cold. Sharik shivered in after him and curled up by the warmth of the stove. His ribs poked through his black and white fur.

"You better get the fire going while everyone's sleeping."

"Are they any better?"

"Viktor's still fevering and the twins have only stopped coughing this hour. I haven't slept all night."

Mitya waved toward me, still wrapped in my feather bed trying to find myself for the day.

"Have you heard from the boys?" Xenkovna asked.

Mitya shrugged his shoulders.

"Philipovna, get some water while Mitya stokes the fire. He has to warm up before he goes to relieve the boys," she said. "Try not to wake *Tahto*. The Comrades kept him up more than half of the night."

Michael and Alexander were out in the woods waiting for Auntie—in fact, we all were waiting for her and we were all afraid for her safety though none of us had the courage to say so. I dragged my feet to the floor. I was getting used to the empty ache in my belly, but the lack of energy was taking its toll. I didn't want to get moving. The day loomed cold and hungry before me. It didn't matter to me whether there was water or not. Still, Xenkovna was my elder and Uncle was asleep so I dared not complain about doing what I was told.

I pulled on my felt boots and headed for the water bucket. As I turned up the path, I stopped to check if anyone was coming. I hoped for Auntie, but was afraid of the army. I always rounded this particular bend with extra care and much trepidation, especially since that morning two weeks before Christmas, when I was sent for water. I had just turned into this very bend in the path when I heard the rumbling of Comrade Zabluda's truck. I dropped the bucket I was carrying and ran back to warn the others. But it was too late.

The bread procurement committee was at our door, right behind me. The Comrades heard rumours that the farmers had food hidden around their homes so they came "either to find the hidden food or put the rumours to rest once and for all," Comrade Zabluda said to Uncle Misha when he and his men barged into our kitchen again. They came into our house with long, steel rods. They poked into the floor, the roof and the walls of our house. They pushed furniture out from the corners and ripped apart our beds. They even tore apart the bedding of the cribs where the littlest cousins slept.

As Auntie gathered the crying Children around her, the Comrades knocked on the fireplace looking for secret hiding places. They opened pots and smashed dishes. But there was no hidden food. We thought we had still saved our secret store of vegetables that were buried in the ground, but we were mistaken. The Comrades went out into the garden and using a grid pattern, stuck their rods into the ground every half metre till they found Uncle's stash. To make sure that we got the message, they made Uncle Misha and the boys—all three of them including Mitya, dig up the vegetables. They dug them up at gunpoint and put them into the army truck while the rest of us were forced to watch, in the cold morning, until all of the vegetables were gone.

"Someone must have opened his yap," Uncle Misha said after the army left. "Did any of you Children tell? I warned you about mentioning that food to anyone. Are you sure you didn't say anything in passing, at school maybe?" He looked hard in my direction and I was terrified that he was going to accuse me. But, Auntie shushed him.

"What good is it to question them? The food is gone," she said.

I sulked away from Uncle. Did he really think I couldn't keep a secret? How could he imagine that I would say anything? Couldn't he see that Mitya was my only friend? Didn't he know how happy I was to be in his house? It was the only place I had called home since my parents died.

Auntie collapsed into her chair and stared at the devastation that had been her tidy home just minutes before. When she couldn't look any longer, she covered her face with her apron. We sat around until the fire was almost out. Viktor complained of the cold that the wind was blowing in through the holes in the walls and thatched roof. It was the only time I ever remember Auntie not crossing herself in a crisis.

Xenkovna and Auntie slowly put what wasn't smashed in order while I swept up the broken glass and crockery. I tried to put the dirt back into the holes the Comrades made in the floor. I did the best I could but its surface remained scarred and bumpy because we could only make the clay finish that made it glossy and smooth in the spring or summer. Uncle tried to fix the holes in the roof but the straw he had wasn't the right kind of straw. It wasn't the time of year for repairing the roof. Auntie cut a couple of the older blankets into rags so that we could plug the holes in the walls. It wasn't the right time of year to fix the clay plaster that insulated our white-washed, wooden walls from the cold, either.

By the end of the day, we found out that every house in our village had had a visit from the Comrades and all had suffered the same molestation whether they had stored food or not. So with our home compromised we shivered through Christmas and the dawning of the New Year, 1932. There was no food for Christmas Eve supper but Uncle brought in a sheaf of straw to spread under the table. Auntie laid out her embroidered cloth and lit a candle. We prayed before sitting down to tea and didn't drink it till the first star appeared crystal in the evening sky.

"We'll sing a few carols," Auntie said. "It is a holy evening whether we eat or not. We have to remember that He suffered just like we do."

"Was Jesus ever hungry?" I asked Auntie.

"Yes. He went into the desert and fasted. The devil tempted Him three times, but He did not give in. I do know that when He was on the cross, he suffered all of the pain that everyone would ever feel. And he certainly would have been thirsty, especially when they gave him vinegar on a sponge."

I didn't feel like singing and neither did the others. But after a couple of half-hearted starts, we all joined in: "God everlasting is born. A Saviour has come from Heaven to forgive our sins ..."

Uncle read the Christmas Story and we prayed again. I was surprised to find that, even though we hadn't eaten a single crumb, the evening felt special and Uncle's guitar sang with the sweetest voice I'd ever heard.

"Do you remember what it was like when we went to celebrate Christmas at *Pan* Kalynowich's estate?" Uncle Misha asked.

"How could I ever forget?" Auntie smiled with the recollection.

"Will you tell us about it?" I asked.

So Auntie told us of how, in 1914, the whole village was invited to the great celebration for St. Nikolai's Day. There was a great feast with stuffed geese, and fish, and even a whole roast pig. Auntie and Mama came to help the Unravelled One peel vegetables, to roll the cabbage rolls and to stuff the *varenyky*. They worked for three days while the house servants polished and cleaned every surface of the great house.

Once the priest blessed the feast and the important guests were served, everyone who helped was invited to join in. They had never eaten such good food, especially the sweet treats that were brought in from Kiev.

"But the dinner wasn't the best part of it," Auntie said. "We hadn't even finished clearing away the dinner when I heard music. The Master had hired a troupe of musicians. There must have been half-a-dozen of them—and could they play! Surely, they were sent from Heaven. It was the first time I had ever heard the bandura."

"The bandura wasn't the only thing you enjoyed for the first time that night."

Auntie flushed with embarrassment.

"Misha, don't tell stories."

"You're the one telling stories," he said. "So go on and finish it."

"Well, the music was so exciting that I couldn't help dancing in the corner from where I watched the Party. Since I was just a village girl—and not even a servant, I didn't want to join in. But, Uncle Misha noticed me. When he asked me why I wasn't dancing, I told him that I couldn't because I wasn't dressed for it. It just so happened that the mistress of the house was near us as we spoke. She said that a pretty girl like me shouldn't worry about what she was wearing. I said that I wasn't fit for mixing with the beautiful guests wearing clothes that had been at the kitchen fire for three days. In the end, the mistress felt sorry for me and took me to her room.

"It was a big room with heavy furniture and a mirror that

showed my whole shabby outfit from my head to my feet. I was so ashamed when I saw my ragged clothes for myself that I wanted to run home. But the mistress was kind. From a carved trunk, she pulled out a beautiful blue woollen skirt and silk blouse, the ones I still wear to church. She said that since it was St. Nikolai's special day, it was fitting to give a needy person a gift.

"I was shy and didn't want to take off my clothes but she turned her back to me while I changed. She laughed when I gave in to my impulse to twirl till the many meters of skirt flared into a huge umbrella and said that it was a pity that such a beautiful girl as me was born into such a poor and low class. She prayed for me as she brushed my hair and tied it with a blue velvet ribbon.

"Uncle Misha couldn't take his eyes off me when I returned. We danced till the morning—and we have been dancing ever since."

I went to sleep that Christmas Eve with an empty belly, yes, but also with a head full of stories and a heart full of hope.

We kept to our house trying to conserve our own heat. We prayed and read the Bible both in the morning and before going to bed at night. On the hardest days, Auntie made us memorize Bible passages to keep our mind off of our hunger pains. She made a ritual out of tea breaks through the day.

"You must drink all of your tea, whether you want it or not," she said. "If you get dehydrated, things will get much worse."

I wondered how she knew what to do. The lack of food was affecting our sense of well-being so we became lethargic and only visited our neighbours for reasons of necessity. Of course, Auntie was called to tend to those who got ill, but once our neighbours heard that the twins were sick, no one came to our home as they were trying not to get sick themselves. Even the propagandists quit knocking. I was excused from going back to school, especially after word got out that Katerina's mother and son had both died from a sickness with the same symptoms as the little twins were suffering from.

Auntie had done everything in her wide experience to cure the twins of the coughing, but they started bringing up white phlegm and continued to get worse. When Viktor woke up with a fever, she finally decided that a doctor should be summoned. Uncle had gone to the clerk's office asking for his papers again.

"It's been more than two months," he said. "My family needs medicine and now that the Children haven't eaten for weeks, they're desperate for food."

"No one leaves the village," the clerk said. "Take it up with the Thousander."

Uncle asked the Comrade at the meeting in the evening.

"Father Stalin's orders," Comrade Zabluda said. "We're not going to bother him about a little sniffle, are we? I hear there's a cold going around. I'm sure they'll survive. After all, they come from good strong peasant stock, don't they?"

Auntie and Xenkovna struggled through three more nights of the twins' coughing. Viktor wasn't improving either. He went from hot to shivering and back to hot in a matter of minutes. His breathing was starting to sound raspy like the twins.

"What should we expect?" Auntie asked, wiping her tearful eyes, "They have no strength to fight with after not having food for so long." It was decided that Auntie would disguise herself as an old woman and go for medicine.

"They won't be expecting me to leave three sick Children," she said to Uncle Misha. "No one has visited for days and Xenkovna can do all of the things I can without real medicine. Make sure you and the boys do everything the Comrades ask of you. I'll be back in two days."

Auntie's transformation was amazing. I sat and watched her put ash in her dark brown hair till it looked gray. She found the oldest ragged coat she could get her hands on. It must have come from the Unravelled One's trunk because I never saw it till that day. She wrapped her head in a black kerchief and wrapped her feet in extra rags before she put on her felt boots. The shadows under her eyes and her sinking cheeks needed no enhancement as we all looked underfed. She wrapped her best embroidery and the little silver spoon that I had found in the river into a small bundle which fit inconspicuously under her shawl.

"Don't forget to say your prayers," she said over her shoulder before she disappeared around the bend where I stood in this gray, miserable dawn thinking over the events of the last two months.

I better hurry, I thought. *Mitya wants to get going to the lookout spot. Michael and Alexander must be freezing by now.* Before Auntie left it was agreed that she wouldn't come straight home. If she were fortunate enough to get some food, we must make sure that it wasn't discovered. She agreed to meet either Mitya or the cousins at the place where the Unravelled One's house had stood. Since the villagers were superstitious, no one would go looking for her there. Even the Comrades were skittish when it came to things that were connected with the supernatural despite their denunciations of God as a fairy tale. Nevertheless, it had been three days since Auntie had gone. The men kept watch for her faithfully since the night before last, but there was no sign of her yet.

A gust of wind caught at my shawl as I hesitated on the path. I picked up my pail and hurried towards the well.

I better go back and fill the other pail too, I thought. It looked like a blizzard was going to blow in. I certainly didn't want to have to go for water later.

"It's about time," Mitya said when I returned to the house. "I hope Auntie doesn't get stuck in this weather. Look at those clouds."

"The weather could be the least of her problems," Uncle Misha said with a yawn. "Put on the tea and we'll relieve the boys."

"Oh Uncle, you shouldn't go out with me," Mitya said. "The snow is blowing in pretty good. Maybe you should stay in and rest."

Uncle Misha coughed and reached for the rags that he used for extra warmth inside his boots.

"Come on girls, get that tea going. I'll not lie about while my sons catch frostbite." So we watched Mitya and Uncle Misha go out into the cold. The morning dragged on as Xenkovna and I coaxed tea into the younger cousins and watched them take turns spitting it back. Their laboured breath was getting shallower as the hours passed by. They hadn't cried since last night. The boys came back and bundled up to sleep by the fire. By noon, the snow was falling steadily. Suddenly Xenkovna dropped Marta and ran out into one of the smaller rooms of the house. She stamped her feet and shrieked at the top of her lungs.

"I can't take this anymore," she cried. "If one of them dies it'll be my fault. Mama will never forgive me."

"Are they going to die?" I asked. I felt my eyes pop in stunned disbelief. No one said a word about anyone dying!

"What—what's going on?" Michael jumped into consciousness. "Who's dying?"

"I don't know," I said through my own deluge of tears. "Xenkovna says that they might die." I flung my arm in the young cousins' direction, but didn't dare say that I thought they were looking a little blue.

Xenkovna was sobbing now. Michael got up and went to his sister.

"What's going on?" he asked gently.

"They're not any better ... I can't help them ... I'm so tired ... Mama will kill me if they die. I'm so tired."

"I'll stay with them," he said. "You go and get some sleep. If Mama comes home and sees you like this, it won't be good. We must be strong. Mama knows that you're doing your best. We all are."

"But Taras ... he's gone and now the little ones ... It's just not right ... I'm so tired ..." Michael held her in his arms as she went on sobbing. When there were no more tears left, he brought her back to the fire where we let her sleep while we tended to the sick ones. Alexander got up when he heard Xenkovna's outburst. He went out to refill the water pails. He stacked wood till there was no more room for it in the house. We sat without speaking till twilight crept in.

"Philipovna," Alexander finally said. "It looks like Marta is turning bluish—or is it the dark afternoon?"

"I don't know," I answered. I didn't bother saying that the Children sounded more like hissing snakes than little ones breathing.

"Light the candle. They'll be looking for it," Michael said.

I found a candle and placed it in the window. We sat without speaking again. There was nothing else I could do. No one remembered to make tea. Although Alexander tended the fire, it didn't seem to be warming the room.

Outside, the wind was blowing harder and the snow was getting thicker. I could feel its draft sneaking through the patched holes in the walls and I knew that if it got any stronger it would have that moaning sound, the one that Taras Shevchenko wrote about in his famous poem about the Dnipro River. The sound of the groaning river and sighing wind not only chilled me to the bone, but would frighten me when I tried to sleep. What if Auntie lost her way? I dared not think about such a terrible thing. Finally Xenkovna woke up again. Her eyes were puffy from crying, but she seemed to be better.

"Do you hear anything?" she said.

We listened.

"Helloooooo, the house!" Someone was shouting in the wind.

"Who's that?" I asked. "Uncle and Mitya wouldn't be shouting like that, would they?"

"Something must have gone wrong," Xenkovna said wringing her hands in fear.

"All of you stay right here," Michael said. "I'll check it out."

"I'm coming with you," Alexander said. "You'll lose your way in this blizzard."

"No, you won't. Someone has to stay here in case it's the Comrades again. I wouldn't put it past them to try to pull another stupid stunt." He lit a lantern but as soon as he opened the door, its light was blown out.

"Ah, fury," he said. "This won't be of any damned use." He banged down the lantern and out he went into the freezing night with nothing to guide him.

We listened again and after what felt like an hour we heard some stumbling at the door.

Alexander jumped to his feet.

"Who is it?" he asked.

"Open up!" a voice called out and its owner thumped on the door.

"Not till you say who it is," Alexander yelled.

"For the love of God! Don't you recognize me—your own father?"

Alexander opened the door a crack.

Viktor started to cry.

Then the wind blew Michael, and Uncle with Auntie in his arms, through the door. Before I could ask about Mitya, he, with two men whom I had never seen before, tumbled in after them. They were dragging a sack. Michael had to put his shoulder to the door and latch it shut against the storm.

Xenkovna rushed to her mother.

"Whoa, not so fast," one of the strangers said. "I'm Dr. Bond-arenko. She may be suffering from frostbite. We need to warm her up slowly. Put some water to heat on the fire—but don't let it get too hot."

Xenkovna did is she was told.

They laid Auntie onto one of the sleeping benches and slowly unwrapped the blanket that the doctor put around her. It looked like she was unconscious, but she reached out her hand when Uncle Misha spoke gently to her.

"You see her cheeks and nose," the doctor said to Uncle Misha. "They're all white. No rubbing, you'll damage the skin. Her eye-lashes are frozen together. We have to bathe them gently with warm water. And don't put her right beside the stove right away either. Is there any tea in the house?"

I jumped up to fill the kettle.

Meanwhile, Viktor's crying got louder and louder. It was only when he started with another coughing fit that the doctor realized that there were any Children in the room.

"Good Heavens! What do we have here? Bring a lamp—now." He turned to the little cousins. "And my medicine bag. He picked Maria up first. Beneath the lamplight her face was a shade of pale lilac. Her breath had developed a sinister whistling sound and she was too tired to cry. The doctor gently placed a thumb on her chin and opened her mouth. Another cough from Maria sent white phlegm flying everywhere. It was the first time I saw the horrible expression of despair that would become commonplace on the faces of the adults in the village as the winter dragged by.

"She has diphtherial croup. She should have been tended to long before this," he said. "I'll give you medicine, but whether or not she will be able to swallow any is another story. It looks like her throat is almost closed with the membrane that grows in the throat with this sickness. Now let's look at the others."

"We couldn't get permission to go for medicine," Xenkovna said.

"Yes, that's what your Mama said before she passed out in the wagon."

He handed Maria to me and went on to examine Marta. She didn't make a sound either. The furrow on his brow deepened as he gave her over to Xenkovna. But it was obvious that the diagnosis was the same. I noticed that Marta's skin had turned that funny shade of lilac too. Viktor wouldn't stay still, but the doctor prevailed and did what he could for him.

Once the medicine was administered and the Children tucked up again, we sat down by the fire. Auntie opened her eyes and slowly wakened. Uncle Misha bathed her face with warm water. He wrapped her in a blanket and sat her in a chair by the fire. Her hands were too stiff to hold her cup so Uncle helped her sip at the tea.

For the first time since they arrived, the doctor's companion spoke.

"We'll sit for an hour and then we must go," he said.

"Yes, Slavko," the doctor said. "I know you risked a lot to bring us here. We can't be caught in this zone."

"But you're a doctor!" Uncle Misha said. "Surely you don't have any restrictions."

"It seems that he does," Auntie said weakly. "Let them rest and I'll tell you the whole story."

"I have no money to pay for the medicine," Uncle said.

"We can concern ourselves with those matters later," the doctor said. "The important thing is that I don't get caught here by the Comrades."

"Xenkovna," Auntie said, "open the sack and boil some porridge. That's all we have to offer."

"Thank you," the doctor said. "We only have time for tea."

We made a place for Slavko and Doctor Bondarenko by the fire. They accepted our hospitality, but Slavko kept his eye on the window.

"It's a good thing you found me on the road," Auntie said slowly. "When I left home a few days ago, I walked to the first checkpoint. I was very scared that they wouldn't let me go through, but I acted like I didn't really know where I was going. The Comrades in uniform laughed and said that if I got lost it wouldn't matter because it was time an old woman like me was on life's final journey anyway. So I smiled back at them and kept on going. The Comrades' reaction made me feel more confident. It meant that my disguise was working."

Between slow sips of tea and pauses for rest, Auntie went on to tell us how she walked to a town which was two towns away because that was where people told her the nearest market was. At the checkpoint to the market town the Comrades were much more thorough. They searched her—pockets, bundle and all. They made her show them everything she was carrying, and as she had suspected the day I first found the silver spoon, there was trouble. They asked for her papers and lectured her for leaving her town without them. They demanded to know about the real silver. They detained her for hours and questioned her as to who gave it to her; did she belong to the bourgeois family whose initials were on the handle of the spoon?

"I believe that they were just playing with me because I was old and helpless," Auntie said.

By the time they let her go, the first day had slipped away. She begged a cup of tea from a woman whose house was at the edge of the village. The woman gave her some bread and butter and let her sleep by her fire.

"I felt guilty for eating the bread," Auntie said, "but she was so kind. She said that I would find Doctor Bondarenko at the edge of the neighbouring town."

The next day, Auntie went to the market. She tried to sell her embroidery, but no one would buy it because there were many folks from all over our area selling embroidery, clothing, jewellery and household goods that they hoped to trade for any food that folks were willing to part with. There were stories about villagers being so hungry that they ate their own animals and sent Children away to relatives under the cover of night. Some of the peasants were getting sick because the animals they were eating were sick themselves and not fit for people to eat. Other people wouldn't buy her embroidery because they were afraid that her house was full of sickness. The market was buzzing with rumours that people were dying of the plague beyond the checkpoints. Why else would the Comrades be prohibiting people from visiting places and family that they had always been able to visit freely?

"I don't understand it," Auntie said with tears spilling out over her frostbitten cheeks. "All of the people in that area have enough to eat. They're walking around, well-fed and warm, while inside our checkpoint we starve and freeze to death. How is it possible that there is no bread for my brother? We are all Ukrainians."

She had almost given up her mission of trading for wheat when she showed her silver spoon to a merchant who was closing up his business for the day.

"Please," she cried, "I can't go home empty handed. My Children will surely die. They need a doctor!"

The man felt sorry for her. He traded her silver spoon for as much wheat as she could carry in the sack.

"God be with you—and with your Children," he said, crossing himself, "and with all of us in these unpredictable times."

So Auntie started walking. She walked around the town the long way so that she could find the doctor and pass without going through the checkpoint again. But that took longer and it was harder to walk carrying the heavy sack of wheat. She decided to pace herself by walking for a while and then resting a few minutes. She went on in that way till she became disoriented, out in the countryside. As she tried circling back to the road that would take her to Zyladyn, she realized that it was getting late and she would not be able to make it back to the agreed upon meeting place. There were no houses in sight. She didn't know any of the shortcuts and couldn't risk trying to cross the countryside. She was getting stiff from the cold.

"I was worried," she said. "I knew that you would be waiting for me, but I knew that I wouldn't get home. I prayed that God would send help." She wiped tears away again and shivered. "There was nothing to do but keep on walking."

The gray twilight deepened into darkness. Auntie plodded on. There were no stars or moon as the clouds were blowing in. She tried to retrace her steps and hoped that she was on the right road. She walked till she lost the feeling in her feet. She wasn't sure where she was, but she was afraid to stop moving because she didn't want to freeze to death. The wind picked up. It was almost morning when Slavko and the doctor found her wandering on the road going in the opposite direction from Zyladyn.

"It was just my luck that the good doctor had to deliver a baby. They asked me to come in," Auntie said. "But I didn't because I knew there was sickness in our house. So I stayed in the wagon, covered up by the blankets till he did his work. Besides, it would be safer for all of us if no one saw me with Slavko and the doctor."

They drove the wagon along the back roads that avoided the checkpoint at Zyladyn until they were as close to the place of the Unravelled One's house as they could go. It was also their good fortune that Mitya was scouting around. Otherwise, they might have completely missed each other in the blowing weather as Auntie had fainted in the wagon. It would be years later that Auntie would tell me and Xenkovna about the piles of the bones of dead people who were frozen or starved to death that she saw lying by the road on the way home.

As soon as there was a lull in the storm, Slavko moved towards the door.

"We need to go while the wind is still blowing. That way the snow will fill in our tracks and no one will ever guess that we've been here," he said. Mitya offered to help him with the horses which were in the barn. The doctor took one last look at the sleeping little Children and reluctantly followed.

"I wish I could do more for you—and them," he said to Auntie motioning toward the Children. He wrapped his thick scarf around his neck and put on his fur hat. "God be with you. You're a brave woman." He shook hands with Uncle Misha and then disappeared into the darkness.

We sat around the fire till Auntie looked like she would faint again.

"Why don't all of you get some sleep," Xenkovna said. "I've

slept all afternoon so I can stay up with the little ones. If I need you, I'll wake you."

I went to my feather bed. I was exhausted but I couldn't fall asleep. The events of the day, the people coming and going all mixed themselves up in my dreams. One minute I was looking at Maria's lilac-tinged face, the next I was looking at the doctor's strange expression. The sound of the wind played its mournful drone in the background and then Xenkovna was crying. I shook myself awake.

It wasn't a dream. She was crying. Sitting in the chair with Maria in her lap and crying.

"What's the matter?" I asked her trying to be as quiet as I could so as not to wake the rest of the family.

"Look," she said, pointing to the lifeless Maria.

I looked at my little cousin. Her face wasn't purple any more. It was blue now. She lay like a waxen doll in Xenkovna's lap and I could see by the peace on her face that she was not breathing at all.

I picked Maria up gently and wrapped her in her blanket. I laid her in her bed and folded her little hands in prayer.

"Come, my sister," I said. "Let's go to bed."

I took Xenkovna's hand and led her to my sleeping bench. It was strange how at that moment we reversed our places. I tucked her under my feather bed and covered her up. I crawled in with her. Then we clung to each other and cried.

We cried for my mother and father, for my little sibling I didn't know, for The Unravelled One and for Mitya's father, for Taras and his brother and now for little Maria. We cried because we knew that Marta was going soon, too, and we cried because we might also be called to join her. We cried because we were hungry and we cried because we didn't know if there would ever be enough to eat again.

We didn't scream or sob like Xenkovna did earlier in the day. We wept silently, with broken hearts whose grief carried us forward on a current as strong as the current of the Dnipro River that rushed by our home and took everything in its way out to the Black Sea. We didn't need to cry out loud; the wind was crying out for all of us, to God, for the Love of God and for all of the forsaken who would suffer after us. As we sobbed together, quietly in the house, the snow fell from Heaven in frozen, sorrowful tears. The wind moaned and howled out our pain in its unfettered fury until both of us had no tears left.

May Day

THE MORNING SUNSHINE was streaming into the eastern window when I woke up. It was so bright in the big room of the house that I blinked several times before my eyes could adjust to the dazzling light. From where I lay on the sleeping bench, I could see the blue sky with not a cloud in sight. I snuggled under my feather bed, staring at the snow-laden branches of our birch tree as they glittered in the sun. The air was cold and still. How could the world turn from the dark and scary place of last night into a beautiful fairyland in such a few hours? The house was very quiet. Could I have dreamed the terrible day that had passed before I cried myself to sleep? But Xenkovna was still lying beside me. I was afraid to look beyond the window to where the twins and Viktor slept. I wondered if Auntie knew that Maria was gone and I didn't want to be the one who discovered Marta—in case she had died while we were sleeping.

A coughing fit from the bed by the hearth got everyone in the house moving. Xenkovna and I almost tripped over each other in our haste to get to Viktor. We could have spared ourselves the effort. From where I lay under the covers, I hadn't seen that Auntie was there all along. She was silently weeping, looking from one dead twin to the other. When Xenkovna reached for Viktor, Auntie

149

didn't move. She tried to stroke Maria's cheek and then Marta's, but she had trouble making her hands do what she wanted. She buried her face in her arms and wept some more.

Meanwhile, Xenkovna patted Viktor's back and helped him cough up more white goo from his lungs. She got him some water and tried to make him drink.

"He doesn't feel so good this morning, Mama," Xenkovna said to her mother. "Should I get him some medicine?"

Auntie silently nodded.

I stood there stupidly. I didn't know what to do. Her eyes had such a dazed look, as if she was in a different world.

"Auntie, can I do something?" I asked.

She shook her head.

"Good morning," Uncle Misha said. "Get dressed and fetch some water, would you, Philipovna?"

He took one look at his wife and rushed over to where she stood. When he realized his babies were dead, it seemed that his sobs would shake the house to its very foundation.

I was relieved to do Uncle's bidding. The fresh air felt sharp as I sucked it into my lungs like someone who has been deprived of air for months. The cold temperature assaulted my nose and cheeks, but somehow, it felt good—at least I was still alive. I breathed in deeply and blew out my breath in white clouds as I took my time retracing my steps from the well.

Xenkovna had the big washing pot ready to fill with water. I made several more trips to the well and then, under Auntie's supervision, I helped Xenkovna bathe the twins. I fought back my tears as we dressed them in their embroidered blouses and braided their hair.

"It's the best I can do," Xenkovna said. "I hope it's all right."

"Yes, daughter," Auntie said, sighing. "I'm so blessed with your help. You're doing a lot better than I can right now. I don't know what I'd do without you."

"They look so thin," I said to Xenkovna. But no one felt like talking.

Auntie was inconsolable and I have no doubt the situation was made worse by the fact that her frozen feet would not allow her to stand and her frozen hands denied her the ability to do the last ministrations for her baby daughters. She never lost her limp and it would take months till her hands healed to the point where she could work again.

At midday, Uncle Misha gathered us under the icon of the Last Supper. He read the funeral passages from the Bible—the one about the many mansions in Heaven where God was preparing a chamber just for us and the ashes to ashes one that we all know so well. I wondered what Mama's room looked like. Did she already have a little corner ready for me? Auntie kissed Maria and Marta one last time.

"I'm so sorry, my darlings," she cried. "I tried to help you, but God took you anyway. Holy Mother! You know I tried."

She went back to her lamentations again. Xenkovna wrapped each of the twins in a clean sheet and then Uncle took them out to the shed. They would stay frozen out there without decaying until the ground thawed and they could be buried properly. When we finally could go to the cemetery in the spring, the Comrades decreed that we could no longer bury family members individually. The crosses and holy monuments were all smashed. So many of the villagers were dying that the Party forced the gravediggers to open mass graves.

"Since our lives are being collectivized in the new order," the Thousander said, "it should be no trouble to be part of a collective grave when we die. Besides, we need the land for growing grain, not for wasting on some insignificant peasant's burial plot."

After Uncle Misha put the twins out into the shed, he turned our attention to the sack of wheat.

"We have to find a place to hide this," he said. "If the Comrades find it here, they'll think of some tax we didn't pay or some fat official who needs to eat. We can't let Mama's great sacrifice go to waste. If we're careful, this wheat will feed us till the garden grows."

We spent the afternoon trying to find a good hiding place around the house. Although we examined every nook and cranny, we couldn't find anywhere that hadn't been already damaged or turned over by the Comrades.

"I don't think we should hide it in the house at all," Mitya said.

"How are we going to keep an eye on it then?" Michael asked.

"We can't. If we hide it on the edge of the *kolhosp* that is right next to the woods, no one will take it. They won't think to look there. I'm sure that the Comrades think we are so scared that we won't go onto their land."

"You're right about that," Alexander said.

"The *kolhosp*?" Uncle Misha said in disbelief. "That's too dangerous."

"I know a few hiding places that I used when Mama and I lived at our cottage," Mitya said. "They weren't part of any *kolhosp* then, but they were good hiding places. If we split up the wheat into small bundles, we can keep a little of it in the house for a couple of days' worth of porridge and then hide the rest in several places. If it is not in the house they can't take it away. If someone finds it out on the *kolhosp*, they can't pin it on us."

"We could fetch one bundle at a time—and take turns so that we don't attract attention," Alexander said.

"Well, if that just doesn't beat my boots," Uncle Misha said, scratching his head. "I didn't realize I had such brave sons."

Mitya's face reddened with pleasure.

"And, remember, we can't tell anyone about it, I mean anyone."

"Who would we tell?" Mitya asked. "The zone is sealed so no one comes to see us anymore."

"I don't know," Uncle said. "Words have a way of slipping out, especially in these crazy times."

Xenkovna and I cut pieces of sacking into squares and sewed them into small bags. She measured the wheat out into three-day lots and we poured it into the newly sewn sacks. It was agreed that no one other than the boys would know exactly where the wheat was hidden.

After nightfall, the boys took it out of the house. They were gone for a very long time. I worried that they had run into some misadventure and Auntie was sure that they were dead. Xenkovna and Uncle Misha kept their heads together so that, by the time the boys got home, a small pot of porridge was simmering on the stove and tea was ready.

Our new routine was established. We huddled in the house all day, reading the Bible and trying to conserve our physical energy and our wood for heating. None of the neighbours were engaging with one another either. They isolated themselves in their homes just as we did.

We cooked at night, long after any propagandist might decide to drop in. Sometimes we had to wait till well into the night after one of the men's mandatory meetings. We ate very small amounts of porridge with no salt or sugar to flavour the boiled wheat. There had been no salt or sugar in the house for months.

"Thank Heavens we still have poppies for our tea. We can't all of a sudden start looking well-fed," Auntie said. "And we can't let anyone smell the smoke from cooking food. That would be an invitation for more trouble. Dear God how we suffer!"

"Woman," Uncle said, laughing, "it would take much more than a few spoonfuls of this porridge to make us look well-fed. Have you seen how we look lately—compared to the fat Comrades?"

Uncle took to spending time in his shed each morning. He never announced that he was leaving the warmth of the cottage, but after a week or so I followed him out.

"Uncle Misha, what are you doing out here? Is something wrong?"

"Ah, you know that curiosity kills the cat, don't you?" His eyes shone with an almost forgotten twinkle.

My cheeks burned with embarrassment.

"Well, you always say what you are doing ... but now you just turn your back and leave us."

"Can you keep a secret?"

"A secret? What secret? Who from?"

"You have to promise," he said. "You can't tell anyone. Promise."

"Cross my heart."

He beckoned me into the shed and shut the door against the wind. On the work bench in front of him sat a perfectly square board. He had carved lines in it so that there were sixty-four squares on the board, eight down and eight across.

"This is my surprise."

"What is it for?" I had never seen a board like that.

"Checkers. I'll burn every other square so that it is black. Then, we'll take these men ..." He dumped out two piles of round coins he had carved. One pile was the colour of the wood they were carved from and the other pile of coins was already scorched black. "The men will move on the squares that aren't burnt ... the white squares. And we'll all learn to play checkers. Don't you think it will help us pass some of these long winter days? I wish I had thought of it earlier."

I could hardly stay still when I got into the house.

"What's going on with you?" Xenkovna said. "You're as skittish as a bunny since you went out after *Tahto*."

"I don't know," I answered. I picked up Auntie's Bible to read for a distraction.

Uncle Misha found out that I could keep my word. After another long week, he came into the cottage grinning. He set the board up on the table with the white men on one side and the black on the other. We crowded around him in excitement.

"Easy does it," Uncle Misha said. "You'll all have a turn. Philipovna, you'll be in the first round because we all know now that you can keep a secret."

I stuck out my chin with pride. We all learned to play. The days passed by more quickly then. Whenever we got restless or complained about being hungry, the checkers came out and we'd have our tournament. I loved the game and became a good player. But I never did beat Uncle Misha.

Thanks to the good doctor's medicine, Viktor's health very slowly improved. The winter days inevitably lengthened and we looked forward to the coming spring. The cold hung in so that it was plain to see that spring would be taking its own sweet time to arrive no matter how hungry we were. Auntie didn't rally. As her hands and feet healed, she resumed her duties around the house, but I could see a hint of the Unravelled One's look in Auntie's eyes. It didn't help that Mitya brought in the last bag of wheat weeks before we could plant the garden.

"Dear God," Auntie said, lamenting. "Does no one in Heaven see how much we suffer? I have no more spoons to trade. How will I ever find anything to feed us?"

"Have faith," Uncle said. "We'll figure something out."

"When? After another one of us dies? Look at how thin Viktor is."

It seems that God was listening. About a week after the wheat ran out, Xenkovna came in with her bucket of water in one hand and her apron tied in a bundle with the other.

"What's in the bundle?" Auntie asked.

Xenkovna had noticed a flock of little birds returning for spring. They were pecking at something on the ground. She tossed her apron over them—not really knowing what she was going to do with them—but thinking that they might be eaten somehow.

"See," Uncle said, smiling. "I told you that God would send something."

"But, they're smaller than sparrows—and there's no meat on them," Auntie said.

"Mama, I'll clean them and we can make soup. I'm sure their bones will have something in them that our bellies can use." Xenkovna was looking tired and anxious too.

So we learned to catch the birds with an apron or cloth and stick them into the snow headfirst till there were enough to cook in a small soup pot. One of us would always be on watch to make sure no one else discovered the secret. As Xenkovna observed, there wasn't meat on the birds to eat but their bones had enough good things in them to keep us from starving. We ate the soup and kept the bones for proper burial in the spring.

One afternoon a loud knocking disturbed the house.

"Put the Bible away," Auntie whispered. She scooped Viktor up awkwardly and motioned to me for a blanket. Xenkovna swept the checker game off of the table, into her apron.

"Good afternoon," Uncle said tersely.

"Comrade," the intruder responded.

The hair on my arms stood on end. I was not accustomed to seeing the snake Asimov standing at our cottage door. What could he possibly want?

"What can I do for you?" Uncle Misha asked.

"It's not me that you can do anything for," the snake replied. "It is the welfare of your Children that I'm concerned with. You have how many school-aged Children under your roof?"

"My nephew is needed to help me with the chores," Uncle answered motioning in Mitya's direction.

"What chores?" Asimov said laughing. "Have you acquired a cow lately—or could it be a horse—or pigs? It's not the stupid buffoon I'm here about. There are just some who can't be taught. He's much better off doing your grunt work. That way he will always know his place."

He looked at me—then at Viktor in Auntie's lap.

My chest tightened.

"Is the young one on the school register yet? He looks about starting age. It's time he was learning about his place in the new order."

Auntie's face turned white.

I moved closer to Xenkovna.

"If things in this village were working right," Uncle said, "he would be going in the spring term, but as they are so ..."

"Are you saying something about how the Party is running the village?"

"We are starving to death and none of the Party is paying attention. Two of my Children have already died and your Comrades won't allow me to send for a doctor for this boy who is barely surviving."

Asimov stepped closer to Uncle Misha, his hand on his holster.

"Look here you ignorant peasant," he hissed. "My business has nothing to do with your belly. I'm here to make your stupid Children come to school—especially that young one. He's too big to be tied on to his mother's apron string. The girl"—his hand gestured in my direction—"has not been to school for weeks and the buffoon, I don't need. I'll be inviting the Comrades to see you unless those two show up for school in the morning. There's no place for lazy brats in the new order."

"But he has diphtherial croup," Auntie blurted out.

"What would you know about diphtherial croup?" Asimov asked. He stepped closer to Auntie and Viktor. "Only a doctor would be able to say something like that."

"Nothing," Auntie answered, swallowing hard. She pulled her little son closer and put her head down so that she didn't have to meet the Snake's unrelenting stare.

"Tomorrow morning," Asimov said. "Or you'll be having a visit you'll not forget."

The next morning, with Viktor bundled from head to toe, I went back to school. As we joined the village Children, I could see that all of them were suffering much the same way as we were. Their cheeks were hollow and there were dark circles under their eyes. They didn't run and play; nor did they laugh or talk as we went to school. Their eyes were focused on the path in front of them or on the adjoining gardens or fields we passed — in case someone had overlooked or dropped something they could eat. Some of them already had swollen bellies. It didn't take long for me to find out that most families had lost a brother or sister over the winter months.

In the classroom, nothing changed. The Snake made Viktor sit up at the front with the little Children where he could be more easily terrorized if he made mistakes or fell asleep from exhaustion as many of the younger ones did every day. The mornings were filled with the usual mathematics, history and reading lessons while the afternoons were strictly devoted to Party politics and brainwashing.

I learned that Asimov planned a festival for Pioneer Day at the end of February. He wanted to set up a Young Pioneer Group for the village Children. The young Pioneers were modelled on the Boy Scout movement, but in those days the Party used them for propaganda and politics. When the Young Pioneers took hold, one couldn't enter a university or get a good job after finishing school if one wasn't in good standing with the organization.

On February 25, which was Pioneer Day all across the country, the Young Pioneers made a brief stop at the school. A Brigade arrived from the city fully arrayed in its light blue dress uniforms with red necktie, kerchief and hat, not to mention the pin that was engraved with "Be Prepared," the Pioneers' motto. They came armed with their red and white posters and banners with their Party slogans "Long Live the Communist Party," "Long Live the Soviet Regime!" and "We Thank the Communist Party for Our Happy and Prosperous Life!"

They performed their marches, songs and flag ceremonies around a big bonfire in the square. I would have liked the Young

Pioneer Anthem had it not been a song that was pushing me towards the Comrades and their Party. I certainly would have liked to look as well-dressed and fed as the energetic Children I was watching. I felt particularly dirty as I compared my unwashed, ragged clothes to their crisp uniforms. It had been months since anyone in the village could get soap, especially since our zone borders were tightened up. The show didn't stay for as long as Asimov hoped. When the leaders of the visiting brigade saw how many of our Children were ill, they moved the Pioneers on to the next village as quickly as they could. Their leader didn't want any of his healthy city Children to pick up any pestilences from "these filthy peasants."

Asimov made no secret of his disappointment. After our poor showing, he was determined to remedy this problem by the coming May Day celebrations which were due to take place in a matter of weeks. He taught us more songs about "living in Paradise, happy and well-fed on our new collective farms." He sang them line-by-line so that we could memorize them by rote. He divided the school Children into groups with the older ones as team leaders and taught us marching drills which we practiced until we felt like collapsing.

"You must look happy," he said. "Put a smile on those ungrateful faces. The Comrades from the city must see how glad you are to show solidarity with them and Mother Russia."

His metre stick was very busy keeping us hungry and tired Children in line.

I could hardly wait for classes to finish. The days were getting warm and the signs of spring were popping up everywhere. The air was sweet with the scent of the thawing earth; the warming sun lifted the pungent smell of last year's decaying vegetation. The grass turned green after the snow. As Viktor and I went off to forage for food along with the rest of the villagers, the nightingales came back and built their nests. They went on singing as if everything was the way it always had been. Somehow, their singing gave us some energy and a renewed desire to help ourselves.

In the river we found tender plants, especially the young reeds. I would hold on tight to Viktor so that he could reach out further over the water's edge and pick the best shoots. I'm sure that Auntie would have been horrified to see us do that. In the forest we peeled off the young bark and newly developing buds from the trees. We collected the mushrooms as soon as they could grow and dug up any roots that looked remotely edible. We tried to keep any new-found patch a secret so that we could come back to it before another hungry villager picked it clean. These excursions with Viktor reminded me of the times Mitya and I had spent in happier days.

The fields were our favourite places for foraging even though we had to wade through the water of the melting snow. We could often find something—mainly root vegetables from last year's crop, preserved by the winter snow and frost. Potatoes, beets and onions were priceless, despite the fact that they were rotten or frozen. Sometimes, we were so hungry we would eat the vegetables right in the field or forest, but usually we brought them home and Xenkovna or Auntie made a kind of potato pancake, mixing them with leaves or even peelings from other vegetables. Other days, they put potato peels, grape seeds and roots all together and cooked it in water to make a soup of sorts. When the potatoes or onions were rotten the smell of the soup made me retch.

"A starving man does not sniff his food," Uncle Misha would say, pinching his nose and swallowing whatever Auntie could put together, no matter how bad it tasted.

"It keeps us alive, if there is enough of it," Auntie said. "If you can find grass, we'll cook grass and remember to thank God for it."

It wasn't an easy task for people weakened by starvation to wander around in the fields hunting for vegetables. Because so many were looking for any scraps they could find, they had to go to faraway areas and this required strength and stamina. A lot of villagers didn't survive. Although they succeeded in getting to a place where there was food they could glean, many of them fell dead in the fields from exhaustion before finding anything to sustain them.

"He's sleeping," I said to Viktor when we found a man who had given up the ghost this way.

"Won't he get cold?" Viktor asked.

"He'll wake up and go home when he does," I said. "Let's not bother him."

Mitya and the cousins took to collecting nightingale eggs and catching birds. On the days they caught a rabbit, we had a feast. Auntie would always cry over the nightingale eggs because it meant that one less bird would sing for each egg we ate.

"After all, those birds are sacred," she said.

One day the cousins came home with a pair of hedgehogs. But hunting for animals proved difficult as anyone who had the strength was fighting for whatever animal could be caught and eaten. It was made worse by the fact that all of the guns, right down to those smaller ones that were just meant for game, had been confiscated by the Comrades. Thanks to the propagandists and their fear-mongering, wherever a man tried to leave the zone to seek food outside his village, he was hunted like a wild animal by the local villagers and then executed as a traitor.

Sharik was never out of Mitya's sight.

"You never know who's going to grab him and eat him for dinner," he told me one afternoon after school.

"Do you really think they would?" I asked.

"What do you think happened to the cats that lived in the shed?" he asked.

"I don't know," I answered in horror. It had been some time since I had seen the scrawny orange cat and her five little kittens that had lived in the shed over the winter. "Who would have done such a thing?"

Then Mitya looked at me—looked in a weird way that I'd never seen before.

"No, no!" I screamed. "We couldn't have—we ..." The realization choked off the rest of my protestation. My stomach heaved and my heart twisted. Which of the little animals that was in our soup was the cat?

I ran out to the river again and didn't come back to the house for a long, long time. I threw myself down on the mossy spot where I had cut the willow branches so long ago and screamed out loud to my mother and father. How could we have eaten those little furry kittens? Couldn't my parents let Jesus know how frightened I was? Didn't He see how hungry I was? I swore I'd never go back to Auntie's house to eat any more cats or other little animals that should be running about in the forest. But the afternoon waned; dusk fell and yes, I was sharply hungry. I had to go home and, like everyone else in the village, eat anything I could find.

May Day finally arrived. Asimov strutted around like a proud cockerel lording over his flock of hens. He marched us into the village with a flourish where we joined the Pioneer brigade that had visited us in the winter. The officials from the *kolhosp* set up a new tractor in the centre of the square. The Comrades were already preaching their propaganda to the villagers who were gathered before a makeshift stage. As one Comrade after another droned on with their platitudes about our "Communist Paradise" and "good fortune to be one of Father Stalin's prosperous farmers," my tummy rumbled. I noticed that there was a large army presence. I saw that the villagers were looking at something that was not on the stage.

Off to one side of the square, the army had barricaded an area where a couple of bonfires burned. Over these fires, hung several large army sized cooking pots and stirring these pots were women from the *kolhosp*. The people closest to the bonfires slowly migrated towards the fires. They remained facing the speakers, but gradually almost imperceptibly they kept sidestepping toward the barricade between them and the women. They moved closer and closer as the speeches dragged on. A gentle spring breeze blew the smoke from the cooking fires towards us and the smell of cooking porridge harassed my nose. I could have pushed everyone out of my way and jumped right into one of those pots.

I was not the only one who felt that way. Just as the visiting Comrade official reached the climax of his speech, a commotion broke out by the barricade. Walter, who was one of the boys that liked to sing songs at the crossroads with my older cousins, couldn't stand the smell of the porridge any longer. He took a running leap at one of the stirring women and tried to grab her spoon. But his heroic effort was of no use. The army commander grabbed him in mid-air and pushed him back roughly.

"That's enough," the official bellowed. "Get to the back of the group. If anyone of you makes another move before you are invited to Father Stalin's feast, you'll find out what real trouble is. Will you greedy peasants never learn your manners?"

The speeches finally finished. The army lined everyone up and the women started ladling exactly two spoons of the porridge into containers which the villagers brought with them. Each person, old or young, big or small got exactly two spoons.

"We have no favourites in the Party," the Comrade from the city explained.

While the line progressed we Children sang our songs about ripening fields and golden harvests and the glory of our motherland —Mother Russia. I could hardly stand the cramps in my belly. I thought I'd faint with hunger. The city visitors from the Young Pioneers joined in the marches and flag raising ceremonies to show solidarity. But they did not eat. When everyone had been served, it was our turn. I don't know where the containers came from, but we all were given a can, a cup or a dish of the porridge.

We sat on the square eating like ravenous wolves. We licked our containers clean like so many dogs and looked to the pots for more. Those who worked on the *kolhosp* were sent to another line for their allotment of two pounds of bread since "they had earned a special consideration from Father Stalin" while the rest of us watched. The city visitors went away; then we were sent home to enjoy the rest of our holiday.

The Empty Harvest

❖❖❖❖❖❖❖

A S THE MAY sun warmed the earth, the *kalyna* blessed us with its white blossoms like it did every other spring. I wandered by the river, not just to see what it might provide for me to eat, but also to escape from the endless weight of a daily struggle for survival.

The dell of forget-me-nots and lily-of-the-valley where I found the silver spoon came to be my own special place. I looked for another spoon many times, hoping that I could bring it home to Auntie so that we might be able to trade it for wheat again, but I never found anything other than pretty stones and tadpoles. Auntie always welcomed the bunches of wild flowers I brought to her. She would set them in a glass as she used to do. I was happy to see her smile. Once in a while, I would convince Viktor to come with me and we went to the river to look for crayfish. I would lie in the fragrant grass soaking in the sun's rays, resting like a scruffy cat.

At other times, I would stare at a particular cloud and picture my Mama floating on it, right above where I lay. I wondered if she sent the silver spoon that brought us that bit of wheat which kept us alive till the thawing gardens and burgeoning forest came to life. I pictured Mama and me sitting on the edge of the cloud and letting our legs swing freely. I imagined us on the cloud eating bread that she baked in Heaven, all different kinds of bread in different shapes and colours, made from all of the different grains that grew around us. I imagined every size of bread from the tiniest of buns to the very large ones with the little birds on top like the loaves of bread that were used for weddings—the kind of loaves that Xenkovna loved to bake. It would be fresh from the oven, warm and dripping with butter that melted into its fluffy centre and run down my fingers so that I could lick it off and languish in its nourishing glory.

I would ask my Mama to help me be grateful like Auntie said I should be, but the truth was that I didn't like the taste of most of the food we ate to survive. I ate because I was hungry, but often ended up with a stomach-ache after eating. The tea that Auntie insisted we keep drinking didn't help with my stomach cramps any longer. I watched the wagons coming through the village every morning to pick up the people who had died overnight to bring them to the mass graves. I wondered when they would come for me. Once I heard Katerina tell Auntie that one of the Children was put onto that wagon while he was sleeping.

"The man putting the bodies into the grave would have dumped the boy in if not for the fact that he cried when they moved him," Katerina said.

After that, I had many sleepless nights fighting nightmares in which I was lost among those bodies. I dreamed of being thrown into dark caverns full of dead people and not able to find my way home.

The familiar path that I took to cross the pasture and go around what used to be Uncle Paulo's orchard seemed different, too. The wind still tickled my nose with the sweet smells of the growing grasses and blooming meadows as I walked, but it didn't feel right. I looked up at sunset and expected to see one of the boys coming back from the fields with the cow. I listened to see if I could hear her lowing. I went into her empty shed and tried sniffing really hard to see if her smell still hung in the warm air inside. I fantasized about drinking her frothy milk and would have gladly put up with the ache in my arms after churning for a taste of fresh bread and butter or Auntie's chiding for a forbidden dip of my finger into the newly-set *smetana*.

"Will we ever have a cow again?" I asked Auntie.

"I don't know," she said, sighing. "We have no notion of what will happen. We can only hope and pray."

The blossoms dropped from the cherry trees. I watched the buds grow and develop into beautiful cherries. The spring was warm and it seemed that the fruit was maturing hourly. I couldn't wait till Mitya and I could get another pail and sneak into the trees again. The fruit, green as it was beckoned to me, begging me to pick it— for just one taste. But I waited.

"Don't eat the cherries while they're still green," Auntie said. "Your tummy is very tender. If you give in, the strong juice will hurt you more than it will help. And, we have no medicine. The last thing I need right now is a sick Child from eating green fruit."

I soon found out that I didn't have to concern myself with the cherries. I was coming home from one of my jaunts to the river and heard the sound of a motor. I rounded the bend at the edge of the orchard and almost walked straight into an army truck. I expected to see Comrade Zabluda, but was surprised to find Uncle Ivan with a half-dozen Party men instead.

"We're here to guard the orchard," Uncle Ivan said when he saw me.

"Guard the orchard?" I spit it out before I had time to think.

"The bread procurement committee has appointed me to make sure that all of the cherries are accounted for. So take care not to be caught in a tree. I won't be as kind as Simon and Paulo were the last time we caught you."

"Yes, Comrade," I said, shivering though it was a warm day.

His nostrils flared like those of a pig as he looked slowly at me from top to bottom. I had the sickest feeling that he wanted some-thing more, but I couldn't put a finger on what exactly that could be. I remembered that he wasn't there when Uncle Paulo and Uncle Simon brought me back home last spring. How did he know that I had been picking cherries? I bolted from Uncle Ivan's lecherous stare and ran home to Auntie as fast as I could.

"I guess we won't be eating cherries this year," Auntie said. "Is there anything that they won't steal away from us?"

Mitya surprised us on the Sunday morning after I met Uncle Ivan.

"Those bastards weren't quick enough," he said. "Look what I have." Somehow, while we were sleeping, Mitya sneaked into the orchard and picked half a pail full of cherries. I was about to squeal with joy but his hand smothered my mouth before anything could come out.

"What about the bells?" I asked.

"What bells?" His eyes had a shadow of the ice blue sparkle of old.

"You know. The ones they had strung on ropes."

"A knife can take care of a rope, can't it?"

So for a few delicious days, we ate cherries with our mush and I was truly thankful.

Uncle Ivan was true to his word. The bread procurement com-mittee arrived just as most of the cherries were turning from pale green to dark red. They stayed for the two weeks that it took for the cherries to ripen. They stripped every cherry from every tree.

One day, as I turned off the path, I heard a commotion by the woodpile. It was unusual as I heard the yelling of men and the bark-ing of several dogs, like the dogs of a hunting Party. There hadn't been a hunting Party around the village for years. Those villagers who hadn't eaten their dog or cat guarded them jealously. What could this be? I cautiously moved toward the sounds and rounded the corner of our house. One of the Comrades raised his gun and shot Sharik right in the head. He yelped and crumpled at Mitya's feet in a pool of blood while the three men with him raised their guns in salute. My screaming drew both Auntie out of the house and Uncle Misha out of the barn.

"Help, help. Uncle Misha, make them stop! Please make them stop. They're hurting Sharik,"

Mitya cried. He bent to pick up our poor Sharik, but one of the Comrades struck him with the butt of his gun.

"What are you doing?" he demanded.

"I'm taking him to my Mama's grave."

"Hold it there, son," another of the Comrades said with a sarcastic grin.

Mitya tried to run, but the Comrade grabbed Sharik by the tail and swung him into a horse drawn cart which was waiting for the hunters on the road and already held a quantity of dead dogs and cats. Mitya bolted from the scene and didn't show his face to anyone for more than a week. I ran into the house and cried into Mama's feather bed till Auntie made our meagre supper.

This is how we were informed the Party had decided that, since people were eating dogs and cats, a hunt for them should be conducted and that they were now a valuable commodity. Father Stalin had need of their furs for the good of the new order. They were brought to the *kolhosp* for skinning.

"What's that smell?" I asked Auntie one evening after I brought in the water pail. "It's so bad I might throw up."

"There aren't enough people to skin the dogs and cats," Auntie said.

"What are they going to do with them?"

"Burn them so that we don't get a plague," she said.

Since the villagers no longer had any arms, the Thousanders in the area were commissioned to do the hunting. They came through, from one end of the village to the other and slaughtered every four-legged creature they could find. Their sport did not begin and end with dogs and cats.

"They're killing the nightingales!" Xenkovna said after going out for water one early May morning in the spring of 1932.

"I don't believe you," I said. "No one would do that."

Each household in the village had its own family or two of nightingales that lived in its orchard or on its tree.

"If a nightingale dies or, God forbid, you should kill it," Auntie said, "something terrible will happen to your family or household."

Though this was a legend, Auntie took it as gospel truth. She lectured all of us as to the sanctity of "God's musical guest," and was especially vigilant when she got wind of little Children planning mischievous tricks that may involve birds' nests. Respect for the nightingale and its nest was drilled into every Ukrainian Child from the time he or she was old enough to wander around the village. It was said that the nightingale's song represented the soul of the Ukrainian countryside. I have yet to hear a concert that compares with the song of that beautiful bird. The Thousanders assaulted our village with their hunting parties morning and evening when the nightingales did their best singing.

"Auntie, why are they shooting the nightingales?" I cried after watching one of these parties stake out our own nest. "You should see how the feathers fly all over when they hit one of them. Poor little things. Why are they doing it?"

"The world has gone mad," Auntie said. "I could understand killing one or two if you were hungry, but to kill them for target practice or just for sport! God have mercy on our people. What would our ancestors say if they could see such a travesty?"

"It's so lonely," I said after the nightingales were all gone. "Will they ever come back?"

"I don't know," Auntie said. She crossed herself wearily and looked at the icon. But when she turned to stare out the window to our empty garden, I could see tears trickling down her hollow cheeks. It would be a good three years before the nightingales returned to their normal ways.

Since it was spring again, it was also time to plant a garden. "What are you doing?" I asked on coming home from school one warm spring afternoon.

"Digging the garden," Michael said. "What does it look like?"

"I thought we had no seeds."

"Mama found a few in her trunk," Alexander said. "And Xenkovna found some rotten potatoes that had enough eyes in them for planting."

Uncle Misha and the cousins dug up the plot where we always grew our vegetables. That is, they tried to dig up enough of the plot to plant whatever they could. I could see that the silver wasn't just at Uncle's temples any longer. His whole head was a dull gray now and his shoulder blades stuck out of his shirt as he stooped. He still had the cough from the sickness that took away Maria and Marta.

"Imagine," Uncle Misha said by the fire that evening. "We used to plough half a field in a day and now I don't have enough strength to plant a few potatoes. I'm in worse shape than a little woman."

"At least you can use your hands," Auntie said, massaging her stiff fingers. "Oh God how we suffer ... and for what?"

We watched that garden grow with great anticipation. Each bud and each leaf was like a new member of the family, welcomed with joy and coddled to make sure that the plant it fed would grow and produce. We also had to make sure that no hungry wanderer would help himself in order to ease his own suffering. It happened often that one of the neighbours woke up in the morning to find his almost ripe vegetables cleaned out as he slept.

The *kolhosp* gardens did not escape the notice of hungry foragers either. It got so bad that the Comrades stationed guards night and day to keep the vegetables in the ground. Half-ripe carrots and beets were dug up; potatoes were stolen and half-grown cabbages were uprooted. Where there once had been a peaceful, charitable community of sharing and hospitality, there now was suspicion and silence. Fights and serious personal injury were now commonplace as hungry people struggled to find food. There were stories of villagers being so desperate that they killed intruders for stealing vegetables and helping themselves to strawberries.

"It's shocking," Auntie said when we heard about a boy from a neighbouring village who had been beaten to death by one of our own hungry neighbours. "It wasn't long ago that he would have been welcomed and fed in someone's house whether we knew him or not. What is this world coming to?"

But as the summer came, everyone's garden grew—not as large or abundant as in normal years, but enough to put some vegetables together for a reasonable borscht or pot of mashed potatoes. It wasn't because of the weather; in Ukraine, where there was no famine, there was a bumper crop that year. The gardens were not as full in our village because either there weren't enough family members to tend them or those who could were too sick to put out the energy necessary for maintaining a good garden. I would sit by the stove, watching the pot boil and salivate over the smell of the cooking vegetables. The beets had a particularly sweet smell while the onions smelled sharp and tangy.

"Go out to play," Auntie finally said. "You're sitting like a hungry vulture. It won't cook the food any faster. Take Viktor out for a game of squash or a walk to the river."

We could make a summer supper of fresh greens, pickles and eventually beets, carrots and tomatoes. There was no bread or meat, but at least we ate food that tasted good and didn't leave us with a sore belly or diarrhoea, though there was never enough of it to feel full. Auntie's hands were still too stiff to work normally so we didn't have all of the herbs that were usually grown for medicine. There was still the occasional visit from the Comrades or bread procurement committee to demand one thing or another, but they must have realized that they couldn't take everything or there would be no one to tend their new collective farm.

I didn't see much of Mitya at that time. He was always far out in the woods, looking for edible plants that I didn't recognize. Other times, he came with mushrooms or wild berries. He looked for a secluded spot far from the village so that he could go fishing or hunting for rabbits or hedgehogs. He would appear from behind the woodpile, bring an offering to Auntie, stay for supper and then disappear again. He became sullen and silent, much like he was when his mother died. He seemed so lost and lonely without his precious Sharik.

The Party's efforts were not confined to the cherry orchard. When it was time to plant the spring grains, they brought in workers from the city. They were sent "to help the peasants and show solidarity." But in practice, it didn't quite work out that way. While their well-fed bodies did help with the physical labour, their work groups were always kept separate from us. They worked beside us in the field, but never left the safety of their group—not even to say a "good-morning" or share a drink from the well.

I watched them turn the black earth and plant the spring barley and buckwheat. When the planting was done, the city workers were moved on to the next *kolhosp* while the villagers maintained the fields and waited for the harvest. It was strange to see the many small farms that used to belong to the village Uncles become just one great field, a part of the new *kolhosp*.

City workers were the first of the additions to the new order. Along with the work groups came the army. They built watchtowers in the field and kept an eye on the work.

"Disgusting!" Uncle Misha said. "We've farmed the land for thousands of years and didn't need an overseer. Now, these city know-it-alls have sent idiots to make sure we do it right."

"Doing it right" was not the real reason for those towers. Once the city workers were moved on to the next *kolhosp*, the villagers were forced to maintain the fields themselves. If one should stop for rest or drop from exhaustion, as many of them did in the summer sun, they were beaten with the soldiers' batons until they stood on their feet again. They were given a ration of bread for their effort on the *kolhosp*, but it was nothing close to the needs of a hard-working man who got up at dawn and toiled till dusk.

Many of the men ate only a small part of their ration and tried to save it to share with the hungry ones at home. Workers and foragers alike would sneak onto the ripening field and break out the eye of the wheat from the maturing plants. If they could collect enough of it, they would take it home and cook porridge out of the green grain.

On a late summer afternoon as I wandered back from the river, I heard a commotion going on in the ripening wheat. I crouched down so that I was hidden by the tall grass that grew by the edge of the *kolhosp* and crept as close as I dared. Everyone stopped working and was staring towards the corner of the field by which I was hidden. What was it all about?

Two of the soldiers held the arms of Stepan Tymashenko, the brother of Oksana, one of my schoolmates. He was about fifteen years old. His thin face was contorted with pain and his eyes were as large as sunflowers. A third soldier took a knife from his belt and slashed Stepan's grubby shirt from collar to belt. A pile of ripening wheat ears spilled to the ground at his feet.

"This is how you treat Father Stalin?" the soldier who was facing the unfortunate boy demanded. "He gives you an opportunity to be part of his glorious plan and you steal the wheat from his field?"

"I'm hungry ... my sister is hungry ... our parents are sick ... my Grandmother just died ..." He sobbed without shame.

Poor Stepan didn't get any farther. The next sound I heard was a crack from the watchtower. With a single shot, he crumpled to the ground just two metres from where I hid and sank into the golden fragrance of the ripening grain.

"Now back to work," the guard barked. No one dared to disobey. I watched the blood ooze out of Stepan's head until I felt like vomiting and then I went on my way to tell Auntie and Uncle what had happened. They sent Xenkovna to tell Stepan's mother. It was after dusk, after the soldiers were safely in their barracks, that the family came to collect the body of their son and take him to the mass grave. In the Party meeting that followed Stepan's demise, the Comrades announced that the grain belonged to the state and Father Stalin. Anyone caught stealing it would be considered an enemy of the people and risked execution by firing squad or, if the state was compassionate upon the judgement, confiscation of their property or transport to Siberia. It was another new law.

Eventually, the grain was ripe. The Comrades announced that the harvest was to begin on a Sunday with a special celebration. I arrived in the early morning to see what would happen. A combine, two harvesters and two trucks stood in the centre of the square. I would have been interested in the new machines at a former time but, this day, all I could do is stand dumbly at a distance like the other villagers.

The soldiers and a group of teachers and students were already stationed at the former church and in the school where Comrade Asimov taught classes. They had been instructed not to speak to the farmers at all. They stood around one of the trucks, the students on one side and another group of city labourers on the other, with a wide berth between us. On the few occasions that they looked me directly in the eye, they did so with contempt. I wondered what I had done to have strangers look at me that way. In their stay, which lasted six to eight weeks, they never associated with the villagers and, to make sure they didn't, the army placed guards around them.

As on the May Day festival, some pots of boiling porridge hung over a couple of fires. Several women from the *kolhosp* stood over them, stirring. I noticed that there were fewer people in the square with none of them sitting or lying around like in May. Most of those had died away and only the strongest ones, those who could stomach anything, no matter how distasteful it was, were left as part of the new order. I stood waiting for Comrade Zabluda to finish his speech, staring at the steam rising from the porridge with my mouth watering like a hungry puppy. It was months since I had eaten any kind of wheat at all.

"Remember how fortunate you are," he said. "We are celebrating this momentous occasion in the most dignified and well-organized fashion. Never forget that you are the luckiest and happiest farmers in the world. Where else would the average farmer have such wonderful machines to do their work for them and who but Mother Russia and Father Stalin would send out workers from the city to make sure that the grain was brought from the fields so efficiently?"

"We didn't need workers and their efficiency before the *kolhosp* was forced down our throats," Uncle Misha said over our simple supper of pickles and potatoes that evening.

Comrade Zabluda announced that the workers from the *kolhosp* would receive two pounds of grain and two hot cooked meals per day for the duration of the harvest.

What about me? I wondered. *And the rest of us?* Since Uncle Misha had not formally joined the *kolhosp*, he and his sons who were over fourteen years of age were not allowed to work on the planting or harvest like those who did. So they missed out on any reward the Party gave out. I thought that the Comrade would go on and on like at May Day, but it seemed that he was more interested in bringing in the wheat.

When he finished, we repeated the same ritual as in May with each person receiving exactly two scoops of porridge. No one dared to ask for any before the speeches were done and no one dared tried to jump the queue. We learned our lesson from Walter on May Day. We moved forward, our heads down, not daring to look the servers in the eye and received our two scoops like the oppressed, humiliated beggars that we were.

With no further ceremony, the combine started moving towards the field. It was followed by the trucks and harvesters. Then the city workers moved onto the fields and the horse-drawn carts and their former owners, some of whom still were licking their porridge containers, followed the military-like procession. The threshing of the grain was underway.

The combines and harvesters roared through the ripe wheat with dizzying speed. The trucks were loaded in no time. It was then that the villagers were told that the grain was going to be taken directly to the train station for shipping to the city and not to be stored at the *kolhosp* as it should be. When the trucks were filled, the horse-drawn carts were ordered to follow the trucks so as not to slow down the process. To make matters worse, the city workers covered the retreating grain with red banners proclaiming that our village voluntarily was giving its grain to Father Stalin and the new order.

"So much for happy farmers," Uncle Misha said over tea that night. "They promised the workers from the *kolhosp* fair payment in beets and potatoes. We'll see how many potatoes they send."

"They wouldn't have to send us potatoes," Michael said, "if we could just keep the ones we grew, like we used to."

For the rest of that week, Viktor, Mitya and I stayed close to the harvesters. We dove for any ear of grain that fell from the trucks and wagons. Since the workers were forced to work at a breakneck speed, there was much wasted wheat. But every villager who wasn't labouring in the fields had his eye on the path which went to the station. I learned to grab the wheat mid-air as it fell to the ground and took care that I wasn't stepped on by one of the workers or trampled on by one of the exhausted horses.

We managed to glean a small sack of wheat over the course of that week. And so the grain was harvested and stolen from beneath our noses. We found out later that the whole harvest was poured out by the railway, covered with tarpaulin and allowed to rot. The men who tried to rescue some for their families paid with their lives as Father Stalin's army kept watch day and night. Nevertheless, Auntie made us say extra prayers of gratitude before the icon.

"After all," she said, "it will carry us through for another little while."

The members of the *kolhosp* waited for their potatoes and beets but, as Uncle Misha correctly predicted, they never came. The nights cooled and our food supply dwindled. To complicate things further, the bread procurement committee with Uncle Ivan as its enthusiastic leader missed no opportunity for confiscating anything that we villagers could manage to hide away. It was uncanny how, just when a small quantity of foodstuffs was secured, he and his scavengers descended onto the unfortunate family, took all of the food and did some damage either to the house or its occupants on the way out. By the middle of October, our gardens were spent; our food was taken and we were back into full famine.

School started again. The class was at least one third smaller than it had been in the spring. Asimov remained his miserable self. No mention was made of the missing students and no questions were asked as to their whereabouts. We all knew that they were in Heaven with their ancestors, but none of us dared to talk about it. The classes resumed with arithmetic, reading and Russian history in the morning and more propaganda in the afternoon. Every piece of paper that was sent home to share with my parents continued to be thrown into the fire.

Viktor walked to school with me every day. He was sullen and did not say a word to anyone until Asimov forced an answer out of him. He fell asleep while he was supposed to be memorizing his lessons. He came home with welts or bruises daily. Viktor stared straight ahead when Asimov beat him, as if he couldn't feel anything, his eyes fixed on a spot far off somewhere. When we got home and Auntie saw the results of the Snake's work, she cried and looked like The Unravelled One used to.

"Please, son," she begged, "Try to stay awake and listen."

"Yes, Mama," he answered.

I could see that Viktor was trying, but there seemed to be something wrong. When he came home, he didn't want to go anywhere with me. He had no interest in skipping stones by the river. He didn't want to look around at bugs and spiders. It was difficult to entice him into playing his favourite game of squash—a Ukrainian game where Children would pretend to be vegetables being picked for a feast. He sat on the sunny side of the house or under the birch tree with his back leaning against the trunk and didn't move for hours, usually not until Auntie called us into the table for our meal. You really couldn't call it a dinner.

"Mama," he asked one day after school. "Can I have a piece of bread?"

Auntie turned to him from the stove where she stirred a small pot of mash made of beets and carrots.

"I'm sorry, son," she said. "I'd give you all of the bread I had— if I had it."

"Please, Mama, I really want some bread. I'm so hungry."

"I know," she said with glittering, suffering eyes. "If I had any, I'd even give you my portion."

"Thank you, Mama," he said. He turned and with his quiet way of late walked out to sit under the birch tree in what was left of the warm fall afternoon.

"I guess I should go to the woods to find some mushrooms," I said.

"I guess you should," Auntie said. "Take Viktor with you. He could probably use a little fresh air. God knows, it's stifling here some days."

"All right," I said. And I picked up my basket.

When I came upon Viktor under the birch, there was no point in asking him to come mushroom picking. I could see by his lifeless open eyes that he had gone to Heaven to break bread with his twin sisters and all of the others who had gone before him. I closed his eyes gently with my finger the way I saw Xenkovna do it when the twins passed on. I went and found Uncle Misha in the shed so that I wouldn't have to be the one to tell Auntie about Viktor.

It was the saddest funeral I had ever seen. Auntie wouldn't let anyone help her minister to her little son.

"I can't forgive myself for not caring for Maria and Marta," she said. "There's no way that I won't do it for Viktor ... And don't talk to me about my frozen hands and feet. I'll die before I let anyone give him his last service."

She bathed him herself and dressed him in an embroidered shirt which was still clean from being stored in the trunk. Xenkovna helped Auntie Xena wrap Viktor in a clean sheet. Michael and Alexander carried the coffin that Uncle Misha made himself and we went to the cemetery by ourselves "with no neighbours who can tell the Comrades what we're doing," Uncle said. Since it was late fall and there were no flowers for picking, I cut some branches from the birch tree that still had yellow leaves on them and some pine branches. I twisted them together to put over the coffin. We buried Viktor with the usual Bible verses and no tears—we were all out of them. The boys and Uncle Misha barely had enough energy to dig the grave. Auntie threw herself onto it when they were finished. She lay on the grave, moaning and sighing.

"Oh Blessed God," she said, hardly breathing. "Why didn't you take me instead? He hasn't even had time to see anything of the world. Oh God—oh, My Blessed God!"

It took Uncle Misha a long time to get her to stand up and walk back to the house with us. We walked home in the pungent-smelling autumn dusk with heavier hearts and one less member of the family, not knowing why we suffered or why God wouldn't intercede on our behalf. It was clear that no one else would or could.

The Orphan

T HE NEXT MORNING, I didn't want to go to school.

"What am I going to say to that awful Snake Asimov?"

"Tell him the truth," Uncle Misha said. "Your cousin has died and obviously won't be a student any longer."

"Why do I have to tell him?"

"Because you are the one who has to go to school. You don't want Auntie Xena or me to have to make the unnecessary trip, do you? We certainly don't need another visit from that despicable Asimov. I'm sure he won't care."

I shrugged my shoulders and scowled.

"Since when does a little girl question what her elders are telling her to do?" He sighed and coughed that cough that had never left him since the twins died. He looked so gaunt and pale that I did not want to argue with him. I walked to school by myself, my legs and arms dragging as if I pulled the weight of the whole world behind me.

As soon as the Children saw me without Viktor, they turned away. I must have been wearing that look, the faraway look with the deep, dark circles around the eyes, the one that lets everyone know that there has been another death. I could feel the tension in my furrowed brow and drawn lips. We all knew what it was and we knew not to ask any questions. I leaned against a tree, without speaking to anyone, until Asimov called us in.

I went to the back of the room to my usual spot and sat staring out of the window at the brilliant fall morning outside. It was cold, but the crisp blue sky beckoned. I wanted to go to the river, to breathe some fresh air, to talk to Mama, to ask her about the twins and the others who were in Heaven with her, to ask her if she had welcomed Viktor and to ask her if she knew when it would be my turn to join the others at the cemetery. I wished I were there, by the river this morning, instead of being stuck in this awful classroom. I was not paying attention to the Snake at all. I wasn't aware of his speaking to me until the wrap of the metre stick on my knuckles brought me back to attention.

"I'm talking to you," Asimov said.

"Yes, yes, Comrade," I said, stammering.

"Why isn't your book open to the lesson?"

"I don't know, Comrade."

"Get on with it. I'll be calling you to recite."

"Yes, Comrade."

I stared at the letters on the page. I saw the words arranged in their paragraphs, but they wouldn't make themselves known to my brain. There was an invisible blanket that separated me from the schoolwork. The Snake seemed to know what was going on as he hounded me all morning. I stuttered and stammered through the little I could remember when it was time to recite. I did not offer any answers in the history lesson. When it was time for arithmetic where I usually executed each sum perfectly, I made mistakes in every calculation.

"How stupid you are today!" the Snake yelled. "When did three times eight become sixteen?"

I stared at the sum on the blackboard. 439 times 287. What was eight times three anyway? I couldn't think. And Asimov would not let up on the pressure.

"Do it again," he said.

I did it again. Sixteen I wrote. I received another blow on my knuckles with the stick and the chalk fell to the floor.

"Write it out fifty times," he ordered.

I picked up the chalk and moved to the left side of the blackboard, the side that was reserved for punishing inattentive students. I wrote the sum over again. I made more mistakes. I tried to correct them. The more I corrected, the more mistakes I made.

"Hurry up already," Asimov said. "You're not usually this idiotic."

"No, Comrade," I answered. I resumed my writing.

"Another mistake!" he said from over my right shoulder. Another blow, this one on the back of my hand. I screamed from the pain and the chalk fell again, breaking into pieces this time.

"Come here," Comrade Asimov said, directing me to the centre of the front of the room. His face was twisted with anger.

"What's going on with you today? Did someone put rocks into your head while you were sleeping?"

"No, Comrade."

"Where's that snivelling little cousin of yours? He should be at school today, shouldn't he?"

"Yes, Comrade, he should."

"So where is he then? Or don't you know that either?"

"He's dead, Comrade."

"Dead? From what?"

"From being hungry, Comrade."

"What nonsense!" Comrade Asimov exclaimed. "We've just brought in a bumper crop of a harvest. Isn't it enough for you happy farmers?"

"Yes, Comrade. but he's dead anyway. We weren't given any of the wheat."

"I guess that's nature's way of ensuring that the strongest survive," he said, brushing me off breezily.

"No, Comrade," I said. "It wasn't nature that killed him."

His face turned red.

"What's that? You dare to contradict me!"

"Yes, Comrade," I answered. I stood as straight as I could and stuck out my chin in the best of the Ukrainian spirit I had left.

"It wasn't nature that killed him. It was Father Stalin and his army. It was Uncle Ivan and his bread procurement committee and it was you, the worst of all; it was you and your metre stick that beat him every day till he didn't want to live any more—till he hadn't enough strength to get water or play with me or go to the river to catch crayfish with me or pick flowers. Now he's in Heaven, with Mama and *Tahto* and Jesus where you or Uncle Ivan or Father Stalin will never hurt him—ever again."

I was screaming now. It wasn't a little Childlike scream. It was a black roar that came from the bottom of my empty belly, that racked my bones, and made my head feel like it might explode.

It didn't take Asimov long to react. He smashed my face with his right hand. My nose started bleeding profusely.

He looked surprised.

"Go home and clean up. I don't need your mess all over my classroom. Maybe, you'll think before you speak the next time."

I found myself out in the cold morning. I sat there, on the stoop violently shaking. That was how Auntie Anna, the sister of our old schoolmaster, found me as she was crossing the square to minister to one of the Babushkas.

"For the love of the Good Lord, Child!" she said. "What has happened to you."

"Comrade Asimov," I answered through my clenched teeth. I couldn't say any more.

"Xena will surely go mad," she said. She helped me to my feet and walked home with me, her arm around my waist so that I wouldn't faint back down to the ground.

Auntie Xena did faint when she saw me. While Xenkovna boiled water and started to clean me up, Auntie Anna tended to Auntie

Xena. Tea was made. I was propped up to try to stop the bleeding. It was a long time before things settled down. My face was swollen for days and Auntie Xena was worried that I would be left with a crooked nose or some kind of breathing problem. But Uncle Misha was angry.

"You know that this won't be forgotten," he said. "Those were serious accusations you made. As a matter of fact, we can expect them to do something. The question is what and when?"

I didn't go to school after that. While my face healed, the month of November set in. It was colder than usual. Uncle Misha and the boys tried to bring in our winter's supply of wood. They went to the woods and carried one log in at a time.

"I don't know how we'll go on all winter with so little fuel," Auntie said. "You just get a log in and split it before we have to burn it for the evening fire."

"We're doing the best we can, woman," Uncle Misha said. "What do you want with no horses or wagons? It doesn't help that we have no energy either. It takes me all day to do what I used to do in an hour not more than two years ago. The boys are helping, but it's all we can do to drag one of those blasted logs home, never mind cutting it into something you can throw onto the hearth. Remember to keep your fire small, just big enough to do what you need or we'll freeze this winter before we can starve to death." He finished with short breath and yet another coughing fit.

"Don't teach me how to build my fires," she snapped back uncharacteristically.

One morning as I cleared the table of our breakfast tea things, I heard the sound of an army truck. No one had to tell me. I knew that the time for revenge from the Comrades had come. Uncle Ivan and some Party men that I didn't recognize emerged from the vehicle and tried to barge into our kitchen.

"Hold your horses," Uncle Misha said as he fumbled with the latch on the cottage door.

"Good to see that you're receiving guests this morning," Uncle Ivan said.

"I issued no invitation," Uncle Misha said.

"We're not here on a neighbourly visit. Get your hat, Michael Ivanowich, and call your boys. Your services are needed for Father Stalin."

"I have no plans to be out today. Nor do I owe any services to the *kolhosp*. I'm not even a member, have you forgotten?"

"No matter. You are raising an enemy of the people in this house so we mean to teach you where your priorities should be."

"An enemy of the people?"

"Yes. An enemy of the people. Did your niece not say to Comrade Asimov that we killed your son? And did she not say that Father Stalin's army was responsible? Did she not say that I was involved too?"

"I don't know. I was here and she was at school. And may I remind you that she is the top student in her form."

"She may be the top student in her form, but she has no manners. She can't keep her mouth shut either. She also has her mind filled with old fashioned fairy tales, does she not?"

"I have no idea what you're talking about."

"She seems to have some notion that things would be better off with Jesus. You should have cured her of that fairy tale long ago. The state is her new Heaven and Father Stalin her ruler."

"Her new Heaven?" Uncle Misha spat at Uncle Ivan's feet. "With the fairy tale of happy well-fed farmers? While two of her sisters and one brother have passed for no reason other than the greed and filth of the Party?"

Uncle Ivan pulled out his revolver.

"Listen here, you stupid, stubborn man. We're cleaning up this village for the good of the new order whether you like it or not. You can hold out and die or co-operate. That is your choice. We'll take

your land, one way or another. But today, I need workers—workers
to bring in the wood for this winter so you're coming or I'll blow
off your head and the heads of your sons if I have to. As for your
mouthy brat, her name is up for examination by the court. The only
thing that is keeping her from being picked up is her tender age. She
should have been off to prison long ago. No one gets away with
treasonous statements like that, so you better stuff her mouth full
of rags if you know what's good for your family."

He gave me one of his lecherous stares and motioned to Michael
and Alexander to move out along with Uncle Misha. What could
they do? He had the gun. They grabbed a hat and jacket and hurried
off into the army vehicle. They didn't return until long after dark.

The next morning, the army truck and Uncle Ivan arrived bright
and early to pick up Uncle Misha and the cousins. They barely had
time to swallow their tea before they were off for another day of
forced labour. Xenkovna and I decided that we would go out to see
if we could gather dead wood from the orchard as a way to try to
build up our fuel supply. It was critical now as we didn't know how
long the Comrades would keep our men in servitude.

"Do you think we can get Mitya to help us?" I wondered.

"Who knows?" Xenkovna said. "He's so strange these days.
I'm afraid he's becoming like his poor mother."

I said nothing more as that thought frightened me. I couldn't
imagine how he would live in the shadowy world of the woods all
by himself with only fairies and goblins as companions. I started
down the path toward the orchard. I was so involved in my mind's
wanderings that I almost bumped into the stooped, old man who
was walking up the path toward me.

"Good day Uncle," Xenkovna said from behind me. "What can
I do for you this morning?"

"Xenkovna, don't you recognize me?" he asked.

Then it dawned on me.

"Uncle Paulo?" I asked. "Is that you, really?"

"Philipovna, mind your manners." Xenkovna stepped up on the path beside me.

We stared at him as if we'd never seen him before. This once solid well-built, robust man with ruddy cheeks and kind eyes looked as if he'd emerged from a grave. His gray skin hung in bags from his cheeks and chin and his eyes had lost their brown lustre. It looked as if every step would be his last.

"Is that really you?" Xenkovna, who usually could control her composure as well as Auntie, wept openly. "Come in, come in. Mama will be glad to see you. I'm sure we'll find a cup of tea—or something for you."

We turned back into the house and found Auntie praying before the icon.

"For the love of God, what have they done to you?" she exclaimed upon recognizing Uncle Paulo. She stopped and took a long look, too.

"I haven't got much strength left," he said. "Is Misha here? I'd like to say what I have to say to the both of you."

"No, he's not. The Comrades came and collected the men to bring in wood today," Auntie said. She proceeded to tell Uncle Paulo what happened over the last winter since he had been here for his chess game.

"Dear God," he sighed and wiped his eyes with his sleeve. "How wrong I was. Please tell Misha that he's right. Though these devils have broken our spirit and taken our land, by the Cross, Misha is right and has been right all along. They will surely defeat us and I say by the Name of our Saviour, they will be worse than any Tsar we've ever known. They preach well-being and prosperity but they'll take everything we have and all we stand for."

The tears flowed freely over his sunken cheeks.

"But we know all of that," he said. "I guess Misha doesn't really need to hear it again. Would you please tell him that I came to ask for his forgiveness? I doubt I'll see the end of this week. I couldn't go to my precious Maria without asking you to pardon me. I should have never given them my land. My heart broke in two when I watched them chase your Children out of my cherries. I used to love to see the joy on all of the faces that my orchard blessed. My dear neighbour, by the Grace of God, I ask for your forgiveness too." He reached for Auntie's hand and kissed it.

Xenkovna and I stared at him in silence.

"I have one more thing to tell you," he said. "Take Philipovna away from here. Take her as far away as you can, so that Ivan can't get his hands on her. After he and Simon found out what she said to Asimov, they've been looking for pay back. I won't say what he threatened as she is so young and still innocent, but you must get her away—at all costs or death will be the least of her trials."

He wiped the sweat off his forehead and finished his tea while we three women sat with our mouths gaping.

"Where should I take her?" Auntie was the first to speak. "Where? Do you have any ideas?"

"But I don't want to go anywhere," I said.

"What you want, Child, is irrelevant," Uncle Paulo said. "What we all want doesn't matter. We want you to survive. That's what matters. If you young ones don't make it, our lives are worth nothing. Our history, our culture, it'll all surely die. I won't make it; but you must! You must. For the love of God, for the love of our land and for the love of our ancestors, you must."

He said goodbye and went on his way. We didn't get up to see him to the door. We were so stunned by what he had come to say. We knew that we would never see him again. His words rang in our ears. Each one of us knew that the others were playing them over and over in our minds, but we didn't have the energy to speak or move for a very long time.

"Come along," Auntie finally said. She got up from her chair and went into the room where Mama's sewing machine was. She pulled out her trunk and started rifling through its contents.

"We have to find something that we can wrap around you under your clothes," she said. "I don't imagine that they keep a good fire at the orphanage. Now put on this shirt under your blouse. It's old, but it will keep you warm." She handed me one of the boy cousins' undergarments.

"Orphanage!" I screamed at her. "I don't want to go. I won't go. I'll run away the first chance I get." I stamped my foot.

"Settle down, Child. Today isn't the first time I've thought of taking you there," Auntie said. "I promised your mother, on her bible—see. It's right here. I look at it often and remember. If no one else survives, you have to—you must. I promised."

Her tears flowed and she clutched the bible in the same way as I remembered her doing on the day that Godfather decided that I should go with her. She put her arms around me with Mama's bible between our chests.

"Do it for your precious Mama, if you can't do it for me," she said, whispering. "God has set you aside for something. I don't know what it is, but I'm sure there is something special that you are being prepared for. Please, Child, do it for your Mama if you can't for me. I promised your Mama and Godfather ... there is no other way. You must survive."

I put on two layers of clothing under my regular blouse; I wrapped my feet with extra rags and stuffed them into a pair of felt boots. Auntie took a small bundle of poppy tea and told me to keep it under my inner clothing.

"Don't use this all of the time," she said. "Save it for those nights that you absolutely can't sleep or when you really can't tolerate the pain. It will stand you in good stead if you can manage it. And, for the love of our Blessed Jesus, don't let any grown-up find you with it. You're smart enough to do this."

She tucked some raw carrots into another small bundle. She found the Unravelled One's coat that she had almost frozen to death in last winter. She put ashes into her dark brown hair, although she didn't have to use as many as last time. She kissed Xenkovna good-bye and waited while Xenkovna hugged me with her tears falling all over my face.

"Tell the men what happened," she said. "I'll be back as soon as I can. At least I won't freeze my hands and feet off this time."

We were off to start another new life. We walked down the familiar path that led around the orchard with its naked branches and wound to the river. We followed the river's bank past the place where we found the Unravelled One by the willows. Their straggly skeletons seemed to be mocking me as they shivered in the cold wind. We crossed the dell whose flowers had long departed and whose grass blew brown and lifeless, as uninviting as the stubble of an empty field. Yet, this was home, the first home that I really participated in, even though it had been prescribed by Godfather and not one that I had been born into like everyone else. To be ripped from its meagre comfort was worse than any death that I had witnessed.

Auntie pushed on briskly. She kept her eyes directly on the path and wouldn't look either to the right or left. We followed the river for about half a kilometre before she suddenly stepped off the path and into the forest. She motioned for me to follow. At first it looked like there was no evidence of anyone ever having walked here but, as I became accustomed to the hard travelling, I realized that there had been a trail here some time ago. It had been neglected and hidden.

"Why are we going this way?" I asked.

"It's a short cut," she replied over her shoulder. "And I doubt if the Comrades have discovered it yet. If they had, there would be a patrol here."

"Where does it come out?"

"At the pasture of the old estate."

"How do you know this path?"

"Your Mama and I visited the Unravelled One here in the evenings when she was supposed to be shut up in her little room embroidering or sewing or knitting. Now stop talking and save your energy for walking."

She pressed on at such a pace that I had no more breath for questions. Within a half an hour, we found ourselves at what was left of a gate in an old, broken-down rail fence.

We didn't go across the pasture. We skirted its edge, always checking for any unexpected company, and by late afternoon, Auntie deemed it safe to go on the road that went toward the town where she traded the silver for wheat. We walked for hours, until the gloomy afternoon deepened into twilight and she started looking for a place to settle for the night.

"We must find shelter soon," Auntie Xena said. "It looks like it might rain."

We passed a cottage that looked inviting with its candle in the window, but Auntie wouldn't knock on the door.

"I'm tired," I said.

"We don't want anyone to remember seeing us on the road. I'm sure we'll find something more suitable," she answered, and we walked on with me dragging my legs as if they were great trunks of trees. We passed by another cottage with a candle in the window.

"Please, Auntie, I'm tired. I can't walk anymore."

She looked back at me with a sympathetic tear sneaking out of her left eye.

"We'll check the barn," she said. "Maybe we can rest here without being discovered."

"Isn't it warmer in the house?" I asked.

"It might be," she said, "but we can't count on the folks being friendly. They might accuse us of begging or trying to steal their food. They might turn us in if the Comrades come asking."

We carefully sneaked around the back of the house. Fortunately, there was a well behind it with a dipper. We took a long cold drink of water. I wished we had some warm tea as the damp day was starting to make itself felt right into my bones. We checked out the barn. It reminded me of the Unravelled One's cottage with its cobwebs and scary shadows which were all the more prominent without a candle. I was sure that the Unravelled One would summon up some demon or *chort* that would put some spell on Auntie and me as we slept. Part of it had already been broken down, not by age or neglect, but I could see that someone had been chopping at the old barn intentionally with an axe or hatchet.

"Why do you think that half of the barn is missing?" I asked.

"They probably needed firewood and for some reason couldn't go to the woods to get it."

"Will Uncle and the boys have to chop apart our barn for firewood?"

"Who knows what we'll have to do, Child. Now eat your carrots."

We found some dirty straw on the floor. Auntie found an old broom and swept it into a pile in the back corner. We sat on the straw and ate our carrots for supper.

"Now get on your knees so we can say our prayers."

She prayed a long prayer, praising His Name, thanking God for my life and hers, blessing those who were left at home and praying for our safety. It was a prayer that I would recite over and over again many times in the coming months. She spread the Unravelled One's coat on the straw and covered us, as well as she could with her own shawl. We huddled together and as the rain began to fall onto the half of the roof that was left on the barn, I fell into a fitful sleep.

My New Home

✳✳✳❖✳✳✳

I WOKE IN the gray dawn, at the time of day when it is between dark and light. I was cold and stiff. I didn't recognize where I was. Auntie was already up straightening her rumpled clothing. My bones hurt from the hard ground. I felt cranky.

"Get up, Philipovna," Auntie said. "Smooth out your blouse the best you can. Hurry with your coat and shawl. We must get walking before someone finds out we're here. We can't take a chance on being reported to the Comrades."

I yawned and rewrapped my cold feet in their rags so that there wouldn't be any lumps in my felt boots. I combed my messy braid with my fingers.

"We'll get another drink of water and be on our way," she said.

We wrapped our shawls over our heads to ward off the morning mist. We tucked our coats around us. I peeked around the corner of the barn.

"I can't see anyone at the well," I said. We cautiously started toward the pitcher that we used last night and its promised cold drink of water.

"Ho, who's this?" a man said, his voice broke the morning silence.

I stifled a scream.

Though the man spoke quietly, his voice startled both Auntie

195

and me as if it were a shot from a cannon. He appeared from no-where, but he must have come from around the other side of the house. He was tall and lanky, a walking skeleton with unkempt graying hair. His coat was as ragged as our clothing was and his feet were wrapped in rags with no boots at all. In spite of my own discomfort, I felt sorry for him. Though his pale eyes were dull and his cheeks sunken, I could see that he had been strong like Uncle Misha before the famine set in.

"Where did you come from?" he asked.

"I can't say," Auntie said. "Please, good Uncle, let us have a drink and we'll be going. Just pretend that you never set your eyes on us."

"But where did you come from? Have you and the Child been walking all night?" His voice sounded kind to me, so full of concern.

"No, good sir, we sheltered in your barn, by the Grace of God. We thank you for it," Auntie said in an unusually crisp manner.

"Have you eaten?"

Neither of us responded. Auntie stared straight at the well.

"A drink is all we need," she said.

"Wouldn't you like to warm up by my fire? I don't have much, but I'd gladly share my fire."

I tried to move closer to the house, but Auntie's hand held my shoulder tight.

"Thank you, sir," she said. "We need to be going. A drink will be as much hospitality as we can accept. And your word that you will say that you never saw us should the Comrades come asking. God bless you for your generosity."

"Running from the Comrades," he said, sighing. "That is a common problem these days. You aren't the first wanderers who have sheltered in my poor barn. Would that we could all run from them and their cursed new order."

He exchanged a hard look with Auntie and he motioned us to-ward the well. We took a long drink as we had the night before. We waved good-bye and with tears in my eyes, I set off behind Auntie.

The walking was difficult because the rain left a muddy trail so we had to avoid puddles and slippery places in the path. I stumbled frequently as the mud clinging to my boots made my feet heavy. We walked all day under low gray clouds and through a fine drizzle which neither turned to rain nor lifted. I was so miserable that I stopped looking where I was going. I had no idea what was around me as we trudged through the soggy countryside. I kept my eyes on Auntie's back and simply put one foot in front of the other until I could hardly feel my toes.

My belly cramped with hunger pains which were stronger than usual because of the energy I was expending to keep up with the relentless pace that Auntie set. I wondered where Mitya was. Was he sheltered somewhere in the woods or did he sneak in by the woodpile to warm up by the fire? Did he think of me or was I as lost to him as poor Sharik? I wished I were by our own fire in Auntie's house with Xenkovna. I wanted to burst out screaming each time I thought of her, but I said nothing and concentrated on following Auntie. When I finally looked up, we were coming to an unfamiliar town.

It was late afternoon and a market day. There were still things left in the stalls. The venders were busying themselves with putting away the goods that weren't sold. I could see that this town was not in the hunger zone because the faces of the people were full with colour in their cheeks. Their eyes were bright with energy. Their clothing was clean and whole as they walked with their heads held high. They avoided looking directly at Auntie and me. They made themselves busy when we got close to their wares. If they did actually look at us, their eyes were full of disgust. We were not welcome.

I stared shamelessly at the pears, the plums and the apples which gleamed with the brightest red and gold that I had ever seen. I was sure that there were no apples more beautiful than these. The blue plums were my favourites. I would have grabbed any of them if I thought I could have gotten away with it. I could feel the saliva coming to the corners of my lips with every inhalation of fragrance from the tangy apples and the floury smell of the fresh bread that still waited for a buyer with a coin to spend for a bite to eat on the way home. Auntie looked over the scene carefully.

"Stay right here," she said. "I'm going to talk to that lady for a minute. I'll be right back." She pointed to an old woman sitting in a corner with a couple of sacks of potatoes and a pile of onion braids at her feet.

I wondered who the woman was, but Auntie was gone before I could ask. It wasn't long before I lost sight of her in the crowd that was moving with last minute buyers and tired venders heading home for their supper. So I stood admiring the squash, and cabbage, the carrots and beets and the few hams and cheeses that were left for the latecomers. I was so busy eating everything with my eyes that I didn't notice a horse and cart coming down the path until they almost ran me over. As I jumped out of the way, I bumped into a corner of a makeshift table and knocked over a nicely arranged pile of its fresh-baked goods.

"You filthy little *Zaraza*," a fat woman with a double chin shouted from behind her table. "Did you have to do that? The least you could have done is begged for some of my bread if you're that hungry. You didn't have to knock it over."

Her jowls scrunched up in rage and she began retrieving her display. A girl about my age rushed out from behind the stall to help the woman. She stared at me for a moment, then turned to rearrange the fallen bread.

"Where do girls like that come from, Mama? And why is she so filthy?"

"You don't want to know," the woman said. "Make sure that you never become one of them."

Fortunately, only two small loaves fell to the ground. I eyed them ravenously, but didn't dare to move toward them.

"Take the bread and disappear." A small man with woolly gray hair and a kind smile who had been standing with the woman behind the table was motioning to me.

"She won't notice if you hurry," he said in a voice which was barely audible in the commotion. "And God be with you. You look like you could use ten of those."

"Thank you," I said, mouthing silently. I scurried under the table and grabbed the loaves out of the dirt. I shoved them into my coat and then ran in Auntie's direction.

"Good grief," she exclaimed as I met her in the aisle between the stalls. "Look at the dirt all over you. What happened?"

"I got us some bread for supper," I answered.

"Good," Auntie said. "The dear Babushka is the woman who gave me bread and refuge last winter. She gave me a small hunk of cheese. We'll find a quiet place to eat and then we'll follow her directions and get you ..." Auntie didn't finish her sentence. We walked off the main path of the market and found a woodpile in a corner of an empty garden.

"No one should notice us here," she said. We ate the bread and cheese in the pale light of the sun that had broken through the clouds of the late afternoon. Then Auntie got down onto her knees and insisted that I do the same.

"I don't want to! I won't go. I won't stay. I don't know anyone there. They won't like me either." My stomach did so many flip-flops that I thought that my precious bread and cheese would come right back up.

"You see how God has provided us this nourishing supper?"

I nodded.

"If you remember to be faithful and pray every morning and every night, I know that He will see to it that you live and that we'll be together again."

"When?" I said, sobbing.

"I don't know, Child. I wish I did." She hugged me close to her boney breast. I could feel her breathing hard and her heart thumping —or was it mine? I didn't know.

"I promised God and your mother," she said. "I've done all that I know to do. It's time to give you back to God and beg Him to keep you safe. It's the only way. And when you get tired of praying to God, don't forget to ask the Holy Mother for her blessing. She lost her son on the cross so she knows what it's like. Now, let's dry our tears. We have to go."

Auntie Xena forced me to repeat every line of the Lord's Prayer after her. My knees ached from the damp ground and my teeth shivered as I repeated those blessed lines mechanically:

"Our Father, Who art in Heaven. Hallowed be Thy Name ..."

Auntie jumped up abruptly. She walked so quickly that I had to run to keep up. As the candles started to light the windows of the townspeople's homes, we marched through the darkening streets of that town whose name I either never learned or have forgotten. I made myself forget many things that happened to me there.

We passed the square with its now empty market. We went by the government buildings. We passed by the smaller clusters of the farmers' cottages at the edge of town and finally turned up the path of one that was not much different from Auntie's own home, though it was in worse repair. As we got to the door, Auntie Xena hugged me hard, one last time. She pounded on the door and waited. When it opened, she gave me a gentle push towards the stranger who stood there. Then she was gone.

A sour smell of sick and unfamiliar humanity greeted me as I looked up into the severe face of Svetlana Ivanovna. She was a spare woman with mousey hair and a gray streak over one temple. Her eyes were hard and small and her voice was as sharp as her features.

"Don't stand there, girl," she said. "I'm not keeping a fire to warm the street. You may as well come in. Did you come alone?"

I was too stunned to speak.

"Do you have a name?"

"Philipovna," I whispered.

"Nikolaiovna," she said over her shoulder, "if there's any porridge left in the bottom of that pot, scoop it up for this new street urchin. We'll find out more about her when she warms up and the food loosens her tongue. Try to clean her up a bit if you can, especially that mud on her feet. She must have been walking for a while by the looks of it."

Ivanovna turned back into the dimly-lit room which corresponded to the main room of Auntie's house and was full of Children, most of whom were younger than me. Their cheeks were gaunt like I imagined mine were and their appearance was just as bedraggled as I knew I was. Some of them were still licking their porridge bowls like little dogs. They weren't going to leave one drop of the porridge in their tin bowls. Others were just sitting quietly on the benches at a long table that stretched from the hearth almost down to the door that had opened to let me in. Not one of them would look at me directly, yet I could feel their eyes looking right through me, straight into my broken soul.

I vowed that I'd never talk to them and that I would never become a part of this place. No matter how much food they gave me, I'd never let them loosen my tongue. A petite woman with dark hair neatly braided and fashioned into a big bun at the nape of her neck came towards me, a bowl of something in her hands. She was much younger than the Comrade who opened the door and had the heaviest eyebrows and biggest brown eyes I had ever seen.

"Sit down, girl," she said briskly. Her voice was firm but not as unfriendly as Comrade Svetlana's. Although her face was stern, I could see that she was pretty.

"Here's the last of the porridge," she said. "My name is Marina Nikolaiovna. We'll find a place for you once supper is cleaned up." She gestured to a tall girl with straw-coloured hair and an angular face at the far end of the table.

"Larysa, get started on these dishes. Gregory, get some more wood for the fire. Mind that you don't make it too big, Father Stalin doesn't like us to waste any precious wood with a fire that's too hot."

A thin boy with lifeless brown hair got up and did her bidding.

"Thank you," I said.

Although I had not long ago eaten bread and cheese with Auntie, I ate every spoonful of that tasteless porridge and licked my bowl in the manner of a little dog, just like the other Children had. I hoped that I didn't eat it too fast as the memory of Auntie's words about my tummy being too small and getting sick whispered in my mind.

"What's your name?" Marina Nikolaiovna asked.

"Philipovna," I said again.

"I heard that one. I mean your whole name."

"That's my whole name," I said.

"What's your mother's name?"

"Mama," I whispered.

"I mean her real name," she said, sighing. "Wasn't that your mother who brought you?"

"No, that was a woman who found me in her barn."

Although Auntie never said that I shouldn't tell anyone who I really was, her secretive behaviour towards everyone we met on our way frightened me so that I didn't want to tell these Comrades anything either.

"So what's her name then?"

"I don't know."

Nikolaiovna shook her head and left me sitting while she went on with her work.

I watched Larysa and another girl gather the bowls and spoons up from the bare wooden table. As they washed, Svetlana Ivanovna moved back and forth carrying trays of various bottles and bowls between the main room of the house and the room that was like the one where my Mama's sewing machine was kept.

"They never send me enough medicine," she said. "How am I supposed to nurse these brats with so little to work with and more of them knocking at our door every day?"

Other Children were lying on piles of old blankets in that room, some on sleeping benches by the walls and others on the floor. Since only one candle lit that room, I couldn't see what Ivanovna or the Children were doing. In time, I learned that this was the infirmary and that most of the Children who went into it never walked out.

While the dishes were being washed, Nikolaiovna and two of the other older girls, who were not much bigger than me, spread out blankets on sleeping benches by the fire that wasn't warm enough to heat the whole room properly. They laid the smaller Children on the benches, like cobs of corn on a table at the market, boys on one side and girls on the other. I squinted hard as the picture of my three little cousins sleeping by Auntie's hearth pushed its way into my brain. Did Xenkovna miss me? Was she happy to have my Mama's feather bed or would Auntie keep it for me the way she had promised? A tear popped out of the corner of my eye.

"Don't cry, Child," Marina Nikolaiovna said softly as she walked past with a scrawny little boy to put by the fire. "You will get used to us."

"I'm not crying."

She shook her head sympathetically and kept going.

Once the smaller Children were settled, the bigger ones were given sleeping places and ragged blankets according to size till I was assigned a place by the draughty door through which Auntie had pushed me earlier in the evening.

"You can share a blanket with Larysa," Nikolaiovna said. "She'll show you how things go here. Maybe you can be friends."

But I didn't want to be friends. I didn't want to lie down under a strange-smelling blanket with a girl I didn't know or want for a friend. My friend was Mitya and the only blanket I wanted was my Mama's feather bed.

"Suit yourself," Nikolaiovna said. "The cold will teach you how to get by."

I lay down as the fire went out. Larysa tried to cuddle close to me but I pushed her away. I felt cold and alone. I hadn't learned yet that sleeping cuddled up to one or more of my fellow orphans was the only way to keep from freezing to death, especially in the depths of the winter that was on its way. The room was full of strange sounds—sounds of breathing, clearing throats and soft sighs as several dozen hungry Children settled for the night. From the smaller room I could hear coughing and rasping and the occasional cry from the sick ones. But that wasn't the worst of it.

This forlorn house smelled bad—not like the house I had grown to love. Auntie's house smelled nice, sweet and spicy from the herbs and onions that had hung in its rafters for years. The fire smelled pungent and welcoming with the residual smell of tea and cooking food even when we had nothing to eat. My feather bed held the essence of Xenkovna whose presence was always comforting no matter what I dreamed or how frightened I was. And though it wasn't always warm enough, I never felt as cold and desolate as I did in this strange place that was brimming with desperate Children who smelled of human filth and vomit.

I tossed and turned under my half of the stinking blanket trying not to touch Larysa who was oblivious in sleep and didn't seem to notice any of my troubles. When the morning broke into another gray gloom, I was fitfully miserable and in no condition to cooperate with anyone or anything that my new home had to offer.

Larysa still lay sleeping, her face down in her blanket. I tried not to disturb her but some rustling movements at the far end of the room caught my attention. I sat up to look around. Nikolaiovna was measuring some wheat into the bottom of a large pot and Ivanovna was moving toward the sick room with her tray of bowls and potions. It's funny how your first impressions of a person lodge themselves in your consciousness. No matter what else Svetlana Ivanovna did after I met her, I always picture her in my mind with a tray of potions and a preoccupied scowl on her face.

I watched her disappear into the sick room. Neither of the women saw that I was awake. I didn't want to lie down again because I felt so stiff and uncomfortable, but I didn't know if I should get up either. As the damp morning oozed itself in, I studied my surroundings more carefully.

The Children's Home, as I found out it was called, resembled Comrade Asimov's classroom. The holy icons were gone, along with anything that made it look like a home except that the stove for cooking still had its accoutrements for food preparations. The walls were covered with tattered posters and banners with New Order slogans and the benches that the Children had used to sit on from around the long table in the middle were now makeshift beds.

I wondered where Auntie spent the night. I wondered if her house felt as empty as this one felt full. I wondered how long it would take for Uncle and the boys to forget that I was ever in their house waking up with them each morning. Then I remembered to pray.

Where would I be able to do that? I looked from corner to corner and realized that I'd never have a centimetre to myself. Everywhere I looked there was someone taking up space. How did Auntie expect me to keep that promise when there was not a spot to call my own and all of the propaganda on the walls to remind me that this was not a place where I would be allowed to pray?

Maybe, I didn't want to pray. If I was a Child of God, why did I have to be here? But the words that Godfather said when I was standing on Mama's sewing machine came back to me. Then there were the words of Uncle Paulo at Auntie's house before we left and the thought of all of those people that had left me to go to Heaven, right from Mama to Cousin Viktor. If I didn't pray, maybe they wouldn't let me into Heaven when it was my turn to go.

I better find a way, I thought. *I will find a way—I must.*

"Larysa, Philipovna, wake up." Nikolaiovna called softly from the stove.

I jumped up. There was no need to dress as I had slept with all of my clothes on. I smoothed my skirt the best I could and made my way toward the fire. Gregory had already brought some wood and was poking at the coals.

"Take the spoon and stir the porridge," Nikolaiovna said.

"But I want to stir the porridge," Larysa said from behind my shoulder. "She can get the water. I'm tired of being the one who always has to bring it. She might as well earn her place the way we all have to around here."

Her green eyes looked at me with icy intimidation. The last time I saw that look was the Easter Sunday that Auntie Lena swore that she would never give me a bite of bread no matter how hungry I was. I felt a shiver go down my back. I stopped with my hand in mid-reach not being sure of what to do.

"It's someone else's turn to get frozen out there every morning," Larysa said. She grabbed the long-handled wooden spoon from a rack on the wall, turned her back to me and began to stir the large pot.

"Larysa," Nikolaiovna said. "You'd be a much better person if you could find a little kindness in your heart."

Larysa glared back at her.

"Kindness? What's that? And whoever shows any kindness to me?"

"You might make a friend or two if you tried. Life would be easier for you if you did."

"I don't need any friends." Larysa frowned more deeply and continued to stir.

"I don't know where the well is," I said.

"Show her where the buckets are." Nikolaiovna motioned to Gregory.

Without a word, Gregory started for the door. I followed his gaunt back to where the buckets were kept and out to the well. Once Gregory saw that I knew where things were, he disappeared back into the house like a shadow. And that's how he was, quietly doing Nikolaiovna's bidding. I never heard him utter a sound in the months that I lived at the orphanage.

The sky was still heavy with clouds and the November air was sharp with the coming winter. Despite the dampness, it felt good. I breathed in deeply, the way I had when I went out for water after the twins died and felt the same cleansing cold reviving me.

I could get water every day, I thought. It would probably be the only time that I would be alone. I could pray as I went to fill the buckets and no one would ever see me.

It didn't take long for me to fall into the drudgery of the Children's Home. I went to the well before breakfast each morning. We lined up for a small serving of porridge and a tin cupful of water. We were given enough to survive, but never enough to feel satisfied. On a rare morning there might also be a piece of bread as well. I remembered the pots at the market place in our village and always waited till the porridge was almost gone before I got my bowl filled. Mitya told me that the porridge was thicker towards the bottom of the pot than the top because it got heavier when it cooked.

After breakfast, the bigger girls put away the blankets, which got dirtier and more ragged every day, and set up the long table for our lessons. Our lessons were taught by a fat, old man with a red face who was a member of the Party. I don't know if I ever heard his name. We called him Comrade Professor. Though his appearance was different from Asimov, his methods and demeanour were the same. The metre stick was often busy at the expense of a crying, hungry Child. There was arithmetic, Russian history and reading in the morning. Propaganda was saved for the afternoon.

"Father Stalin doesn't want his Children to be ignorant," the Comrade said.

Those who were relatively healthy were assigned to help with the chores of the house or caring for the sicker Children.

"You might as well learn that, even though Father Stalin considers each and every one of you to be his own, he expects you to earn your keep," Ivanovna told us.

I always chose to do the chores that separated me from the others even those that might be more difficult or those that would take me out into the cold. I believe that being out in that cold killed much of the sickness that weakened the rest of the Children. If I was sweeping, drawing water or bringing in wood, I didn't have to talk to anyone. I also learned that if I pasted a half-smile or absent look on my face, Nikolaiovna would leave me in peace and not try to convince me to be a better person the way she always tried with the sulky Larysa.

A second pot of porridge was made at seven each night and the bedtime routine of the first evening that I arrived was played over again. Occasionally, a Child would be carried out of the sick room and sent to the cemetery. Since I never made friends with any of them, I never knew who they were. They would disappear without an explanation or a prayer. We were never told what really happened to them in that room.

When new Children arrived, which they did regularly, I stayed away from them, especially the smaller ones. I learned to look through people and to turn off any feelings I had left inside. When I prayed, the words seemed to come of their own accord. I often wasn't sure if God heard me, but I remembered my promise so I continued praying. When I thought of Auntie and the others, I choked the thoughts out of my mind as well as I could. When I wasn't being ordered around by one or the other of the Comrades, I sat alone and stared out of the window.

Time had no meaning. Each day was like the one before with no future in sight. And so the endless days of the fall of 1932 blurred past my ninth birthday and into the particularly cold winter of 1933. One day as I returned with my full water buckets, I was surprised to see that Nikolaiovna and Larysa were covering the long table with newly laundered sheets. Where could those have come from? We hadn't had any soap in the house since my arrival.

"Aren't we having breakfast?" I asked Larysa as she smoothed the sheet at her end of the table.

"Don't you know anything, you stupid girl?" she said. She stuck her thin nose in the air as if she knew something really important that I should know but obviously didn't.

I shrugged my shoulders and walked away. Why should I listen to that viper? I saw that a pot of porridge was boiling on the stove. I put the water buckets into their customary place and headed for my secluded corner to wait for breakfast as usual. I had no energy to care about what was going on. I'd find out soon enough.

The time for lessons to begin passed. We still were not given breakfast. The little ones started to fuss as they were hungry.

"Marina Nikolaiovna, why can't we have our breakfast?" one of the little boys asked.

"Because we are waiting for a special visitor. It's a surprise."

"What kind of surprise?"

"Don't ask so many questions," she said. "Suck your thumb till he gets here and you'll feel better."

It was almost noon when Comrade Professor arrived with two fur-covered Comrades from the city. They came bustling in with the falling snow, a big wooden box between them. The smaller Children moved in closer to have a good look, but Nikolaiovna shepherded them back.

"Let the Comrades in," she said. "We'll sit down for lunch and then you'll see what the surprise is."

Instead of lining up to get our bowls as usual, we were instructed to sit at the table like "civilized Children." Nikolaiovna and Larysa brought each person his porridge, starting with the visitors, while Ivanovna dished it up. As we ate the visitors took turns talking about how fortunate we were to be in this home and how well we were being taken care of by Father Stalin, especially as most other Children whose parents died were left out in the world to fend for themselves. Comrades Ivanovna and Nikolaiovna took it all in with satisfied smiles.

"And just to show you how special you are, we brought you a present," the taller of the city Comrades said.

The Children whispered excitedly around the table while the Comrades from the city opened their wooden crate and handed out the most beautiful orange fruit I had ever seen.

"What are these things and why do we get presents today?" one of the smaller boys asked.

"They're oranges. You peel back the skin and eat each section one at a time," Nikolaiovna said.

"In the Old World, it used to be Christmas Day on this day," the shorter Comrade from the city said. "People used to believe in that religious fairy tale and they did things like praying to please a father God that doesn't exist. Father Stalin wants to show you that we don't need to pray or do those things any more. No one prays these days. Enlightened people know that Father Stalin will give them everything they need. Those old fairy tales are only good for western farmers whose food and cattle are stolen from them by the capitalists. To show you that he is more important than God, he sent you a present."

"But Comrade," Larysa said from our end of the table, "I know someone who prays every day."

"You do?" he answered. "It must be an older person who's lost her mind and can't see common sense any longer."

"Oh, no, Comrade," Larysa said. "It's someone very young." Her face lit up in a smirk of satisfaction.

"How can that be?" Both of the city Comrades looked curiously at Comrades Ivanovna and Nikolaiovna. "I didn't think there were any believers in the home. You must get about town then."

"No, Comrade," Larysa said. "There's someone right at this table. I see her praying by the well every day."

Every eye in the room assaulted me. They all knew that I went for water and spent as much time as I could alone.

"Is this true?" Svetlana Ivanovna's sharp eyes were trained on my face like a pair of guns ready to blast my head off.

When had Larysa seen me praying? I always checked around me before I knelt. If I suspected even a faint movement in the wind, I stood and prayed invisibly — so I thought. Had Larysa been following me out? Had she watched me through a window? How did she know? And why was she doing this? I had tried to avoid her. My chest cramped till it hurt to breathe.

"Yes, it is." Larysa pounced on me like a cat that has finally captured her prey.

"Is it true?" Ivanovna said.

I nodded.

What followed amounted to a mock trial. I was questioned and badgered for hours till I admitted that I prayed by the well every day, that I believed in God and in Heaven, that I was going to see my dead family there some day, that my Auntie taught me to pray and that I could see my Mama's face in the centre of the flame of a candle because that's where one's soul was seen if one believed.

Comrade Professor's laugh was the loudest.

"Do you see a soul there?" the taller Comrade from the city asked.

They lit all of the candles they could find, looking for souls and laughed at me until one of the candles was knocked over in their merriment and almost set the house on fire. The Children were encouraged to denounce me in turn and some of the more aggressive ones even made up crude rhymes about my plight. In the end, I cried so hard that I fainted from exhaustion. They put me to sleep on a bench in a corner. I never said Auntie's name or who my family was.

I don't know how long I lay there. I woke up some time the next day with a head that felt as big as a pumpkin and red eyes that could rival those of a town drunk. My only consolation was that I never said the name of my family so I knew that, for now, I didn't cause them more grief. Comrade Ivanovna gave me extra propaganda pamphlets to memorize and took away all of my duties that gave me the space I had enjoyed before. She assigned me to help her in the sick room where she could keep an eye on me.

Larysa walked around as proud as a peacock. But Comrade Nikolaiovna sent sympathetic looks my way whenever she could see that no one was looking. She saved my orange for me and gave it to me while Ivanovna was gone out on an errand.

"Eat it slowly," she said. "It's sweet and tangy at the same time. I even like to bite off little bits of the peel because they taste bitter like the sunshine. Try it and see for yourself."

Ghosts in the Twilight

BEING RELEGATED TO the sick room changed my life as dramatically as if I had been sent to another country. A row of sleeping benches was lined up with their heads against the long wall of the room. They were so close together that I could hardly fit between them. It was my job to care for the Children who languished on these benches, especially when they had a fever.

"Try to make them drink as much water as they can," Ivanovna said. "Give them a small sip at a time so that they can keep more of it down. And clean them up when they vomit."

This was a very hard thing to do. Though the Children were underweight and small for their age, many of them were so weak that they couldn't lift their limbs and were surprisingly heavy. I was worn out by trying to support their bodies as I helped them eat their tiny serving of porridge or drink their few sips of water.

"Take care that they are lying back to back or heads on opposite ends so that they don't vomit all over each other," she explained. "Two or three together under a blanket keeps each of them warmer for a longer time. Pull up the covers as soon as you notice that they throw them off ... nothing we can do about these lice though." She scratched at her armpit trying to be discreet.

I shivered in sympathy and looked away.

"What is making us all itchy?" I asked. "I never was itchy before I came here."

I wondered why we all scratched at our groins and armpits.

"No need for shame," Ivanovna told me since we had no choice but to share beds, blankets and clothing with no soap to launder them, even the two Comrades suffered from body lice constantly.

"It's one of the hazards of being assigned to one of these uncivilized outposts," she complained.

I opted to keep my old sleeping spot with Larysa as it got me out of the Sick Room at least for a few hours each night. I fought with the memories of long winter nights snuggling under my Mama's feather bed with Xenkovna's arm around me and my face in her sweet-smelling hair. It didn't matter now anyway—or did it? Would God protect me? Would he bring me back to Auntie or would I die here with these outcasts? Would Mama and *Tahto* still want me after I spent so much time in such a terrible place? Maybe God wouldn't let me into Heaven after all. I was too filthy. I did Ivanovna's bidding.

As the winter progressed and the cold intensified, only the sickest were put on the beds while the stronger ones were put onto extra dirty blankets on the floor at the foot of the benches. In the end, the blankets would be so full of waste or vomit that there was nothing to do but throw them into the fire. Ivanovna argued with the authorities for more supplies. Many were promised, but few were ever delivered.

"For a nine-year-old, she's pretty strong and capable," I heard Ivanovna say to Nikolaiovna after they thought I had fallen asleep. "I couldn't manage without her. There's too many of them getting this horrible thing. Not enough nourishment for them to really get strong enough to fight the sickness. And never enough medicine or food for these Christian degenerates. I can't wait till this assignment is over so that I can go back to my decent hospital in Moscow."

"Ivanovna," Nikolaiovna said, "they're Children. As innocent as our own. What do they know about the Party or the New Order?"

"What good is their nationalist fervour now? Look at them. You keep on bleeding for these lousy brats and see how far you get. It's my politics that got me into this wasteland in the first place. Pay attention if you don't want a worse fate. Their ignorant parents should know better by now. Father Stalin will break them no matter what they do. I won't say that I heard you sympathizing with them, but don't expect anyone else to stay quiet. If you don't want trouble, I'm telling you to keep thoughts like that to yourself. Have you forgotten what the little witch Larysa did to Philipovna at Christmas?"

I shuddered at the memory.

The south window of the sick room which could have been letting in sunshine and light was covered with a sheet that once was white but was now a dirty yellow. I could tell whether the sun was out or not by the intensity of its dingy glow. I longed to be out in the bright sunlight on the other side of that sheet no matter how cold it got.

"The light will hurt their eyes and make them blind," Ivanovna said when I tried to pull the sheet aside one day. "Sick people need to rest. Cold air will let in bad things from outside."

"But it's so dark in this room. And it smells bad. I can't breathe in here." I never got used to the smell of vomit and, even after all of this time, I still retched when I had to deal with it.

"Stop your whining. Breathe through your open mouth and not your nose. You'll smell less of it that way."

So I learned to breathe through my mouth.

"Now hold his head while I give him some medicine."

I went to the bench where a boy who was about twelve lay. He had shrunk down to where he was smaller than me and was crumpled up into a shaking ball with stomach cramps, a common symptom of starvation. I grabbed his boney shoulders, holding him tight against me as Ivanovna pinched his nose with one hand and poured a spoonful of horrid smelling liquid down his crying mouth with the other.

"Don't you dare spit that out," she ordered as the boy gagged on the stuff.

I felt the tears wanting to squeeze themselves out from the corners of my eyes.

Ivanovna used the same spoon for giving all of the Children their medicine. Those were the days before we knew about sharing spoons and glasses with others when they had contagious diseases. But even if we had known about that, there weren't enough to go around and no soap to wash them with.

"Let me cover you up now," I said and patted the boy's matted hair as I laid him back down onto the bench. I didn't ask the sick Children what their names were. I learned to close my ears so that I wouldn't hear them moan and I learned not to look into their eyes so that I didn't have to see their pain. But we were all in pain — so much of it that if one didn't learn to shut down her mind, one could not survive.

Some of the Children just went to sleep — they closed their eyes at night and didn't wake up in the morning. No cramps; no sighs; just a quiet resignation, a quiet surrender like Viktor when he went out to die beneath our birch tree.

I learned to recognize it by the blank look on their faces. I was sure that I didn't look much different myself, especially as I felt more and more tired after helping the Comrade each day. I wrapped the dead Children in the blanket they lay on and then the silent Gregory would come and put the body at the side of the house where someone took it away at night.

I don't know where the bodies went or who took them as there were no wagons that hauled away the dead like in our village. This was a healthy town where things like this were not supposed to happen, I found out later. I wondered how long it would be before all of us would die and there would be none left.

Occasionally, one or two Children would wander in on their own asking for a piece of bread or be pushed through the door by a relative, usually a woman as desperate as Auntie had been when she left me here. It was like a never-ending procession to the grave, but rather than having the music of a choir to sing the Children's last rights, they were accompanied by a whispering dirge of coughing, crying and moaning. There was no parent to mourn their passing and no priest to bless their journey as they returned to the bosom of their ancestors. There was certainly no hymn of Memory Eternal either.

Whenever I was left to wrap a dead Child on my own, particularly if I was sure that no one could see me, I would fold his hands in prayer the way I had folded little Maria's in our cottage so long ago. I wondered if God could see us suffering Children. Some days I was even angry that he had "chosen" me as Godfather had said. Why should I be the chosen one? Why did I have to suffer?

I no longer attended any of the classes that were held in the big room.

"I'm supposed to teach every one of these orphans," Comrade Professor said to Ivanovna on one particularly dreary January afternoon. "She's on the roster. When the Thousander comes to check, I'll have to answer for her lack of progress. Besides, she's probably the most intelligent one of the lot and stubborn, too. Remember even a good paddling with the porridge spoon didn't get her family name out of her. Someone has been doing a good job with her studies."

"Tell the Thousander to send me a good nurse so that you can have her back," Ivanovna said. "I can hardly do my job with not enough medicine or blankets never mind that they don't send a decent nurse. My term out in this uncivilized wasteland can't be finished soon enough. Besides, why should you put yourself out for her? You know that once she's been in an orphanage, she's marked for life. She'll never be accepted as a complete person. She'll be put in one place like this or another so she might as well get the practice she'll need to survive. You know they're called Father Stalin's bastards in real society."

"Well, just maybe, this is one of the poor wretches who has the brains to make it out, and she's very, very pretty." He lingered over the last sentence and looked me up and down the way Uncle Ivan had when I last saw him.

I winced.

"Why don't you take that sour one over there? She's much bigger and much stronger." Comrade Professor motioned toward Larysa. "She's as dumb as a post and as miserable as an old witch. If she catches something from the others it really would be no loss."

"If she's a poor student, what kind of nurse do you think she'd be?"

So my chance for relief was only at mealtime, if one could call a meagre spoonful of porridge a meal. I continued to wait till close to the end of the line for my daily serving. I could choose my place as none of the healthy Children wanted to be near me. I would see them exchange knowing looks or turn their noses up when I got too close to them. Whether I smelled badly or whether they were afraid that they would get sick from me, I never knew.

I sat or stood, rubbing my feet which were often numb from the cold. I had nothing to say to my fellows. I didn't want to think about most of what I had to witness each day. I kept my ears open for Ivanovna's next command hoping that it wouldn't come when I was trying to eat. I did her bidding like some automaton, looking straight ahead, not thinking or feeling lest some unseen monster would pounce on me and rip me to shreds. But the monster was real and right there in front of me. It wasn't a person or an animal. Yet, the spirit of poverty and deprivation was a force that beat on my soul worse than any metre stick or fist of Asimov's.

One evening, as I waited for the others to get their spoonful of porridge, there was the customary knock. This knock was barely audible, not like the usual sharp "let me in so that I can drop my precious burden and run away" knock that relatives often used.

"Let the wretch in, Philipovna," Ivanovna said from the stove. "My hands are full. Marina Nikolaiovna, see to the new street urchin. What else could it be on such a cold and nasty night?" She pushed past me with her tray of potions as she went on to her usual duties in the sick room.

I opened the door. A small woman wrapped in a beet red shawl and carrying a bundle was blown in by a blast of the winter wind.

"Close that door," Nikolaiovna said. "We'll all freeze at this rate." She motioned for Gregory to help me.

He lifted the limp woman while I disengaged the bundle from her stiff fingers. I didn't have to look to know that beneath the layers of blanket there was a Child. I unwound the *platok* that the poor mother wrapped around the Child's head. I noticed that it was made of very fine wool and hand printed with an exceptionally beautiful flower design. Auntie Lena showed me and Xenkovna one very much like it that she brought from Kiev when she and Auntie Liza had gone there.

"Where did these two come from?" I said.

"Who knows?" Nikolaiovna said. "You should be asking where we're going to get more porridge to feed them. Bring the baby to the fire. The sooner it warms up, the better."

"No," I said. "Look at its cheeks. They're white. Doesn't that mean they're frost bitten? Shouldn't I let it warm up a little bit at a time?"

"How did you know that?" Ivanovna asked, going back to the stove with her empty tray.

"A doctor told us once — once when Auntie went ... well it doesn't matter where she went. The twins died anyway." How could I have almost blurted out such a thing? My stomach twisted as all eyes in the room focused on me. How could I almost let our family's biggest secret slip out so easily? I held the bundled baby against me and slid down to sit on the floor. My face must have given something away because Gregory took the woman's red shawl and awkwardly put it over my shoulders.

"Ho," Larysa shouted. "That's not hers. Why does she get to wear something nice like that? I'm the one who has to go out in the cold for water. I need it more than she does."

She bounded across the room with her hand positioned to grab the shawl.

Gregory stuck his foot out just as her fingers touched its edge.

Larysa tripped and fell face first to the floor knocking Ivanovna's replenished tray from her hands as she was making her way back to the sick room.

"What do you two think you're doing?" the enraged Comrade demanded. "You've spilled the whole tray of medicine! I don't have enough of it as it is. I'll teach you uncivilized animals how to behave."

I hugged the bundle in my arms and rolled out of the way into the sick room as Ivanovna's quick hands found the broom and administered a vicious beating to both Larysa and Gregory while the others numbly stared. Larysa fought back howling and crying like a wounded wolf, but Gregory stood there, like Mitya had in the school room with Asimov, staring into space without making a sound or shedding a tear. I wanted to cry myself, but my chest was so tight that I couldn't breathe and I wanted to vomit even though there was nothing in my belly to bring up.

When the dust settled, I was allowed to keep the shawl as it was clear that its owner was dead. Ivanovna ordered Nikolaiovna to take some of the dead woman's clothing so that it could be used for one of the orphans. This was not a surprise to me as I had seen her take off usable clothing from other dead Children in the sick room. It was usually done out of our sight and the recipient never knew where the clothes he or she was given came from. Sometimes, the Child hadn't even quit breathing before the Comrade was salvaging a shirt or pair of pants for another of her living charges. There was never a pair of stockings because all of our feet were wrapped in rags ripped from sheets or blankets that were wearing out or torn. It reminded me of the night Auntie tried to put the Unravelled One's shawl around me. At least this one was red, not black like a Baba Yaga's shawl, there were no insects in it, and I was too cold to care.

The baby woke up and started to cry. I took my first good look at it. She turned out to be a little girl about the age of Maria and Marta when they died. Her cheeks were hollow with circles under her big eyes. I could see that she was once a beautiful Child. Then she looked right at me. I had to turn away. Those hazel eyes! Which one of the twins was she? I could swear that it was Marta or Maria coming back from Heaven. I scrunched my eyes shut and shook my head. I looked again.

She cried some more. Her face changed. She was not one of the twins any longer. I sighed in relief. I tried to give the baby to Ivanovna.

"What do you expect me to do with it?" the Comrade said. "Can't you see my hands are full?" They were. Ivanovna had retrieved her tray and was mixing, measuring and pouring as usual. She motioned to Larysa.

Larysa hissed something at me down her swelling nose and cleaned up the supper bowls. I turned towards Nikolaiovna.

"I have to get the little ones to bed," she said with a sympathetic smile. "I'll thin out a little porridge and you can feed her."

I stiffened in horror. Xenkovna did such things. What did I know about feeding babies?

"It's not that difficult. Take very small spoonfuls. Put a little into her mouth at one time. I'm sure she'll eat it because she's probably very hungry. You'll be a little mother in no time."

Truer words were never uttered. Since the Comrades were always busy, the care of the new arrival fell to me whether I wanted it or not. It was determined that, though the Child was tiny, she must be about two and a half years old. Once she got warmed up and accustomed to the orphanage, she ran about like other toddlers her age.

The surprising thing was that she attached herself to me. Whether it was the recognition of her mother's shawl from her point of view or those hazel eyes that looked so much like those of my dead twin cousins from my perspective, I never really knew. But we became inseparable. Since we didn't know her name, I called her Malenka, meaning Little One. In turn, especially when one of the Comrades was irritated with me, I was called Little Mama. Nevertheless, I slept, ate and worked with my new charge attached to me as if she were another appendage.

At first, I resented Malenka, but she always brought back the memories of the twins. I never let her cry for long. I remembered all of the times I refused to play with Marta and Maria, the afternoons I lingered in the woods with Mitya, instead of caring for them while Auntie and Xenkovna were busy with supper preparations, and the times I ignored the twins' tears if they fell down. Perhaps God sent this little Malenka just for me.

"Please, God," I said. "I can show you and Mama that I can be really nice to little Children." I doted on every smile, every little giggle and every new word Malenka learned. She was the little sister I should have known, the doll I never had. The Comrades didn't mind when I took a few minutes out of my work to play with her. Caring for her gave me more energy and made the otherwise endless days move a little faster.

Soon after Malenka came, I was wiping her face and neck after feeding her porridge. I almost cried out in surprise when I discovered a little gold cross on a fine gold chain tucked beneath her under clothes. I was glad that no one was paying attention to us. This little girl must have come from a well-off family as her mother's shawl was soft and warm. But what if she didn't? Maybe, the cross was passed down through the generations like the cross Mitya had in his wooden box that was recovered from the Unravelled One's cottage. Either way, it was Malenka's inheritance like the beautiful *platok* and red shawl that I wore.

I knew that I should save them for her, if I could. But it was so cold that any article of clothing that was put down anywhere was immediately picked up by someone else. The cross was someone's promise to God—a promise to take care of this Child in the parents' stead. I knew all about that from the day I stood on my mother's sewing machine on the last day in my father's home. Maybe this was God's reason for keeping me alive. Maybe, I should be her Godmother since she had no one else to take care of her. I decided to do the best that I could.

"Don't worry," I said to her sleeping angel face. "I won't let anything happen to you—just like Auntie never let anything happen to me."

I would hold the little cross between my fingers as we fell asleep each night. I silently prayed for my living family and for the protection and guidance of my dead ancestors. I prayed that I would find my way out of this terrible place and that, some day, I would bring Malenka home to Auntie and Xenkovna so we could drink tea and eat freshly baked bread. I wouldn't let myself think of the smell of it when I prayed.

The memory of that smell haunted me many nights as it was. I dreamed of the day when I could show Malenka off to Uncle Misha and the big boy cousins. I cried when I realized that she would never play with Viktor and the twins. I dreamed about how Mitya and I would take her to the river to pick mushrooms and how we would lift her up into the cherry trees. That would be the very best—to see her little hands and face dripping in sweet red cherry juice and to know that we would never be hungry again.

But dreams are dreams, fleeting moments of imagined desire that draw the sufferer into a future that is dark and vast, like the carrot that pulls the hopeful horse forward when his legs can no longer lift themselves to put one hoof in front of the other.

The day came when the diphtherial croup took hold in the orphanage. Ivanovna blamed it on a little boy who wandered in by himself several weeks after Malenka arrived, but the truth was that we never really knew who got it first. One morning, as I was stretching my cold legs, I heard it.

"*Bark, bark.*" A sound you never forget. It came from one of the littlest Children.

"That sounds like the cough from the croup," I said without thinking.

Ivanovna's look could have struck me down dead.

"We don't have such things in our homes," she said. "That only goes on in your villages and farms because Ukrainians don't know how to care for sick people. Their doctors aren't as well educated as us Russians."

"It sounds like the croup."

"What would a little snipe like you know about the croup anyway? You think that you're some kind of doctor."

"No, Ivanovna. I don't know a lot about the croup, only that Children die from it. My Auntie—she's the one who's the healer. People come from all over for help and she knows about herbs and ..."

"These herbs and potions you people use are from the dark ages. They're old wives' tales and have nothing to do with science. Do you know how many years I studied before I could call myself a doctor?" She scowled at me.

"No, Ivanovna."

My tongue ached from holding it still and not shouting back at her. I knew that she was wrong. There were many folks who had come through Auntie's door for healing. Auntie was well known for making them recover from all kinds of illnesses without having stepped one foot into any Russian school. My bones already shivered from the thought of how we were going to suffer and die. Yet, I stared glumly ahead and continued to do what I was told. What else could I do?

Meanwhile, the days dragged on. At first it was the little boy who *barked* with the cough. But gradually, those who slept around him or who played with him also began coughing. Ivanovna's demeanour changed too. The furrows on her brow deepened. She said less and frowned more. Finally, there were so many sick Children that Larysa was ordered to help us in the sick room while other girls were put to work in the rest of the house.

"Can't you keep these urchins quiet?" Comrade Professor said one afternoon. "How do you expect me to conduct my lessons with this racket going on?"

It had been a difficult morning indeed. Due to the spreading illness, we could all feel the growing tension in the house. The smaller Children cried at any word from Comrade Professor. His impatience with their tears brought on the metre stick and things seem to disintegrate from there. One of the older boys coughed so hard that Comrade Professor ordered me to take the "spluttering brat" away. And none of the other students could do the recitations without forgetting or stumbling. His usual tactics lost their hold.

"They're sick!" Nikolaiovna said. "What would you have me do with them?"

The little girl that she was holding began to cough and choke. A cloud of phlegm spewed from her gasping mouth and showered Comrade Professor's jacket.

"Get that dirty pig away from me!" His jowls quivered in purple rage. He wiped his chin with one hand and slapped at the Child's puffy face with the other. Nikolaiovna dodged his hand, enough to save the Child, but not enough to avoid a sound crack across her own cheek.

"You filthy tub of lard!" she screamed. She dropped the little one and charged at the man with nails aimed at his eyes. But he was too quick. He grabbed Nikolaiovna by her braided bun. He punched her with a full fist. Each time a blow landed I could hear the Comrade gasp and I cringed with each thud. I could not do anything as I already had my hands full with the hysterical Child that Nikolaiovna had dropped.

Ivanovna came rushing from the sick room. She started pulling at Comrade Professor's arms and kicking him to try to break it up.

"Stop, stop! What are you doing? You're going to kill her!"

But the man didn't stop. Some of the blows landed on Ivanovna as well. The Children all began screaming. The door burst open and Gregory flew in. His armful of wood scattered in the doorway. He grabbed Comrade Professor's metre stick and smashed a re-sounding whack onto his head. In his surprise, Comrade Professor let Nikolaiovna go. She fell into a heap on the floor. Ivanovna knelt to help her.

"You spawn of the devil," the madman roared. He tried to grab the metre stick out of Gregory's hands but the boy was quick and snapped it in half. He threw it across the room. Comrade Professor, shockingly agile for his size grabbed Gregory and slammed him against the wood stove. He held the boy there until I could smell burning cloth and cooking flesh. Then, some unknown force took over my body. I passed the crying little girl to Larysa.

"*Zaraza*! *Chort*! Let him go. Let him go. He didn't do anything to you! Let him go! *Zaraza*!" I was screaming like a mad woman. I grabbed at the buckets of water that had just been filled. I started throwing them at the Comrade. The first one missed its target and hissed all over the wood stove creating a cloud of steam that made the Children scream louder. It took three bucketsful to get him to stop. When the schoolmaster let go of Gregory, the boy collapsed onto the floor beside Nikolaiovna.

"I'm out of this den of maggots until you two get it under con-trol. Some doctor. You can't even cure a simple cough. I'm reporting it to the Thousander. I'm not taking my life into my hands for the sake of a handful of degenerate brats."

"A single tear of one of these brats is worth more than one hundred of you," Ivanovna shouted from her position by her fallen colleague. "May their God strike you dead or make you blind! You've ruined both of my best workers, you filthy scum. Now take that stinking ass of yours and get out of my sight."

"You'll regret this," he bellowed. "Just wait till I get a hold of the Thousander. Your next job will take you out into Siberia, if you're lucky."

Comrade Professor packed up his books, his chalk and slate, his posters and his broken metre stick. Dripping wet as he was, he walked off into the winter wind. I never saw him again.

"Larysa," Ivanovna said. "Put the Child down—never mind that she's crying. Get more water. We're going to need it."

I bent over Gregory. The shirt was completely burned and stuck onto his skin. Where the shirt had ripped off, his back was like an over cooked piece of meat. I could see exposed bones on the places that Comrade Professor had pushed against the side of the stove. He lay unconscious on the floor as still as death.

"What are we going to do with him?"

"First I need something for bandaging Nikolaiovna. I have to stop her bleeding. Bring me a clean sheet—if you can find one—Hurry! Larysa—the water!"

"But what about Gregory?"

"He'll have to wait. He can't feel anything when he's unconscious. We'll have to regroup somehow. Give me a moment to catch my breath."

The rest of that day was a blur. I was pulled from all sides. If it wasn't a crying, coughing Child, it was Ivanovna with another order —"cut the sheet—hold her head—bring some water." Nikolaiovna's injuries were messy because of the bleeding.

"You have nothing serious to worry about once the swelling goes away. You'll have some nasty bruises and plenty of pain, that's for sure," Ivanovna said.

"Men!" Nikolaiovna said through clenched and loosened teeth. "You can't get away from their fists no matter how far you run away."

"Did you run away from a man?" I asked.

"My dear, you're too young to hear about all of that. Remember, you can't trust them so don't get too close. Even when you don't want them they're all over you." Her eyes took on a vacant look. I could see that she was going inside, somewhere far away where I was not welcomed. I didn't want to go there with her anyway. I just wanted to lie down and go to sleep.

"Larysa, Philipovna," Ivanovna said. "Get a blanket and help me take Gregory to the sick room."

Gregory was coming back into consciousness. He groaned with pain. I remember thinking that his groan was the only sound I ever heard him make. His arms and legs flailed involuntarily while his face was a contorted mask of suffering. We couldn't roll him onto the blanket on his back because of the injuries. We couldn't pull him across the floor on his belly either because we would hurt his face. It took all three of us a long time to manoeuvre poor Gregory across the floor from beside the stove and onto a bench in the sick room.

Larysa's awkward movements and reluctance to help also slowed us down. The other Children were so frightened that they tried to get as far away from us as they could. They huddled into groups which piled themselves under blankets on the sleeping benches or in the corners of the big room. Nikolaiovna fell asleep. It was eerily quiet.

"We have to cut away his clothes," Ivanovna said. "Hold down his arms so that he doesn't bump my hands. I will have to take some of the flesh ... I have no choice ... the poor boy." She sharpened her knife.

What? I thought to myself. *Is she really crying?* And she was. As she cut away the burned clothes and the occasional patch of skin where the two had melded together, Ivanovna's forearm would swipe across her eyes to keep her tears from falling onto Gregory's back.

"Hold him still!" she said as Larisa's grip relaxed from holding on for so long. Larysa was retching and crying, too.

The smell of the burnt wool and linen that comprised Gregory's ragged clothes mixed with the smell of his seared flesh was making me sick. I fought with the gory sight of his back, his flailing limbs and the gagging reflex. My arms vibrated with the effort.

"Philipovna!" Ivanovna said. "Don't you dare faint! I need your hands ... don't you dare."

The world started spinning, but I willed my arms to stiffen like frozen logs and hung on.

"I'm almost done. For the love of God, don't faint. I need you."

Thankfully, Gregory succumbed to the shock and pain and lapsed back into oblivion. I don't remember clearly seeing Ivanovna finish her ministrations. For the next while, I sat on the floor slumped over in exhaustion.

"Come Philipovna," I heard Ivanovna say. "I know you're tired, but I have only you and Larysa to help now. Try to keep going. It'll be a day or two before Nikolaiovna can do things again."

I was confused by the change in Ivanovna's voice. She wasn't tossing out commands or yelling. She was actually speaking to me, speaking like a normal person. Her face had softened somehow. Larysa was sent to start cooking the evening porridge.

"Get some of the stronger ones to help you. Philipovna has to stay here with me," Ivanovna said. "We still have the other sick ones to care for."

Larysa sulkily obeyed.

"I don't know what I'm going to do." Ivanovna stood over Gregory wringing her hands. "There's no morphine ... I have no more carbolic soap ... and they never send enough antiseptics or anything else I need either. I'd like to know what your precious Auntie would do in this situation. He'll probably die of infection."

"Do you really want to know?"

"I wouldn't be asking if I didn't."

"There is one thing she would do," I said. There were really two things that she would do, but I knew that Ivanovna wouldn't want to know about the praying. She gestured for me to go on.

"When someone gets a bad burn like this, Auntie gets someone to urinate into a pot and, using a clean cloth, she washes the burn with urine."

"But urine is your waste."

"Yes. But Auntie says that it's perfectly clean especially if you let the first little bit go before you collect the rest into your pot. The men used to do that when they were wounded at war and it saved many of their lives."

"All right then. Get a pot."

I did her bidding.

"Now lift up your skirt and go," she said.

"I can't," I said. "I peed after you fixed Gregory. I always have to do that when I'm upset."

The doctor picked up her skirt; peed a little on the floor and then emptied her bladder into the pot.

"Do what you saw your Auntie do," she said. "I'll believe it when I see it."

"It stings when you first put it on," I said.

"It doesn't matter. He's unconscious. He's going to die if we don't do something."

"When it dries and the skin starts to heal, it gets crusty."

"We'll see," she said.

I could see that she was sceptical. I dipped a ripped piece of a sheet into the Comrade's urine and washed Gregory's back. My stomach heaved each time I touched him.

"This may take care of the infection," Ivanovna said, "but it won't take care of the pain. He'll hurt himself more by throwing his arms and legs around in those spasms. And when the skin crusts as you say it will, it will pull and crack. He'll be in so much pain. I wish I had some morphine."

"Would this help?" I reached into my clothing with my hand that still smelled like the Comrade's urine. I tugged at the bundle of tea that was still tied into my under shirt, the last precious thing that I had from Auntie. I didn't want to give it to Ivanovna, but Gregory's back looked so terrible that I wanted to do something, anything that could help.

"What's this?"

"It's poppy tea. My Auntie grows it in our garden every year. She gives it to us when our tummies hurt and we can't sleep." I fought back the tears and the memories.

"It's not morphine," Ivanovna said, "but it will certainly help. The poor boy could use anything that will put him to sleep. Make it exactly the way your Auntie did."

I went out into the big room. As Larysa stirred the porridge, I made Gregory's tea. The Children were getting ready for supper. Nikolaiovna was sitting up. She was not able to do anything, but she was already giving the girls instructions. So the house slowly came back to a sense of order.

Farewell

I CONTINUED TO do Ivanovna's bidding. She resumed her command voice and brusque manner, but she was also more patient than she had been before Comrade Professor's departure. Her problems were compounded by the fact that her medicine was running out. She was reducing the doses and giving it only to the Children who looked strong enough to survive. I would watch her eyebrow rise in frustration as she pondered over a Child, examining him or checking her. I could see that it was difficult for Ivanovna to play the part of God as she decided who would live and who wouldn't. She often asked for my opinion when she was thinking out loud about what to do next. I held my tongue until I was pressed for an answer.

Why is she asking me? I'm not an adult and I'm not as wise as Auntie, I would think.

The rest of the house was adrift. The loss of the schoolmaster meant that there was nothing to do in the long day that dragged out before the Children each morning. Larysa took on Nikolaiovna's jobs. Meanwhile, Nikolaiovna sat on a bench and directed the goings-on. The cold in the house did not encourage healing. She became stiff from the bruising.

"I feel like an old baba," she said. "I can't move my right arm. Are you sure it's not broken?"

Nikolaiovna's face was very black and swollen. At first the distortions frightened the little Children so that only the bravest ones would come close to her. After a few days we made sport of watching how it shrank back into place and how the bruises faded from black, to blue, purple and then green and yellow. The good-natured Nikolaiovna indulged our antics. She planned a little celebration for the morning when her face would return.

"It always does, you know," she said with a painful grimace. "I'll do a dance for you when I'm back to myself again."

"You shouldn't talk like that to them," Ivanovna said. "It's a serious matter."

"I know it's a serious matter. But if I cry, they'll be afraid of every man they meet. Would that be better? Maybe they should be afraid. So far, the men that have crossed my path were men I should have stayed away from. Ask Gregory. He would tell you if he could. Why do you think he doesn't speak? His father loved his horse better than he loved Gregory."

"You mean you're his Mama?" I said, blurting it out.

"No, my poor unfortunate sister was. That horrid man of hers drove her into the ground."

I could see tears standing in her beautiful brown eyes. So that's why Gregory stayed in this awful place. Other boys of his age would be out proving themselves rather than hanging on to a woman, even if they worked for someone else or survived on their own in the woods like Mitya did, unless they were like my cousins and their father had a place for them to labour.

There was not much time for small talk or my personal reflections. Gregory's back crusted. Ivanovna was hopeful because it looked like Gregory was improving. But as the skin dried, it shrank and cracked. It bled the way she had feared it would. In the end, the infection set in. I felt sick at the sight of the blackened scabs and the weeping, yellowish mess that came oozing out from the fissures on Gregory's back. There was no penicillin or any of the drugs we are used to today. They hadn't been discovered yet. Even if they had been, Father Stalin wouldn't have thrown them away on some poor orphans in an obscure home in the wasteland of the Ukrainian countryside.

"There's too much flesh missing," Ivanovna said. "There's not enough to grow back over those bones."

"He'll be a monster," Nikolaiovna said through her tears. "No one will ever want a man who can't speak, never mind someone who looks like he will. He used to be so beautiful before the hunger. It might be better if he were dead. It's a good thing his poor mother didn't live to see this. What will he ever do if something happens to me?"

It was dreadful to watch the poor boy suffer. I prayed for him to die. I begged Mama to tell God to take him to Heaven so that I would not have to look into those pain-filled eyes. But the days dragged on and Gregory languished. The nights were a little better for him as I managed the bundle of Auntie's tea carefully. I was so grateful when, under its influence, his eyelids got heavy and slowly shut as he retreated into sleep. Fortunately, he wasn't coughing yet.

The croup didn't let up its assault either. It was hard to sleep at night with the noise of the coughing. We were always on watch because we never knew when one of the little ones would choke on the phlegm. Ivanovna let me sleep first and then woke me when she couldn't keep her eyes open any longer. I did the same for her.

The sound of that cough gave me nightmares. It reminded me of the nights Xenkovna and Auntie would spell each other off when the twins were sick. But every now and then we wrapped another unfortunate in a piece of sheet or blanket and Ivanovna laid him or her out by the back wall to be taken away. I was glad when

Nikolaiovna could take back her regular duties and the sullen Larysa could help in the sick room again.

"What are we going to do when there's not enough space for all of them in here?" Larysa asked.

"We'll cross that bridge when we come to it," the Comrade said.

I knew we'd never have to worry. Larysa was oblivious to the fact that Children kept on dying. The one thin wall that divided the two rooms also created a barrier between those in the sick room and the rest of the house. It never ceased to amaze me at how separate those two worlds seemed to be.

Nikolaiovna got tired of the restlessness that set in when there was no school to keep the healthier Children occupied.

"They need something to do," she said. "I'd send them out for a good game of Big Bear's Den if there was enough clothing to dress them properly. They could use a breath of fresh air."

"It's just as well," Ivanovna said. "Our neighbours don't want to see sick orphans wandering through their healthy town. The other Children wouldn't play with them anyway."

"I don't have a husk of corn to make a doll out of or yarn and rags to make any clothes for it either. There's no book to read or slate to write on. No wonder they pick at each other. The ones who have given up sit staring off into Heaven. They'll die of boredom before they starve."

"I'm not a Baba Yaga that can pull things out of thin air," Ivanovna said. "I'm already expected to do that with the sick room. You'll have to figure this one out by yourself."

Nikolaiovna made a game of bringing in the wood. She drew lots for those who could help with the chores and organized the girls into groups that swept the floor, folded up blankets or washed the few dishes we had.

"I'd like to see a good game of *Baba Kutsya*," she said another time. "But there's not enough room for all of them to run away from being tagged."

"Try a game of shepherd then," Larysa said. "Half of them have to be the sleepy sheep so only the thieves get to actually move around. And Lazy Hrits is just lying about anyway."

"I wish I would have thought of that one," the Comrade said.

So they pushed the long table to one side of the room with the benches under it and played a game of Shepherd. The part of Lazy Hrits was easy to find a Child for. The more energetic Children were enthusiastic so she could get the first group of thieves to steal the sleeping sheep, but after that the game fell apart because the rest of the Children were either too lethargic or too sick. Others complained that they were too cold.

"You'll feel better if you move around," Nikolaiovna said.

Finally, she decided to play at spelling words and reciting times table games with those who could pay attention. It's not that they didn't want to play games; the plain truth was that the Children were so hungry that they were lethargic and stupid. If three or more would not respond, the game was very short, but if they co-operated, she rewarded the whole group with a story.

It wasn't long before all of the able Children were involved and trying to please Nikolaiovna, not only in the word play and the times tables, but also in any chore she needed them to do. I found myself pushing through my work too. I would sit in the back of the group cradling Malenka and listening. I even caught a glimpse of the stern Ivanovna lending an ear when she had a break in her duties.

Nikolaiovna was a walking bookful of stories. Though she was Russian, she knew many Ukrainian fairy tales. There were strange ones like the three sons who were expected to look after their parents' grave. The two older ones didn't do their duty and pushed it onto the youngest son. The youngest was a faithful son. He brought the bread offering to the grave as was the custom in the old days. In return, he was allowed to visit his dead parents in the other world and talked with them through the burning of three candles. When he re-emerged, it was three hundred years later as the burning of each candle represented the passing of a century.

In a strange way, this story comforted some of the Children whose parents had died. They all swore that they would be like the good son and would take care of their parents' graves when they grew up so that they, too, might earn a visit with their lost ones.

"What happens if we can't find our Mama's grave?" a quiet little boy from the corner by the stove asked. "The Comrades took my Mama and threw her into a big hole with a bunch of other dead people. Then they covered it up with a machine. We weren't allowed to say good-bye."

"You'll just have to find a nice place that your Mama might have liked and remember her there," Nikolaiovna said. She dabbed at the corner of her eye with the edge of her shawl.

My favourite was Nikolaiovna's version of Ivan, the Dragon Slayer. None of us could believe how stupid the dragon really was. His stupidity was so silly that, though the dragon and his mother were hideous and terrible, none of the Children were afraid of him. They laughed at Ivan when he fooled the dragon by squeezing rivers of whey from the *varenyky* which he had stuffed into his pants and shirt.

"Could anyone really make such a scary dragon believe that Ivan was squeezing water out of the big rock?" one of the little boys asked.

They cheered when Ivan thumped the dragon between the eyes with a rock and clapped their hands when Ivan outsmarted the dragon's attempt at burning him alive. But the best part was when the dragon went away. Ivan could live in his peaceful village and grow up to be a farmer. No one ever said a word, but I could see the shadows on the Children's faces and feel their longing for home every time Nikolaiovna told the story.

She asked if we knew any of the stories from our own family. She said that if we could remember them we should, since it was one way we could always hang onto a small part of our parents and grandparents. Some of the older Children told stories that they remembered from around their own hearth, and sometimes the memory of those tales brought on tears. I liked telling the one about the fox going to market and meeting all of the small creatures of the forest as he went.

"Why does a Russian lady like you know so many Ukrainian stories?" I asked the Comrade.

"Because my Mama was Ukrainian and only my Papa was Russian. My *Babusya* told me the Ukrainian stories and my Papa told me the Russian ones. We had such good times, my sister Natasha and I. She was so little and beautiful with her black curls and hazel eyes. Papa made a big swing that hung in the tree at the front of our house where we sat and 'told lies' for hours, especially after Mama died. Natasha's favourite was the one about *Tsarevitch* Ivan, the Firebird and the Gray Wolf. Do you know that one?"

"No," I said. "No one has ever told me a Russian story."

"Have any of the rest of you heard a Russian tale before?" she asked.

None of the others had heard one either. So she agreed that the next day we would work extra hard before we gathered and she would tell us about *Tsarevitch* Ivan, the Firebird and the Gray Wolf.

"Aren't wolves dangerous?" one of the smallest girls asked. "Don't they eat chickens and little Children? I'm already scared."

"Not if they are magic wolves," Nikolaiovna said. "You'll have to wait and see. It's a long story so you will all have to get ready sooner tomorrow. And if there's any fighting or grumbling ..."

"We know," one of the little girls said, grinning, "there'll be no story."

The next day felt like a holiday. Our enthusiasm must have infected Ivanovna because she started the day with the hint of a smile. The wood was brought in; the floor was swept and the blankets were folded for the day in no time. By noon, the smaller Children were impatient. I found myself hurrying through my chores.

I helped Ivanovna with the medicine in the morning as usual and fed some of the sicker Children their porridge. I tidied up the blankets and tried to make their cramped beds a little more comfortable. As I was giving Gregory his mid-morning drink, one of the girls came in with Malenka.

"She's so crabby this morning. We can't do anything with her. Nikolaiovna told me to give her to you since you're her Little Mama."

She plunked Malenka at my feet and went out to the other room heaving a sigh of relief. Malenka sat staring at me with dull eyes and a fitful face.

"You have to wait," I said.

She sat on the floor, pouting until I was finished. I picked her up and cuddled her for a while. She clung to me the way she usually did at bedtime.

"Now go play like a good girl," I said. "I have a lot to do. Pretty soon we'll listen to a story. You can sit with me then."

I took her out of the sick room and settled her to play with the others.

As Nikolaiovna was getting ready to tell her story, I took my usual place by the door of the sick room with my ragged blanket around me. It took Malenka a long time to get comfortable. Usually, she would lay her head in the crook of my arm or against my shoulder and fall asleep but today, she squirmed and fussed. Her arms and legs were jerking about as if someone had wound them up with springs. I quietly hummed the lullaby I heard Auntie sing to the twins while Nikolaiovna put more wood into the stove and stirred the fire.

"Come on, Malenka," I said. "I want to hear the story." I stroked her red-gold hair, the way I did when I tried to get her to sleep on a restless night. I couldn't resist sticking my fingers into that mass of shiny curls as tangled and wild as it was.

"Are we all here?" Nikolaiovna asked.

The little ones crowded around her like a flock of chickens

around a mother hen. It reminded me of Xenkovna with our own little ones. The room grew quiet as she began:

"Once upon a time, there was a very rich *tsar* named Vyslav. He lived in a palace which had a beautiful garden, the most beautiful garden in the world. The trees of this garden bore fruit made of sparkling jewels. But his favourite was the one which grew apples made of gold. He had three sons, *Tsarevitch* Dimitri, *Tsarevitch* Vasilii and the youngest, *Tsarevitch* Ivan."

I was impatient with Malenka's restlessness. I wanted to listen to Nikolaiovna's rich voice with its exotic accent. She told how the firebird came at night to steal the golden apples, with its shining crystal eyes and feathers as bright as the brightest moonlight. But Malenka kept on fussing.

"Nikolaiovna," one of the littlest girls asked, "what is crystal?"

I was happy that she asked because I didn't know what crystal was either.

"It's the most sparkling glass you've ever seen," she said. "It's made with lead and melted into beautiful things like glasses and vases. When it comes off of the glass blower's wand, it has to cool and set. Then, someone cuts pretty designs in it that send rainbows winking all around a room when candlelight hits the glass or vase."

Nikolaiovna told us how the two older sons fell asleep when their father commanded them to watch for the thief who stole the golden apples and how *Tsarevitch* Ivan pricked his own thigh with his dagger in order not to fall asleep. It was so exciting to imagine what the crystal eyes of the bird would look like with their glinting rainbows and the glowing feather that *Tsarevitch* Ivan finally grabbed out of the fire bird's tail and wrapped in his handkerchief to prove to his father that he had really stayed awake to watch it come.

Malenka got crankier. I noticed that her breath had a funny smell. Maybe she was thirsty. I finally slipped into the sick room and gave her a little drink of Gregory's tea.

As Nikolaiovna went on to tell about how the brothers were sent out to look for the firebird, the tea started to do its work. Malenka's limbs slowly stopped their flopping and, like a rag doll, she finally fell asleep. I was glad. I could get lost in the tale at last.

Would the brothers find the firebird? I wondered who put the stone in the green meadow and who could have written the strange messages on it. I held my breath as *Tsarevitch* Ivan pondered over his choices. I cried with *Tsarevitch* Ivan when his horse died. How did the wolf know who *Tsarevitch* Ivan was after he had wandered all day through a strange forest? Oh, of course, he was a magic wolf. I held my breath with anticipation when *Tsarevitch* Ivan climbed onto the wolf's back to fly to the firebird's palace. What would it be like to really fly like that? Wasn't it amazing that the wolf knew where to go? And how could it be possible that, after getting the firebird, the golden bridle and falling in love with the beautiful *Tsarevna* Helen, *Tsarevitch* Ivan was cut up into pieces by his brothers?

Malenka was deeply asleep now. She seemed to be heavier than usual. When I moved her because my left arm was feeling numb from her weight, I noticed that her cheeks looked a bit pink. But Nikolaiovna's story was moving forward so I shifted Malenka's weight to the other shoulder and listened on. The gray wolf found *Tsarevitch* Ivan who had been cut up into pieces and brought him back to life after he made the crow fetch the waters of life and death. There was a stir of disbelief among the Children.

"Can someone really come back to life like that?" one of the little boys asked.

"My Mama said that Jesus did," one of the little girls said.

"Shhhh," Nikolaiovna said. "You can ask questions later. Don't break the magic spell."

And she went on to finish. She told how the wolf brought *Tsarevitch* Ivan back to the palace in the nick of time before the marriage of Helen to the false brother could take place. Nikolaiovna told how Helen the Beautiful related to *Tsar* Vyslav that the older brothers cut *Tsarevitch* Ivan into pieces while he was sleeping and threatened her with death if she ever spoke a word about what had happened.

We were all so relieved when the two older brothers were put into prison. We were thrilled to hear about how *Tsarevitch* Ivan came back to life. We hung on every detail of the fantastic celebration when *Tsarevitch* Ivan and Helen the Beautiful were married and could finally live happily ever after.

As the Children asked Nikolaiovna their questions, I tried to get comfortable with Malenka. She seemed so heavy and hot.

Hot? I thought. *It isn't hot in here. It isn't even warm! What's happening?*

Malenka's face wasn't pink any more. Her cheeks were flushed red with fever. I jumped up.

"Ivanovna! Look at her! Why is she so hot?"

I knew before she could take one look. Malenka's breathing was shallow. She had the croup.

"Calm yourself," Ivanovna said. "Little Children can have fever for any reason, even a little cold or tummy ache. She's healthy as things go and she has shown no sign of running nose or coughing. I need you to keep your head."

I couldn't keep my head. I tried to do what I always did yet, as the afternoon crept into evening, I kept making mistakes. I spilled some of the precious medicine down the front of one of the sick Children. I forgot to make Gregory's new batch of tea. I earned a cuff on my ear from the impatient Ivanovna when I didn't hear Larysa call me to help her move a bigger girl until she dropped her onto the floor.

"Will you keep your mind on what you're doing!" Ivanovna said. "Since that Malenka got sick, you're useless."

"She looks like she has the croup. Her face, her breathing. The twins looked like that too. And then she's going to sound funny and spit up phlegm and sound like a snake and turn purple. And then she'll die! She'll die ..."

Smack! I didn't see Ivanovna's hand coming. I sobbed louder.

"You're right," she said. "She may have the croup. That doesn't mean you can fall apart and terrify everyone else. Even if she dies, you have to keep your wits about you. What's the matter with you? Someone is dying here every week. I have no one else and Niko-laiovna has even less help than I do. We're doing as well as we can."

I slumped onto the floor by Gregory's bed and sobbed. The Comrades didn't do anything to stop me. Larysa stepped over and around me trying to keep things going. I sobbed and sobbed until I fell asleep there.

When I woke up, it was night. The house was as quiet as a house on a funeral day. Ivanovna was sitting by her candle with Malenka in her arms. Malenka's breath was raspy. As I quietly approached she looked straight into my eyes and tried to smile. That horrible cough caught her mid-smile and that familiar sound ripped at my heart as if someone had swiped at me with a jagged piece of glass.

"Ivanovna," I whispered.

She acknowledged me with an exhausted stare.

"Ivanovna," I started again. I knelt at her feet.

"If I begged you, would you get Malenka some good medicine from the doctor in town?"

"Child, if I had the means, I would do anything to get good medicine. But you know yourself, I only have what the Party gives me—and"—the tears were trickling out of her exhausted eyes—"you know there's never enough and that they don't care about us."

"I know how we could get a little bit of good medicine. If we could even just get enough for Malenka, and, and maybe for Gregory ..."

"Child." Her tears were streaming now. "No medicine will help Gregory. If he lasts a week, he'll be lucky; the suffering will just drag on. He's too weak, too tired and doesn't have enough food to re-cover from a mosquito bite, never mind a catastrophe like that.

Don't waste your tears on him. It's just a matter of time. If God is as merciful as everyone says, He'd take the poor boy this minute!"

"Ivanovna, if I tell you how, would you get Malenka some medicine? If any is left you can use it for someone else."

"Child, is the cold numbing your brilliant mind or what? Don't let your roof slide off its beams or I'm really in trouble."

"My roof is still nailed on. If I tell you a secret and show you something, will you go for good medicine?"

"What secret could a little urchin like you possibly have? And what would you know about getting good medicine?"

I felt as if I was bargaining with Mitya again. I had one good shot at getting what I wanted. I either would have to tell her or forget about it. If Malenka had any chance of living, I'd have to do it. I got up and reached for her clothing.

"No, don't give her to me," I said. "Not yet. I want to show you something."

I revealed the little cross.

"Look at that!" she said, her eyes wide with surprise. "I never thought you could keep such secrets. You're much tougher than you look. If anyone survives this misery, it will surely be you."

"It's a small cross. But it's heavy and, if you take it to the old woman who sells onions at the market, she can show you where the doctor is."

"It's beautiful," Ivanovna said. "It looks like it may be very old and expensive. You're not from this town. How would you know about the woman at the market and how would you know where a doctor would be? I'd be risking my own skin. You know we're not allowed to mix with the villagers even though we work for the Party. We're not supposed to talk about what goes on here."

I had no choice but to sit at Ivanovna's tired feet and tell her about the day that Auntie risked her life by walking through the snowstorm. I told of how she begged for bread and traded her silver spoon for wheat and how she was rescued by the doctor.

"If I tell you his name," I said, "please, please don't tell anyone. I know he'll give you medicine. I saw his eyes when he tried to save the twins and Viktor. He wants to save Children, all of them, just like you do."

She promised that she wouldn't tell. She said that she would think about taking the cross and trading it. So I took the fevering Malenka from her. I watched Ivanovna settle herself onto her sleeping bench. As I sat through the long, dark hours of that early spring night, I was frightened.

Would Ivanovna keep her word? Would she tell the Party men? Would they put me on trial like they did at Christmas? If they did would it be a simple but shameful round of harassing me? Or would they send me to Siberia this time? I was older now, and I could hear Comrade Asimov's words in my head: I should know that the old ways were dead and that we should obey Father Stalin if we were to be good little Russians. I knew that the punishment would be meted out according to my supposed sins and that I already had several close calls. Except for the Grace of God, I couldn't keep on being lucky. As young as I was, I had the sense to know it well. I stared at the candle as it burned to a stub and prayed to the imagined face of my Mama in the heart of the flame.

"Mama, Please let Malenka live. She's so beautiful. If I die, please let them do it quickly. It might be easier to come to you, and Viktor and the twins and ..."

I must have succumbed to a fitful sleep. Ivanovna was shaking my shoulder and the sheet over the window was faintly glowing yellow with another cold dawn.

"Give me the cross," she whispered in my ear. "You know how to do the medicine. Not a word to anyone about where I'm going. Tell Marina Nikolaiovna I'm on an errand and nothing more. We'll both catch it if anyone knows where I've been. And if she doesn't know, she can't be held responsible."

I unfastened the gold chain on Malenka's neck. Ivanovna

snatched the cross almost before I could refasten the clasp. Then, she was gone.

Her absence was immediately noticed and the porridge line buzzed with speculation. Nikolaiovna must have come to her own conclusions because, to my great relief, she never asked me a single question. She went on with her day as if it were normal. But Larysa was a different story.

"You have to do what I say," she said. "I'm the older one so I know better."

"Ivanovna told me what to do."

"She's not here now. And what if the Comrades catch her where she's not supposed to be? What's she doing out there anyway?"

"She didn't say."

"You have to tell if you know anything."

"She's a doctor. She can go where she wants. Why don't you just shut that big mouth of yours! She gave me instructions before she left." I was screaming now.

"You have to tell me what they are then. I'm bigger than you are, and older."

Nikolaiovna intervened.

"Girls, stop the fuss. Get on with your work. Sick Children don't need to hear you're arguing. It will make them feel worse."

I was about to complain that it was Larysa who was the problem when Malenka started coughing violently.

"Larysa, have you forgotten the last time you crossed Ivanovna's path? Do you need another beating? And Philipovna, mind that Child before she chokes. No more of this nonsense. I don't need the two biggest girls in the house making problems. I can take the broom to both of you if I have to."

And so the dull gray day dragged on. Every chore was a challenge. Either Larysa had a complaint about how I was doing it wrong or I would have to stop to check on Malenka. By noon, two more of the little ones were showing signs of the fever.

To make matters worse, Gregory wouldn't drink his tea. His eyes looked straight through me and he wouldn't drink.

"What should I do with him?" I asked Nikolaiovna. "I don't think he can hear me or see me. Look at him."

She came in and held his hand.

"Please darling," she said softly. "Auntie Marina is here. I'll help you. Please darling."

But he wouldn't drink for her either. His eyes looked through her too. She was teary and quiet through that whole damp afternoon. She would drop what she was doing to sit by his side or stand over his bed for a moment or two and then go on with her duties. But Gregory's condition didn't change.

Malenka coughed harder. By mid-afternoon the first signs of the white phlegm appeared. There was still no sign of Ivanovna.

Maybe, the old woman wasn't at the market, I thought. *Maybe there wasn't even a market today.* I didn't know what day of the week it was. The days always blurred together.

"I'm so tired I feel dizzy," I said to Nikolaiovna. "I'm going to drop soon."

"How is he?" she asked.

"He hasn't had a sip of tea since last night," I said. "I think his breathing is getting funny too."

She stood at Gregory's bed staring down at his bluish face and then she did the most amazing thing I had ever seen. She knelt by his side and took his hand.

"Gregory, my darling Gregory," she said in a barely audible whisper. "If it is too much for you, let go. Go to Natasha and *Babusya*. My darling, I see your suffering. I'd gladly trade places with you. I wish it were me so that you could go and live your young life, but God isn't letting it happen that way. You have my permission to go to your Mama. Let her guide you. I'll be all right."

She laid her head on his filthy blanket, right by his face. Her tears washed both of their cheeks. I had to leave the room. I pulled Larysa out with me and to my great surprise, she didn't resist.

When we were in the big room again, I noticed that the gray day was getting gloomier. Twilight was setting in. Larysa must have noticed too.

"I'm going to start cooking," she said.

"Go ahead."

"Do you think Nikolaiovna will be cross?"

"No. She'll probably be glad."

"How long do you think she's going to hang around him like that?"

"Till he dies."

"Is he really going to die?"

"Yes."

"How do you know?"

"Ivanovna said that it would be better if he did because there's not enough flesh on his burned bones and because we don't have enough food for him to get well."

"Where is she anyway?" Larysa said.

Her eyes were shining bright green with tears. She started to cry. She grabbed the water pail and began slamming the porridge things. She didn't look at anyone or talk for a long time but as the porridge was made she stirred and crashed around the stove like a bear with a sore paw. The rest of the Children just sat and stared. They knew better than to ask any questions. Their blank faces and dull silence built a protective wall so that they could stay as far away from the crisis as they could. They dumbly lined up for their meagre supper. They sat and ate without talking and waited—waited for Gregory to die, for Nikolaiovna to reappear from the sick room and for Ivanovna to come home.

The twilight deepened. I lit the candles. Nikolaiovna didn't come out.

"I have to go in to look after the ones in the sick room," I said to Larysa.

"Don't bother Gregory," she said.

"I won't."

"I'll put everyone to bed. It's too cold to do anything else anyway, and no one feels like stories without Nikolaiovna."

I went in and ministered to the sick ones. Malenka had been sleeping and seemed to be a little better for it, although her breathing was starting to come with that familiar hissing sound. I picked her up and sat in the chair where Ivanovna had left me. Malenka started to cough. Since Gregory had not drunk the tea I had made earlier in the day, I slowly let Malenka drink it.

She might as well be as comfortable as she can, I thought.

I felt so tired myself. My throat had an unfamiliar scratchy feeling. There was nothing for me to do now but sit and wait.

I must have fallen asleep again because through my fog I heard some movement. When I looked up, Nikolaiovna was on her knees beside Gregory's bed on one side and Larysa was on the other. They were wrapping him in his blanket and crying.

"Farewell, my pet," Nikolaiovna whispered. "No one will ever harm you again. I'm sorry I couldn't take better care of you. Tell Natasha I'm sorry. Farewell, my pet. Farewell."

"May I please do it for him?" Larysa asked in a small and tender voice that I had never heard before.

I watched as Larysa closed his eyes and gently kissed their lids. I could see her thin shoulders spasm with the effort it was taking not to sob out loud. My own chin shook with silent grief. They each took an end of Gregory's wrapped body and carried him out to where he himself had laid so many Children.

Reunion

THE NIGHT LOOMED large before me. I shifted Malenka's weight from one shoulder to the other and reached to light another candle. How was I going to stay awake until Ivanovna returned? My throat was dry no matter how much water I drank. It was no longer just scratchy, it was getting sore. My eyes teared from the effort to keep them open. My cheeks burned. My head dropped. I jerked awake again. Was that a sound I heard?

I laid Malenka down on my sleeping bench and went to investigate. Nikolaiovna and Larysa were dozing by the stove. I tiptoed past them so that I could see what the sound could be without disturbing the house, but everything looked the same as I had left it. I gently lifted the latch and went out into the cold night.

A sliver of the early spring moon was peeking out between the breaking clouds and a wind was blowing. I took a deep breath, my first breath of fresh air for months. But instead of feeling cold and refreshing, it made my chest hurt. My shallow breath came out in hot bursts and floated in small white puffs. I stood shivering as I looked around the quiet cottage.

I could see nothing out of the ordinary out there either. Yet the feeling that things were happening wouldn't leave me. I wasn't sure if I shivered from the wind or from the fear that was creeping up my bones. I looked among the shadows. Ivanovna stood between two men, whispering by the wall where we laid the dead Children. They had found Gregory. I tiptoed closer although I wouldn't have been heard as the wind was rattling the ice-covered branches of the frozen willow by the wall. Ivanovna was telling them what a wonderful boy Gregory had been and how he had been so terribly injured. I could hear her sniffling.

"That damned Party will be the death of all of us," the taller man said roughly. "Imagine, a brute like that beating a defenseless Child!"

"Slavko," the other said. "No one will tell you what to think. But watch what you say. You should have learned that by now. I won't be able to protect you if some *cholera* turns you in. You never know who you can trust."

The man called Slavko shrugged.

"I wonder how long he's been out here," Ivanovna said.

"Only a couple of hours," I said.

Ivanovna swallowed a scream. The two men turned on me as I stepped into the shadows.

"What are you doing, sneaking around out here?" Slavko said. His big hand clapped down onto my shoulder like Uncle Misha's had on that last Easter Sunday when Mitya and I discovered the men around the campfire.

The sudden gesture brought a flood of tears. "Is anyone else with you?"

"What have you heard?" the other man asked.

"Nothing—nothing just your talk about Gregory," I said.

In the dim light of the crescent moon the men seemed familiar. Could it really be Doctor Bondarenko and his driver? Could I be lucky a second time? I shivered violently again.

"Philipovna? Is that you?" Ivanovna asked, recovering her composure.

"Yes, I was almost asleep and heard a sound. I had to see what it was." A tear slipped out. I jabbed at it with a cold finger.

"We were being quiet," she said.

"You were. I was listening for you."

"This is why I wanted to come so late. I needed to be sure no one was out on the street," the man who looked like Doctor Bondarenko said.

"I wasn't out on the street," I whispered.

"I can't be too careful. You never know who is watching or who will give the Comrades a nugget. The last thing I need is for my patients to find out that I was visiting a filthy orphanage."

"Let's go in," Ivanovna said. "We're better off talking inside."

Slavko's hand was still on my shoulder. Where did he think I would be able to go? I was taken into the house behind Ivanovna and the doctor who gagged and covered his nose as he entered.

"What do you expect when we're not given any soap or supplies not to mention any medicine for at least the past six weeks?" Ivanovna said. "Breathe through your mouth. It's not so bad that way." She closed the door behind us. "Let her go already. She's one of the orphans, and my good helper too. If I had a couple more like her, my life would be much, much easier."

Slavko's hand slowly released me, but his eyes didn't look away.

Nikolaiovna and Larysa started up.

"Where were you?" Larysa said.

Nikolaiovna acknowledged them with a nod.

"All will be told in good time," Ivanovna said with an impatient wave of her mittened hand. "These gentlemen have some things to do. We'll talk later."

I realized that I had never seen her thick mittens before. I wondered where she got them. Could she have traded Malenka's precious cross for things to wear? Or did she give it away for a good meal for herself?

"Doesn't this one look familiar," Slavko said, still studying me.

"As a matter of fact," the man who looked like Doctor Bondarenko said, "she does."

"But we've seen her somewhere else," Slavko said.

"Do you know this man?" Ivanovna asked.

I swallowed hard.

"Answer the question," Slavko said.

"She doesn't have to," Dr. Bondarenko said. "I know who she is. How are the twins?"

I looked down.

"And the older Child?"

I shook my head.

The doctor patted my unruly hair. My muscles all stiffened when he touched me. It was months since anyone had reached out to me with a kind gesture of affection. I choked back a sob.

"Maybe it's better that they are gone to Heaven," he said. "It's a terrible time for Children, especially the very sick ones."

"They aren't the only ones that are gone," Nikolaiovna said.

Ivanovna faced her for the first time since we entered the house.

"We found him by the wall. I'm so sorry."

Nikolaiovna started to cry again.

"He would have never stopped suffering," Ivanovna said. Her eyes glistened. "Truly Marina Nikolaiovna, it is for the best."

"Let's see the cross again," the doctor said.

I breathed a sigh of relief. We still had the cross. Ivanovna was true to her word.

"My father's brother was a goldsmith so all of our crosses have the same markings. Do you see that?"

He took Malenka's cross from Ivanovna. He held it in one hand, pulled a bigger one from beneath his shirt and motioned for me to step up to him. He held it close to one of the lighted candles and carefully compared it to Malenka's. He made me recount how I found the cross, what I did to hide it and explain why I didn't tell the doctor about it earlier.

When I came to the telling of my thoughts about how God wanted me to be Malenka's Godmother, his eyes filled with tears.

"I'm sure He will have something very special for you in Heaven. Imagine, someone who still needs a Godmother of her own and you've cared for her. Let's see this Little Malenka. I must not stay too long."

Slavko placed himself on watch by the window that looked out onto the yard as he had done at Auntie's house.

I followed the doctors into the sick room.

"Is this all of the light we have?" Dr. Bondarenko asked. "I can't see anything in here. How do you work in these conditions?"

"We haven't had kerosene since last winter," Ivanovna said. "Philipovna bring some more candles. It's the best I can do."

The light must have disturbed Malenka's sleep. When I set the extra candles down, she began to cry. The crying got her cough going again. I picked her up and patted her back to settle her. I turned away from the doctor so that the phlegm wouldn't be sprayed on him, but his hand grasped my arm as he stood looking down at us, tears streaming down his cheeks.

Ivanovna's eyebrow was raised in that familiar look of exasperation that I knew well. But the doctor stood staring at the Child.

"She looks just like her—just like little Olya!"

"Would you please get on with what you need to do?" Ivanovna said. "I don't have all night."

"Did you see her mother?" He turned to me.

"Yes, Good Uncle, I did."

I described the night of Malenka's arrival. I pointed out the beet red shawl which was now discoloured by months of constant use and told him how Gregory had given it to me. I told him that we had wrapped Malenka's mother in an old blanket and how Gregory put her by the wall where we always placed the dead. I pulled out the *platok*. The doctor gulped down his breath.

"My sister painted this," he said. "It is a copy of the design from Kiev that she did especially for all of her nieces." He grabbed the crumpled *platok* and pressed it against his heart.

"Have you noticed anything unusual about Malenka?" he asked.

"You mean her beautiful hair?" I said, taking a guess.

"No. Any unusual marks?"

I stopped to collect my thoughts.

"You mean that little mark under her neck that looks like a little berry from the *kalyna*?"

"Yes," he whispered.

"I thought it was some kind of a scar."

"No. We all have one." He unwrapped his heavy woollen scarf and pulled the collar of his shirt open. "Look here."

Ivanovna stepped in close behind me to look over my shoulder. I could hear her inhale with surprise. There, below his collarbone was the same birthmark I had wondered about often as I wiped Malenka after a meal.

"What is it? I thought that she might have been hurt somehow."

"No, Child, our whole family has one. It's our own sign."

I gaped.

"You mean ... you mean you're family?" I stammered.

"Yes, I am ashamed to say that I am."

Ivanovna and I stared. What kind of a way was that to claim one of your own? In our village, a lost one would be a cause for rejoicing.

"Ashamed?" I asked.

"It's a long story," the doctor said, sighing. "I shouldn't burden you with our troubles. I could have done more to help. And I should be moving as quickly as I can."

"But I want to know. She's my little Malenka."

"I'll have Larysa make you some tea," Ivanovna said. "Surely, you have a few moments to answer Philipovna's questions. Besides, you promised to give me some medicine. You have more than the value of any cross with the recovery of the Child."

I put Malenka down and went to make tea myself. Larysa was still despondent and didn't look like she could be trusted around a fire or hot water. Marina Nikolaiovna was no better as she sat weeping quietly into her apron. I slowly filled the tea kettle from the almost empty bucket and put it onto the stove to heat. I was feeling hot and light-headed. Slavko watched me struggling with the bucket.

"Let me go out and fill it for you," he said. "You don't look so well yourself."

"I'd be surprised if you found anyone that looks good in a place like this," I answered.

"Would that the Party should listen to its Children," he said, smiling wryly. "I should scout around and make sure that no one followed us to this Godforsaken hovel."

I put the kettle onto the fire and found the tea things. Slavko quietly went to fill the bucket. I nodded my thanks.

After he returned with the fresh water, he took on the job of bringing wood in from the shrinking pile outside. He even stoked the fire. I could hear the doctor and Ivanovna's muffled voices rise occasionally and caught the few words that let me know he wasn't parting from his medicine easily. They seemed to be arguing for a long time. My head felt hot and foggy so that I couldn't listen in on their conversation from a discreet distance as I had learned to do when I really wanted to know what the Comrades had in mind.

The tea was well steeped when they came out of the sick room. The doctor's face was sullen.

"I know this is costly for you," Ivanovna said. "But at least you can go and get more medicine. Not like me. I just have to sit and watch the Children die while the Party debates over who gets what."

The doctor had opened his overcoat and stuffed Malenka in—right next to his chest, as filthy as she was and would have kept on walking right out of the door had I not darted over and clung to his sleeve.

"You promised," I said. "I've made you tea. You can't go without telling me something about her Mama. How will I know who and what to pray for?"

Ivanovna looked hard at the doctor.

"She's right. You owe her that much before you go."

He acquiesced, brushing me off like an unwanted fly.

"Quickly then. Pour your tea. Just let me alone."

We retreated to the benches by the stove.

"Here it is; the simple truth," the doctor said as he blew the steam away from his hot cup of tea.

"Olya, the woman who died here, was my niece. A sweeter Child I have never met. She was quiet, obedient and smart. She was like a little fairy—even the cow came to her for milking without her calling to it. Snap her fingers and her work was done. Send her to the well and the water was there. Before you said the floor needed sweeping the broom was dancing with Olya, her golden curls flying behind them. I never heard a sorry word come out of her mouth. Once she was finished, she'd find a book. I'd often see her sitting in the corner or under a tree, embroidering the *kalyna* onto a *rushnyk* or shirt, lost in her own world. To see her was to love her. No wonder then, that when she grew into a fine young woman, there was no lack of suitors. Everyone called her *krasawitsya* as she really was a beauty.

"Of course, the young men of the village flocked to her door. She'd welcomed them graciously as was expected of her, but showed no particular interest in any of them. Finally, my brother-in-law decided that this had gone on long enough.

"'It isn't right to let a girl, even one as lovely as you, my dear Olya, to remain an unmarried old maid,' he said. 'I would rather you choose a husband, but if you won't, next summer, you should expect a wedding.'

"Since she wouldn't choose, her father decided that the miller's son would be the lucky man. It was truly a match made in Heaven. He was very handsome and, since everyone in the town comes to him for grinding their flour, she'd never want for anything. 'If the two of you work hard and continued to manage the mill as your father has, you may even get rich someday,' my brother-in-law said when we all raised a glass to the lucky couple.

"Olya smiled but said nothing. While she didn't complain, she didn't seem happy either. I only came to understand what was going on the day that she and my sister, her mother came to me.

"As she sat silent, her mother told me how Olya had come to know one of the Russian Party members. He had lured her off. Any innocent girl's head would be turned by a handsome young man, especially one as nice as he was, despite the fact that he was a Communist.

"Olya wouldn't say how long this secret affair was going on, but it must have been happening for some time as she had discovered that she was pregnant. Her mother wanted me to help her get rid of the baby.

"'You know that having it will be the disgrace and ruin of her. After all, no one has to know,' she said. But Olya wouldn't have it. She wanted the baby and its Russian father, too. When my brother-in-law finally found out, he was out of his mind with rage. 'How could you?' he roared. 'It's bad enough that you'd ruined yourself but with a Russian—a filthy Communist!'

"The girl had no peace. When her brothers found out, they beat the Russian so badly that he was sent back to his parents in Leningrad. I fixed him up the best I could, but we had to lie low for some months till it blew over. I can't imagine how the Party didn't figure it out. I don't know how the poor fellow made the journey home.

"Olya went into mourning and finally decided to leave her father's house. She went from aunt to aunt. She stayed with me for some months till the baby came. I even helped her have Little Nina, whom you call 'Malenka,' baptized with my *Babusya's* cross. But the shame, the disgrace would soon follow. People talked; they whispered; they pointed. She finally ran away with Nina. We looked for her, but as soon as we contacted her, she would disappear like the fairy Child that would dance away with her broom. Then we heard that she was in the sealed-off zone. Since then, I asked for her in every village I was called to, but there was no finding her. I never dreamed that she would turn up, right here practically under my own nose."

His shoulders shook. He sipped at his tea trying to swallow his grief.

"I can promise you, Little Godmother, that nothing will happen to what's left of our Little Olya. I will take her Child as my own. With all that is going on around here, people will soon forget and Nina will live well. I promise, and to prove it to you, her name will be Malenka from now on. That way, her unfortunate past will stay buried with her poor mother. You have done well. I hope that you can take care of yourself as well as you have taken care of her. God knows you deserve a Heavenly hand of your own."

He stared right into my eyes for a long, long time. I'll never forget the pain in that tortured stare. He drank his tea.

"Say your goodbye," he said. "We have worn out our welcome. If I can ever help you again, come and find me. But wait a while, if you can. If you come too soon, it may cause some suspicion."

He opened his shirt. I wanted to grab Malenka and squeeze her to my heart as hard as I could, but she was floppy as a rag doll in her sleep. No doubt the doctor's strong, warm chest was comfortable. I ran my fingers over her luscious curls. I kissed her face—her eyes, her nose and her fevering little mouth. My tears fell on her cheek. I couldn't look at anyone else. I ran to the sickroom and threw myself onto my sleeping bench. My sobs wouldn't stop.

Eventually, I cried myself to sleep. But there was no relief. The dreams took over my head. My nightmares churned with memories. I shrank back in fear as Auntie Lena's face came towards me reminding me that she would eat every crumb before she would give me one bite of bread. I saw the army trucks with all of our wheat, Uncle Misha's bleeding wound, the pile of wheat on fire and then poor Gregory slammed against the stove.

He wasn't quiet in my dreams either. He called my name,

screaming for me to help him. I was afraid that I would burn up with him. When I tried to run away he followed me with the stove clattering behind him, its fire roaring and smoking monstrously. He chased me for what seemed to be hours, with me just being able to stay out of the reach of his burned and boney fingers. It was so hot that I wanted to pull off my rags and run away naked.

Then I found myself lying on the grass beside the twins' grave and watching as the earth opened and the scrawny hand of Mitya's mother slowly clawing towards me.

"Come," she called, as I lay shivering, "Viktor and the twins are waiting. They want Malenka to see the nightingales in Heaven. Come and listen. They sing so much better up here."

I tried to scream, but my throat was closed. I tried to wake up. I couldn't move. Everything hurt, especially my head. It was so cold. I could almost hear my bones rattling. I thought I heard the Comrades talking. They whispered about how ill someone was.

"Will the medicine help?" It sounded like Marina Nikolaiovna's voice. I thought I caught a foggy glimpse of sunshine coming through the sickroom window.

"She always wanted sunshine in here," I heard Larysa's voice say.

"I guess it can't hurt her now," Ivanovna said. "If she makes it, I'll go back to church and thank God myself. Come and hold her shoulders up so we can get her to swallow some of this tea. Maybe it'll stay down this time." I felt someone raise me by my shoulders.

"Just a bit higher, Nikolaiovna." It sounded like Ivanovna. "She's going to pass out again. Let's make it worth her trouble."

The tea was held to my mouth, but my throat burned so that I could only take a couple of swallows. I was very tired. Someone covered me with a blanket. Then I faded off into darkness.

I dreamed again. But this time I was with Mama. We sat on our cloud with Viktor, the twins and Malenka. Somehow, Mama was holding us all and singing. I could smell Xenkovna's baking bread again. Mmmmmm. ... My mouth watered. I looked down on my little dell on the riverside where forget-me-nots and lily-of-the-valley were blooming. A warm wind tugged at my clean hair. I heard Auntie calling me.

I tried to turn toward the direction of her voice.

"Hush, Child, hush," it said. "Xenkovna and I will take good care of you now. Drink this tea and lie still."

"Auntie?" I managed to croak out.

I felt someone wrap me in a blanket before the spinning in my head made me flop backwards into a foggy limbo. I dreamed I was moving, a gentle rocking motion like that of a rolling wagon behind horses that walked at a steady pace. I saw glimpses of blue sky and puffy clouds. I couldn't concentrate for long as when I tried to look at anything it would start spinning and I would have to close my eyes just to keep from vomiting. The gentle swaying of a wagon rocked me back into a blissful unconsciousness. It seemed like I was there for a long time.

When I woke up, everything was very quiet. It was so strange to hear no coughing or breathing around me. I wasn't cold either. It felt as if someone had wrapped me in my Mama's feather bed. I slowly opened my eyes.

I was wrapped in a feather bed. The room was oddly familiar. The walls that looked like they were once whitewashed were patched and broken. I could see an icon of the Last Supper hanging in the corner. A hearth with its few cooking implements occupied one of the walls. A table was pushed under an open east window and I could smell the scent of cherry blossoms. In the corner, with the pale pink blush of the dawning morning lighting her face, sat a woman.

Strange, I thought. *She looks like Auntie.* I shut my eyes.

You're dreaming, I told myself. *Wake up. It can't be her.*

I opened my eyes again. I tried to sit but I couldn't. I could just manage to prop myself half up on one elbow. I lay staring at the woman. She did look like Auntie—well, maybe more like her mother.

Her skin hung in loose wrinkles below her chin. Her dark eyebrows, which once must have been beautiful, were going gray and her hair was gray, but the rest of her thin face could pass for an older version of Auntie. She sat sleeping upright with an open Bible resting in her lap. I closed my eyes again.

"What kind of tricks are my eyes playing on me, God?" I asked of no one in particular. When I rubbed them open, my hand smelled like carbolic soap.

"No tricks, my darling," a voice that sounded like Auntie said.

I looked again. The woman got up from the chair and came to me. She wrapped her arms around me and held me close to her thin shoulder. It was Auntie Xena!

We wept.

As she sat on my sleeping bench motionless with her arms around me and me clinging to her, our tears mingling on each other's cheeks, the door opened with a rush of warm spring air.

"Oh my God, Philipovna!" Xenkovna almost dropped her full water bucket. She rushed to Auntie and joined in the embrace. "I wasn't sure if you would ever come back to us."

"Hush, Child," Auntie said. "You must never speak like that. I knew that if we gave her back to God he'd let her come home some-day. I just didn't think she'd suffer so. Look at her."

Xenkovna looked.

"God have mercy on us! If it wasn't for those eyes that are so much like Auntie Barbara's, I'm not sure we'd recognize our Little Philipovna."

I stared at Xenkovna for the same could have been said of her. She was gaunt. The hair that was so beautiful just two years ago lay thin and limp around her face. Her eyes were still hazel but the twinkle in them was gone. While her face was full of love and con-cern, it was old so that she looked more like I remembered Auntie did before the hunger. I wondered what I really did look like myself.

"Am I really here?" I asked. "How did I get home?"

"Doctor Bondarenko," Xenkovna said. "He told us how you saved Malenka. So did the Comrades."

"The Comrades?"

"Yes, the Comrades. The Comrade doctor was very sorry to lose you. She told us about how you tried to help Gregory and how brave you were to throw the water all over the nasty schoolmaster."

"You mean you were at the ..." I couldn't say the word.

"Yes," Xenkovna said, pushing the hair out of my eyes. "Doctor Bondarenko sent Slavko to take us to you. He figured that if you could risk your life in order to save his niece while the zone was closed, the least he could do is to make sure you could be returned to us as soon as it was open again."

"You mean it's over?" I asked.

"I guess they realized that if all of us died there would be no one left to run the *kolhosp*," Auntie said.

The New Order

AS THE SPRING of 1933 swelled into summer, I convalesced. The pneumonia I contracted at the orphanage slowly went away. I grew into my new life of keeping the house and tending the garden plot which every member of the *kolhosp* was allotted. Although there was never the abundance of food we had enjoyed before the hunger, there was enough for the three women that remained in our household to get by. Thanks to the blessing of a healthy ancestry, I regained most of my physical strength.

The matters of the heart are another story. Xenkovna warned me not to discuss things with Auntie. She told me that Uncle Misha was the first to die—on Christmas Day, God rest his soul. Michael lasted one more week and Alexander died a few days later. They had lived through a bleak winter indeed.

Only a shell was left of the Auntie that I used to know. She was always tired. I would often catch a glimpse of The Unravelled One's expression in her dull eyes as she sat by the hearth staring at the icon with its dusty *rushnyk*. I even saw an occasional tear drop from the corner of her eye when she thought that nobody was watching. I longed for the warmth of the Auntie I remembered. She brightened a little on Wednesday evenings when her friends came to read the Bible and pray.

"Aren't you going to get into trouble?" I asked as I watched her prepare tea for one of these gatherings.

"Oh no, Child. There are only worn-out old men and poor women left. The young people are working at the *kolhosp*. What other choice do they have? The Party has all it wants. They won't care about us few believers because we really can't do anything to them anymore. They can have the little I have left if they want it."

"Then why should you pray? Everyone is gone."

"Memory Eternal. We can't bring them back, but we can pray for their souls. May they rest in peace." Her jaw quivered as she crossed herself. She was overwhelmed with guilt for surviving.

I found some comfort in the old prayers and the readings from the Bible, many of which I had memorized by the fire with Uncle Misha and the boys. I listened to the gossip over tea under the birch tree when they finished their devotions. I learned that Uncle Simon had moved up through the ranks of the Party and was now a big official in Kiev. I heard about the time that Uncle Ivan was accused of cooking children in order to survive and was shot for it though there was no evidence or trial. And I must admit, I wasn't sad about that—though when I said so to Auntie, she chided me for my un-christian attitude. I heard their pity for Katerina who went mad when she found out that her daughter had suffocated herself by closing the damper in her chimney after all of her five children died.

"What choice did she have after her little children were gone?" one of the *Babushkas* asked, wiping the tears from her eyes. "They were bathed and dressed in their finest embroidered clothes too."

"It's best not to talk about these things," another said.

And that is how it was. We stopped talking about it. It was as if the famine had never happened. Folks would look at Xenkovna or me, cross themselves and go on their way.

In the fall, a nine form school was organized in the same house where Asimov had taught us when the Comrades arrived. All of the children of school age were obliged to attend. The teachers taught the same way as Asimov had, but none of them were ever as mean. There was a good deal of catching up to do in order to make up for the months I spent at the orphanage. I studied hard and paid attention. I didn't want to be left behind my form or be humiliated the way Asimov had humiliated me ever again. I stayed in that school until I graduated.

I didn't have many friends. I was the orphan, the stigmatized, untouchable one. Father Stalin's decree that all of the orphans were his children didn't help me. Ivanovna was right. "Stalin's bastard," they would say among themselves when they thought I couldn't hear. When one of my classmates came to school in a newly-knit sweater or a pair of new shoes, I felt painfully left out. So I went home directly after school to do my chores where I didn't have to see the children who still had mothers or fathers.

Since I had the run of the house after school, I rooted around in the spare rooms. I found some old cloth and thread in one of these forays and, by taking apart some old embroidery, I taught myself how to make some simple cross stitch designs.

"What a clever little pigeon," Xenkovna said when she discovered me working on them one evening. "You've always been full of surprises. I never know what you'll come up with next."

We took to sitting in the colder small room and, over the coming winter, she taught me the stitches that Auntie taught her when she was a little girl. We decided that I could learn to make a simple little square.

"If you work hard at this," Xenkovna said, "you can present it to Mama at Easter. We'll need a smaller cloth for a smaller basket anyway. She'll be so surprised. If you keep at it, you will embroider your own red and black table cloth someday. Remember, the red is for love and the black is for sorrow."

"We've sure had enough of sorrow."

"Hush, Little Sister. There's no point to talk about it. We can't help anything now." She brushed a tear from her cheek with the back of her hand and reached for the black embroidery thread.

"I'm going to use as little black as I can," I said. "The red is prettier anyway."

"That may be true, but you must learn our village's special design. Did you know that the women in each village in Ukraine have their own way of embroidering?"

I liked those evenings when Xenkovna had a few minutes to spare for me. I uncovered my Mama's sewing-machine. I turned the wheels and pushed the treadle. I played with the bobbins, but I didn't know how to make the machine work. In time, Xenkovna would meet Luba at the *kolhosp* and learn how to sew. It seems that she inherited the practical skills from Mama for her sewing was as exquisite as was her baking of bread. So it was that, without saying a word, I relinquished my treasure and the sewing machine that had been my mama's became Xenkovna's machine.

I dug through Auntie's trunk and found the old embroidered outfits and her precious blue wool skirt that was given to her by the old mistress of the estate. I tried it on and imagined how I would look in it when I grew up. I would spin in it till its ten metres flared out like a huge umbrella. I would stop only when I was dizzy and felt like I might fall over. I was glad that Auntie couldn't sell it in the famine because I knew that my Mama might have worn it sometimes, too.

I tried to put things back neatly so that Auntie wouldn't know I was rooting around in her special place. Because she never said anything about it, I guessed that she either didn't look into the trunk anymore or didn't have enough strength to care.

Once after Xenkovna learned to sew, she pulled me into the room where the sewing-machine was. The blue skirt flowed over her arm and there was a strange expression on her face.

"Ask Mama for some of her skirt," she said. "She always lets you have anything you want from her."

"What do you mean?" I asked.

"I want to take this apart."

"But why? It's beautiful as it is—and it's Auntie's special gift."

"I know, but we don't have clothes to wear and no warm material to make anything with. If I carefully take it apart, I can use one of the flare panels for you and one for me to make us each a skirt. Then I can put the rest back together for Mama. She'll still have lots of flare left."

"But we have no blouses," I said.

"We'll raise silkworms in the spring, like the other girls at the *kolhosp* do. The trader says that girls like us raise them from as far away as India, Persia and China. We can earn enough silk from the silk traders to make a blouse. If we do well, Luba says we'll have a new blouse for Christmas. You can help me raise silkworms."

So we learned about silkworms. After I tended the garden each day, I cut up the mulberry leaves and spread them on the trays of dark babies that the trader would bring at the beginning of each month. I watched the worms get lighter with each shedding of their skin until the fourth time when they turned the colour of cream. Then, we would set up a pot over a fire in the garden to boil the worms out from their silken cocoons. We tried not to do it in the house as the smell of those worms rivalled the memory of the smell of the sick room in the orphanage. I always tried to get Xenkovna to do that part. I felt so sorry for taking the coats of silk off of those little worms even though I knew there would be a blouse for me at the end of it all.

The best thing I discovered in my rooting around the spare rooms of our cottage was Uncle Misha's guitar. I didn't let anyone know I found it. I would rush home, do my chores and sit with it by the fire. I would turn the keys on the end of it till the sound was right. I didn't know that I had perfect pitch then. I plucked the strings the way I remembered Uncle Misha doing it.

"Don't you dare let her catch you with that!" Xenkovna said

when she came home early from the *kolhosp* and found me strumming by the fire one day. "She will become unravelled."

I decided to take the guitar out into the barn so that Auntie wouldn't hear me. I found one of Mitya's ragged blankets and wrapped the instrument in it for safe keeping. I was afraid at first, always expecting the ghost of the Unravelled One to appear. But the music from inside the guitar would drive the ghosts away and the familiar songs from the evenings at the fire with Uncle Misha slowly came back to me. It was like reuniting with a steady old friend.

When I could play a song straight through, the tears would come and I would pray to Mama asking if I was playing it well enough. Other times, the memory of Uncle's kind smile overwhelmed me and I'd have to put the instrument down for a while until I could breathe again and get myself past the pain in my chest.

We also learned some songs in school—Russian songs that were about propaganda. I didn't like those, but occasionally, the teacher would teach us something from his school days or a folk song that his father taught him. I liked the way the Russian language tickled my tongue when I tried to figure it out. But the desire to play the guitar and sing any song I could remember drew me to the instrument and pushed me out into my hiding place in the barn. I could spend hours there.

I learned to keep my eye on a certain beam that was cracked and hanging loose. I figured out that, if the shadow of that beam crossed over the floor in front of me, the sun was low enough that it was time for me to go into the house. One afternoon Xenkovna came looking for me because she had come home early from the *kolhosp*.

"You should go and play that with the young people who sing in the village in the evening," she said. Her eyes glistened with the memory.

"Do you really think I could?"

"Of course. You sound like a little nightingale." She bent to kiss me. "You can't be shut up in this cage forever. You must grow up like everyone else."

"They don't think that I'm like everyone else," I said.

"Who are they?"

The words choked in my throat. "The others in my class. They call me 'Stalin's bastard' when they think I can't hear."

"Don't worry, when they hear your music, they'll forget. We all must live past it someday. After all, we're all Ukrainians. We've always sung and danced in the square. Our families have lived here together for over a thousand years."

She was right. I did go to sing with the boys and girls. Though I got a curious but cool reception, the shock of finding out that I could play the guitar and pick up a melody quickly crossed the abyss between us. Music does that. It puts a song into a sad heart and lightens one's step wherever life might take them. It is a leveller in so many ways. But my heart ached for my lost friend. Would I ever see him again?

When I asked about Mitya, no one knew where he was. It was as if he had fallen into the river.

"One day he appeared from behind the wood pile with a rabbit," Xenkovna said, "and the next thing I knew, he was gone. He didn't even stay to eat with us."

I scoured the woods and riverbank looking for Mitya. I waited at his Mama's grave and I searched for clues by the place where his Mama's cottage used to stand. I longed to have just one more look into those wild blue eyes. I prayed to God and my own Mama to please send him back to me.

One warm October afternoon, after I was dismissed from class, I heard someone calling my name. The voice sounded familiar but I couldn't see anyone.

"Philipovna. Over here," the voice called from behind the corner of the school.

There, in the afternoon sun, on the side of the schoolhouse away from the path, sat a scraggly boy. In spite of the filthy clothing, matted hair and thin face, I recognized those steel blue eyes.

"Mitya!" His name choked in a sob as I took in his appearance. "Where have you been?"

"The Comrades put me to work in a sugar factory," he said. "I worked till I couldn't stand up. I fainted at the place. They took me to a Children's home. I stayed there till I thought I'd be strong enough to walk back here. I didn't think I'd make it. The bastards will probably come to find me soon. They'll put me in jail for being absent from work."

"You look terrible." I reached to put my arms around his boney frame.

"Don't touch me." He pulled away. "I've got dysentery. My stomach hurts."

He leaned against the building.

"What can I do?"

"Nothing. I came home to die."

"You can't die. I've just found you again." It took all of my strength to keep from screaming.

He slid down the side of the schoolhouse to the ground.

"I'm so cold. Can you get a blanket? My stomach ... it hurts so much." He doubled over, hugging himself in pain.

I touched his forehead. It was burning up.

"Can you walk home with me? I'll help you."

"No. I just want to sit here."

"I can get Auntie Anna. Everyone else is at the *kolhosp*."

"No. Don't get anyone. They'll get into trouble. I need a blanket."

I ran home to fetch a blanket. I tried to take my Mama's feather bed, but it was too heavy; so I took one of Auntie's lighter blankets from the hearth. As I was going out of the door, I saw the Unravelled One's black shawl hanging over the back of Auntie's chair. I grabbed it too. I ran back to Mitya.

"Here's your Mama's shawl. That should make you feel better. Should I get you a drink of water?"

He nodded as I wrapped his shivering shoulders in the shawl and covered him with the blanket. I brought him a drink from the well behind the schoolhouse. Everyone was gone by this time so I didn't have to worry about being caught. I held the dipper as he took a sip.

"I will tell my *Tahto* that I really tried. I tried to get the bastards who killed him. I just didn't have time to grow up enough."

"What are you talking about?" I asked through my tears. "Have another drink. You'll feel better."

"I want to be with my Mama and *Tahto* and Sharik, wherever they are. I'm so tired."

"Please Mitya, don't talk like that. You're scaring me."

"There's nothing to be scared of. This isn't nearly as scary as the stuff they did to me."

I didn't ask what they did to him. I didn't want to know. I had seen enough of what the Comrades had done. I sat beside him and held his hand. His eyes closed as the sun dropped down into the evening sky.

"I'm going home now," I said. "I have to tell Auntie Xena."

He didn't answer; he was asleep.

I ran home to find Xenkovna. We met each other where the path to our house broke away from the main path of the village.

"Slow down," she said. "You look as though you've just seen a ghost."

"Almost," I said. "Mitya's home."

"God have mercy! We'll have to celebrate."

"No, he's too sick. He said he's come home to die." My tears burst out again. "Do something, please. He says he's come home to die."

"Oh, Philipovna, let's hope it's not that bad," she said. "There's been too much of that. We do have more food now. I'm sure some warm tea and a little care and he'll be getting better. He's a tough young fellow."

By the time we got Auntie Anna and one of the old Uncles to help us bring Mitya home, he was dead. We each held a corner of his blanket and took him straight to the cemetery. We buried him next to his parents and his dog Sharik. He still lies there in peace.

Auntie kept her promise to my Mama and my Godfather. I often wonder if more of my cousins would have lived had she not made that promise. But what do we the Children know of our Father God's plan?

I had to find my way as my Godfather had predicted so long ago. I thought I'd be like all of the others, finish school, find a man to marry and have a family just like my ancestors did for generations. Little did I know that the tide of war would sweep through that village on May 29, 1942 and set my life into a whirlwind adventure. So, by the Grace of God and with the lessons of perseverance and love from my Auntie, I found my way through Europe, across the ocean and into Canada where I could live in peace. I finally understand the meaning of *Tahto*'s lesson of the ducklings so many years ago. I couldn't really live unless I was free.

Acknowledgements

I'd like to express my sincere thanks to the following:

The Ontario Arts Council for bestowing the Writers Works in Progress grant at its maximum amount in 2012.

Dorothy Bull and her late husband Robert for financial assistance with editing.

David Chilton for many hours of help with editing, which were complicated by the fact that I'm totally blind, and many more hours for support and encouragement.

Daniel and Andrea Leising for listening to years of discussion and struggle as this project came to fruition.

Grace Luke for her constant faith in me.

Without their help I would not have been able to fulfil the promise of writing my mother's story.

Vera Philipovna Kyslenko, I trust that you are in the peace that you've always longed for.

About the Author

Born the blind daughter of Ukrainian immigrants in Hamilton, Valentina Gal was educated at the Ontario School for the Blind in Brantford, which is now considered an institutional school. She graduated with a Master of Arts from McMaster University. In 2015, Valentina was a finalist in the Writers Union Short Prose Competition for Emerging Writers. In 2012, she was a finalist in Creative Nonfiction Writing for Diaspora Dialogues, Toronto Public Library, where she was mentored by Andrew Pyper. Also in 2012, she was awarded a Writers' Works in Progress grant to help her work on *Philipovna: Daughter of Sorrow*. In 2011, she served on the Toronto Writers Co-op Editorial Committee. In 2008, she was a finalist in the Writers Union Postcard Story Competition. She now makes her home in Fergus, Ontario, where she continues to write.